THE GLENBERRY WIVES

A NOVEL

THE GLENBERRY CHRONICLES
BOOK 2

LEE CAREY

SOME KID PUBLISHING

PART I

$$1$$

July 2019, Mid-June.

Ally traced the gold stencilling on the red leather with her fingertips: 1959. She pressed her hand to her pocket, feeling the letter through the fabric of her dress. Fragile cream paper, tucked away in the attaché case for sixty years.

The sound of her father-in-law, Sandy, on his ride-on mower drifted in from the Great Lawn. Through her mental churn she had concluded only one thing: the letter had to remain a secret. From Sandy. From Alec. From everyone. This was something she had to keep strictly to herself until she could find out more. Sharing it with anyone in the family would detonate a bomb that had been buried, ticking, for sixty years.

She shuddered to think how this would have landed with Alec today. That morning, her normally mild-mannered husband had stormed out of the castle, seething about Ally's encounter with Derek Leslie. So much for her calming walk.

Sandy had tried to calm Alec down. 'Son, now isn't the time to go round confronting Leslie, when you're in this state.'

'OK great, Dad, so Leslie just gets away with accosting my pregnant wife on her morning walk? On her own property?' He had paced and ranted until they finally persuaded him that, apart from anything else, if he tried to go and find Leslie, he'd miss his flight.

It was hard for Ally to believe that she ended up being the calmest person in the room, when her legs had been like jelly all the way back to the castle after the ugly exchange.

Ally had become an early riser in her pregnancy, at first reluctantly, because she had to be up and dressed before the builders arrived with their questions about the renovations. But she had come to enjoy early morning strolls around the estate, trying to picture where Alec would be building dens and rope swings in a few years with their twins. She had been doing exactly that this morning, spotting a particularly good spot for a swing over the burn, when she noticed Leslie up ahead.

At first she expected the same curt, flat enquiry about the land dispute she'd endured on other occasions. But then she noticed the old Ordnance Survey map in his hand, along with a measuring tape and a ball of string, and her heart sank. This had the hallmarks of a longer ramble about the boundary agreement he claimed was made back around 1960.

'Morning,' she called, trying to keep the wariness and weariness out of her voice.

Derek Leslie didn't answer. He stood with his back to her, elbows jutting out as he bent over the map spread across a fallen tree trunk. He probably hadn't heard her, he must be in his eighties after all. Resisting the opportunity to simply turn back, she made her step heavier and cleared her throat as she got closer.

He turned suddenly and practically snorted when he saw her.

'You're up early this morning,' Ally said, already in placatory mode.

'Well someone has to figure out this damn thing out – who owns what on this side of the burn.'

'Oh great, straight into it today,' Ally thought.

'Mr Leslie, I –' she began.

'You what? You thought you could ignore me, and I'd just forget all about this? So your damn illegal musical festival can go ahead again, causing all sorts of trouble for the area in its wake.'

Ally didn't know where to start. They'd already been over the legality of the musical festival, which debuted last year, a dozen times, and today he seemed more irrational than ever.

'Mr Leslie, sorry, but you know that's not true. You know it's not illegal. You also know that ninety-nine percent of locals think that the festival is a positive thing for Mid-June. I haven't been ignoring you at all, in fact, this issue has been taking a lot of my time. Our solicitors have been investigating your claims and haven't been able to find any evidence at all of the variance you say you agreed with Glenberry.'

Leslie gave a dismissive snort. 'Taking up a lot of your precious time, am I, Little Miss Lady-of-the-manor?' he said with ugly sarcasm. 'Well, I'm sorry to cause any bother, m'lady, but my family has lived in Mid-June for centuries before it was even known as Mid-June, so we know the land better than any of your pimply lawyers! And I've told you before, the deal was done on a gentleman's handshake.'

Something was off with Leslie today. There was an edge in his voice, a desperate look in his eyes.

'I understand you're frustrated,' she said carefully. 'But you have to understand that a gentleman's handshake is hard to –'

'Well, if it's hard to prove, it comes down to my word against yours. And, my word is that the border is here.' He pointed to a fence post, which held two rows of barbed wire, his voice rising in frustration. 'And unless you can prove otherwise soon, I'll go ahead and deforest this whole strip of land on my side of it. Where will that put you with your festival permits, I wonder?'

Ally should never have provided him with all her permits, and the accompanying forms. She had thought it would put paid to his objections, but instead it had added fuel to them and forced him to grasp at straws.

She looked Leslie in the eye. She felt her pulse elevate at the seconds-long, yet interminable, stand-off. She knew it was in hers, and the babies' best interests, to draw this to a close.

'I think you know fine well what taking down all those trees would do, and I don't appreciate being threatened. I'm going to go now, Mr Leslie. I'm sorry that you're obviously not having a good day.'

As she turned to leave, he yanked her back by her shoulder to face him again, making Ally gasp in shock, and by reflex push him off her. Leslie stumbled back and grabbed for something to steady him, unfortunately finding the barbed wire, grasping it hard. There was a loud angry growl as he fell to the ground. Ally instinctively stepped forward to help, but Leslie's head snapped up from staring at the blood starting to flow onto his palm, and his rage was startling. It was her survival instinct that kicked in now, and she turned and left in a trembling march, Leslie cursing and ranting from his helpless position.

SANDY HEARD MORE of the detail of the story from Ally than Alec, principally because he listened more than Alec. He joined Ally for some tea in the library. Its soaring windows got any afternoon sun and its immense, battered old Chesterfield sofas were perfect for her post-lunch naps, away from the noise of construction in their rooms at the other side of the castle.

'The trouble is Ally, how do you prove a negative? We can't prove that something didn't happen, but it seems like that's what we have to achieve to finally get Leslie off our back. His threat about the trees – what's that again? Is that for the noise control permit?'

The Glenberry Music Festival, or GMF, was very much 'Ally's baby'. An impressive line-up had been the easy part as, thanks to the bizarre circumstances in which she and Alec had met, they were good friends with Sir Rod Stewart, who had been their surprise headliner. But it had been a gargantuan effort to get it approved through a long and complicated permits process, with no precedents to refer to. Leslie's threats put more than one of those permits at risk.

'If Leslie could somehow prove ownership of those strips of land that border the two sides of Festival Field, our acreage vs attendees statistics would no longer stand up, and we'd have to reduce the number of people at GMF. That's bad enough, but if he went ahead and took those trees down, legally or not, we'd be scuppered, because they provide noise reduction *and* protect the Dark Skies Area from light pollution. If they're gone, for any reason, we lose a key sound and light barrier that got us the go-ahead in the first place.'

'Gotcha,' Sandy said. 'Sorry Ally, you're a victim of your own success on this one, that you're the only one that really knows this thing. And you do know it inside-out.'

'Well, it's not getting me very far at the moment. As you said, how do we prove a negative?' Ally wondered, sipping her tea.

'Well, my father never mentioned anything to me about this – very convenient for Leslie – "gentleman's agreement". But in the scheme of things, compared to the size of the estate, it's not *that* big a deal, so maybe he forgot, and no one thought to record it.'

Sandy sipped his tea too. Then: 'Hang on. All those red cases there just caught my eye. Do you know what they are?'

A few banks of the towering library shelves were colour-blocked crimson with stacks of leather attaché cases. They were all identical in shape and size, though in the slant of the light, Ally could see subtle differences in the shades of red, signifying handmade quality. They were placed handles out, marked by year with subtle gold stencilling.

'Not a clue, though I can't say they haven't caught my eye. They look like politicians' despatch boxes. But you can't exactly just pull one out for a look. I just could picture them toppling like Jenga on top of me.'

'Oh God, no, don't try that,' Sandy said quickly. 'They belonged to our dear estate manager, Iain Watson. He kept ledgers and notes all his life. He also had terribly endearing delusions of grandeur, and filed them in red despatch boxes, which look exactly like the Queen's – no accident I assure you.

'I've never looked in them – somehow it would have felt like an intrusion, even if I'd had cause. But you have cause now, as well as a degree of separation, so you could go ahead. I'd bet that if a significant deal was "made on a handshake", Watson would not have relied on the handshake – he'd have written it down.'

Sandy put his tea down and went over to the shelves. 'When did Leslie claim this happened? What dates am I looking for?'

'Between 1959 and 1962. He says he knows that because it happened while he was at uni,' Ally replied. She didn't get up to help. She was too comfortable in the deep sofa.

'Well, good news and bad news. This column here ends with 1959 at the bottom. But I'm afraid 1960,' he craned his head upwards, 'must be away...up...there!'

He pointed to the top of the next bank of shelves, practically two storeys high, and only reachable by the elegant but precarious sliding brass ladder.

'I'm afraid with my bad knees, I'm not going up there, and

of course you are forbidden from doing so and putting my grandchildren at risk.'

'Sandy, don't be ridiculous, I would never. Those can wait for Alec if we need them. Feel like getting 1959 out for me though?'

It took some unpacking and re-stacking, then Sandy placed the despatch box on the coffee table in front of Ally.

'I'll leave you to it, but if Glenberry has any deep, dark secrets,' he said, tapping the top of the case three times, 'this is where you'll find them.'

ALLY ENDED her lap of anxious pacing at the window and watched Sandy contentedly riding back and forth across the lawn. It was his favourite estate task, and this was the final cut before the Strawberry Fair, so his straight lines were particularly pristine.

The calm of it all jarred. She found herself reaching for the letter in her pocket.

Just one more time, she told herself, for the third or fourth time.

12 Rose Street,
London,
S.W.16
30 December 1959

Dear Alexander,

It seems foreign to address you so formally after so
many more affectionate notes between us in days gone by.
Can you believe it has been more than eight years since we
ceased such exchanges? I have thought of you often,
wondering how you might react if I were ever to contact
you again.

Now I feel the time has come to do so, and I write with some news you will find momentous: our time together in London, our wonderful romance, produced a son.

My darling Charles is a healthy, handsome boy, newly eight years old. I enclose a recent photograph of him, taken on a visit to Hamley's to see Father Christmas. He has been brought up with the help of my parents, but he is of an age where he is starting to ask questions about his real father. Therefore, I decided it was only fair to both of you that I should write.

I have made enquiries about the journey to Scotland and, if I have remembered the local names correctly, I believe it is possible to travel to your estate by train. I would be willing to do so, to allow you to meet your son and to discuss with you the path ahead for him, and for your place in his life.

I can be reached at the address above, and I look forward to hearing from you soon,

Yours Sincerely,
Elsie Morris

From the desk of Iain Watson, Glenberry
Tuesday 31st March, 1959

In just a few days the waiting will be over: the castle will have its Laird back, and we shall finally learn what lies in wait as regards the new Mrs Alexander Douglas-Lauder, née Amelia Johnson, preferred name, 'Mimi' [sic].

Glenberry has been host to only ghosts and yours truly for too long, and I look forward to it warming up into a home again, but I cannot help but feel a degree of apprehension.

The arrival of the new Mrs Douglas-Lauder has had the effect of making me see the castle through a newcomer's eyes. The old pile has been my companion for so many years that it is like a good friend whose foibles and eccentricities you only notice when introducing them to a new acquaintance. This happened to me last year when a friend came to stay expecting enchanted turrets, but was dreadfully disappointed to find out that even the Victorian additions to Glenberry predate that Queen's penchant for Baronial frippery. Mrs Douglas-Lauder may be expecting Walt Disney's gleaming castle, and will be greeted by Glenberry: grand, stoic and with no pretensions. Worse still if she is expecting all modern conveniences.

I simply have no reason to believe that ~~a Yank~~ an American will have any understanding of what it means to take on a house of this age and its unyielding temperament. The castle will not bend itself to her whims, and if she expects otherwise... well, she will have to adjust those expectations.

Still, best foot forward and all that. Mrs Law and I, aided by her husband whom I recruited as an extra set of hands, have done our best. Walls have had their annual wash of warm water and vinegar, as per the old family method, instead of the repaint they really need. The carpets have been beaten and aired on the Great Lawn, despite the March wind threatening to carry them over the woods to the Leslie Estate. Having the chimney sweep visit has helped deal with the smell of old soot which was beginning to dominate the entrance hall.

The newlyweds' sleeping quarters have already been warming for a few days, to combat the damp. Mrs Law has laundered and pressed the bedding, as well the canopy for the bed: its four posters have been tended by a carpenter, as good as new for another hundred years.

I shall hope that first impressions are made in what we have done, rather than many things we couldn't do.

Subsequently, I will be honest with Mr Douglas-Lauder about the many upkeeps that were neglected in his absence. In fact, I will welcome the opportunity to be frank. Hopefully his own desire to make a home for his new bride will spur him towards an improvements plan, ~~within firm limits, of course,~~ in keeping with tradition and history, of course.

Overall, I am attempting to stay open-minded about the impending Mrs D-L. The photograph Mr D-L sent showed a bright, smiling woman in her thirties. (A relief after some of the much younger companions he's been snapped with in the society pages in the past. An immature novice would have been troublesome.) Mr Alexander speaks of her with genuine affection. He claims she is kind and lively, with a quick mind. I hope that is so. The house has been far too quiet since he left, and activity about the place will do it as much good as a fresh coat of paint.

I am mindful, too, that my first duty is to him: if she brings him happiness, I shall give her every courtesy.

These quiet years have afforded certain freedoms, such as the occasional weekend visit from a friend. With the Laird's return, those will naturally become rarer, but on the other hand I'll be less shackled with being Glenberry's sole occupant and will be able to make more frequent trips up to Glasgow.

And so there remain only the final tasks: checking the over-mantel in the Kite Room, supervising some (small) flower arrangements (which Mrs Law will then rearrange to her satisfaction), and a final dust down of the Grand Hall, so it looks its most welcoming. As I say, best foot forward.

Postscript: Must remove the dead pheasant from the west porch before they arrive. Mrs Law blames the fox, but such a welcome would not do.

2

April 1959, in the area of South-West Scotland not yet known as Mid-June.

Alexander squeezed Mimi's hand as they made a sharp left onto the long driveway. The soaring pines either side of them were already stealing the afternoon light. Mimi wondered if the trees could be described as ancient. Nothing in suburban Long Island was ancient, and certainly nothing in Manhattan, with its lustrous new skyscrapers. London had old stuff, yes, but Mimi craved the feeling, and the reassurance, of permanence. Scotland must be steeped in it, and Alexander's ancestral home of Glenberry Castle, in the Southwest of the country, must surely be positively oozing with romantic ancientness.

Alexander had teased her about how she would adapt to the countryside, as well as what the locals would make of her and her bold It Girl glamour.

'I'm not the city slicker you think I am. My end of Long

Island is very different from the one you know from your summers knocking about the Hamptons.'

'Well, you had embraced an urbanite air by the time I met you in London.'

'Oh honey, I'm bluffing lots of the time. But I'm sure I'll do just fine at Glenberry. I just can't wait to set eyes on it for the first time.'

'I know you're going to be perfectly fine too. And you won't be disappointed in the old homestead, I promise.'

THE JOURNEY HAD TAKEN two days and everything had surpassed her expectations so far.

The view from the London to Glasgow train had been captivating: from the smog of the city, through dense suburbs, and then further out, to where signs of human settlement gradually thinned out among the patchwork fields and hedgerows. As they reached the Lake District, the vistas became more sweeping and quietly romantic and Mimi nudged Alexander with an excited smile.

'You ain't seen nothing yet, doll,' he said, with a playful attempt at her own accent.

Sure enough, her delight turned to awe, when at the border, the land suddenly unfurled into dramatic hills and windswept moorlands. The sky dropped lower, but stretched wider, a washed-out pewter, that gave everything the brooding intrigue of *The 39 Steps*.

Alexander sensed her wonder and squeezed her hand. Mimi was too overwhelmed to speak. She squeezed back, then turned to him, tears welling in her eyes.

'Told you you'd love it,' he whispered.

When they reached Glasgow Central Station, she marvelled at its, surprisingly beautiful, immense glass-and-iron roof. The bustle reassured her that a taste of city life was only a train ride away from Glenberry, as she admired impeccably dressed office workers, and shop-girls rushing for their trains, in far-from-sensible shoes: women after her own heart.

They had dinner at Rogano, which had the Art Deco sophistication of a transatlantic liner, then drinks at the champagne bar of the Central Hotel, where they were spending the night. They chatted to the barman, though Alexander sometimes had to translate his heavy accent for Mimi. He boasted that the first ever long-distance television signals had been sent to the hotel by John Logie Baird, long before his time of course. Laurel and Hardy had stayed there, also before his time, but he had met Gene Kelly, and made him a Tom Collins cocktail, when he was in Glasgow promoting *Singin' in the Rain*.

'No way!' Mimi said smacking him on the arm, the champagne making her familiar. 'My husband met him at the New York movie premier!'

'Is that so?' the barman asked Alexander.

'If you think that's a coincidence, wait until you hear the rest of the story,' Alexander nodded to Mimi, who was about to continue anyway.

'The thing is, I still lived on Long Island then, and some girlfriends and I got the train into the City, to wait outside Radio City Music Hall to try to get a glimpse of him and Debbie Reynolds. We did see him leaving, and the chap that he was walking out with – and chatting away quite the thing – was none other than Alexander. Gene Kelly had bummed a cigarette off him outside the restrooms.'

'Nae way, yer pullin' ma leg.'

'What?' Mimi asked.

'He thinks you're kidding him on, darling,' Alexander translated.

'Is that how yous met then?' the barman asked.

'No! That's what's so amazing – we met much later, in London. I mentioned that I'd once seen Gene Kelly in the flesh,

Alexander one-upped me, and we figured out we had been ships that passed in the night.'

Mimi had gone to bed tipsy and happy, brimming with anticipation. She wondered why Alexander had felt the need to move all the way to London to find sophistication, since Glasgow seemed to have plenty of it.

The train to Glenberry this morning brought them West, then South, and again Mimi just stared out the window, enjoying the scenery and pointing things out to Alexander.

'Who'd have thought a wee lassie from Long Island would end up here, eh?' he teased.

Wow. As their car eased through two enormous stone pillars, Mimi caught her first glimpse of her new home on the left. She gave a small gasp and turned to her husband, her jaw still dropped, and Alexander grinned back. It was a dream. Mimi's brain couldn't comprehend the scale: was the arched stone entrance way with heavy double doors twenty feet tall, or forty? Same for the symmetrical run of elegant leaded windows on the upper floor: if someone was standing in the window for scale, would they take up half the height, or just a third? She could only just see the ramparts atop the beautiful facade by craning her neck and pressing the side of her face against the car window.

'Ready?' Alexander asked, tapping her thigh and gesturing to the welcome line-up. Mimi smiled, feeling wave of warm familiarity, because Alexander had anticipated and described the scene before them to a tee.

At the foot of the stone steps to the giant front doors, stood a man in his fifties in a tweed suit, that Mimi knew must be Iain Watson. Beside him was a stout lady, who must be Mrs Law, the cook, less because of her uniform, more that she looked like a cook from a picture book. Lastly a young woman in a maid's uniform, her face pale and frozen with nerves, who must be the 'new girl'.

Alexander gave Mimi one hurried last note: 'It would be very kind of you to act impressed, my darling. Watson will be squirming in embarrassment at the paltry number of staff in the greeting party. It's not good for his ego that times have changed and he manages so few people.'

'Honey, there's no acting required. I'm absolutely bowled over by this place already,' Mimi assured.

Alexander introduced Mimi to Watson first. She shook his hand then handed him one of three immaculately wrapped turquoise packages, which the lovely girl at Fortnum's had adorned with a small tartan ribbon and sprig of heather.

'It's only small. Alexander tells me it would be described as just a "wee minding". He's been trying to introduce me to Scottish phrases – I hope you'll bear with me as I'm trying them out.'

'Perfectly put, Mrs Douglas-Lauder,' Watson replied. 'There was no need, of course, but a wee minding is very thoughtful of you, thank you. May I introduce you to Mrs Law? And this is our new girl, Hattie.'

For some reason, in saying, 'Pleased to meet you, Hattie,' Mimi mimicked the way Watson pronounced the name: with sharp British t's, *Hat-tie*, as opposed to the soft t's of her own accent, *Haddie.* She heard a soft chuckle from Alexander behind her.

'I'll let you do the honours, Mr Douglas-Lauder,' Watson gestured towards the entrance. 'I'll start bringing your luggage in.'

'Thanks Watson. After you, darling.' Alexander in turn gestured towards the steps.

Mimi held her breath, ascended the stairs, and took her first steps into Glenberry Castle, her marital home.

A chill crept over her shoulders. Apparently, the castle itself hadn't been notified about the warm welcome. Outside was still bright, but all warmth and light from the sun disappeared as she entered the cavernous hallway.

Her eyes gradually adjusted to the indoor light, or lack of it. On the walls she made out intricate arrangements of old weaponry, with cold steel swords fanned out in decorative circles, and sharp, parallel rows of bayonets and daggers. They were interspersed with pictures of horses in the unearthly flying-gallop style of earlier centuries, and in a watchful row above it all were stags' heads, their glossy black eyes fixed on their new mistress with a sinister wariness.

Whoever had overseen the decor, clearly disagreed with Coco Chanel's 'less is more'.

With every step that echoed across the cold, tiled floor, Mimi's heart sank. All buoyancy left her, and something name-less and heavy settled in her chest. She was glad that Alexander was behind her exchanging pleasantries with Mrs Law; she knew her face was betraying her.

A wide staircase loomed up in front of her, the worn carpet runner too narrow to soften the hard grey stone, if that had been the intent. It split into two at halfway, each side leading up to a gallery that wrapped three sides of the upper hallway high above her. She was beginning to grasp the scale that she couldn't from the car; it unnerved her, made her feel tiny. Swallowed up. Lost.

The windows behind her, high above the front door, stretched several storeys upward. How could such vast windows be letting in so little light? Why was everything so dark and austere? The cold floor, the wood panelling, even the black backgrounds of the stern portraits she could just make out along the upper gallery – another grim stroke of décor genius – all seemed to swallow what little daylight there was.

Alexander's bright voice punctured the gloom. 'Mimi – come back here! I forgot to carry you over the threshold in all our excitement.'

Mimi took a split second to plaster a wide smile on her face before she turned around and walked back to the black, backlit figure that was Alexander, his tall lean frame dwarfed in the massive doorway. He scooped her up, carried her into the centre point, marked by a mosaic rose, and twirled her around twice, before putting her down and wrapping her in his arms.

'Welcome home, my darling. I knew you'd love it here,' he said.

Mimi just squeezed him tighter, saying nothing, her head held tight against his chest.

'Are you ready for the tour?' he asked.

'Actually, could I freshen up a bit first?'

'Of course.'

Alexander turned to Watson who had stacked their suitcases just inside the door. 'Give me a couple of those Watson, I may as well take them up while I show Mrs Douglas-Lauder to her room.'

Watson tried to protest, but Alexander picked up two pieces and said, 'We've talked about this Watson. I'm all for rolling my sleeves up now that I'm back. I wouldn't want to be waited on hand and foot, even if we could afford the staff to make that possible.'

'Can I at least take Mrs Douglas-Lauder's coat and hat?' Watson asked.

'No!' Mimi answered a little too quickly. Take her coat? It was only draped over her shoulders, but she fully intended to put it on properly, *and* button it up. She was freezing. As for her fur hat, she might never take it off.

'No, thank you, Watson, I'm all right for now, but that's very kind of you. I'm very glad to be here and to finally meet you all, but I think I need to put my feet up before the grand tour.'

Preferably under the blankets. Would it be rude to ask for a hot water bottle?

3

—————

Ally slowly gathered her detritus from the stately oak desk where she had settled to get her bearings among the contents of Watson's despatch box. The library had been his office, so she was probably going through his meticulous records in the same spot that he'd, well, meticulously recorded them. As well as boring estate stuff though, there were journals penned in beautiful cursive. Watson was formal, even in his journals, but they did seem to give some human insight.

Pushing back her chair, she placed her hands on the scratched and divotted desktop to ease herself up. Elsie Morris's letter was tucked safely back in her dress pocket and she was going to take the despatch box back to the apartment with her.

As she was turning off the reading lamp, Susan phoned, which was the accepted way of reaching each other in their rambling abode. Even though it was just on their regular phones, in a joke that had stuck, Sandy referred to it as their walkie-talkie system, mystifying guests when he'd say, 'radio me later', or, 'you can catch me on the two-way'.

'I've made that seafood pasta you like and a salad. Are you

feeling up to joining us or would you rather pick up a plate and have it in peace?' her mother-in-law asked.

'Will anyone be offended if I choose the antisocial option?' Ally asked tentatively. Only one of Alec's sisters was home, but even just a dinner for four, small in Glenberry terms, felt taxing.

'Of course not! I thought you might like that, with Alec being away. I still remember what it's like, how tired you are by the end of the day, even though my pregnancies were a long time ago.'

'I know, thanks for understanding.'

'Where are you now?'

'Just leaving the library.'

'I'll do you one better and meet you at your door. I'll not even come in'

'You're an absolute star, thank you so much.'

'See you in five. Over and out.'

Alec and Ally had inherited the private apartment within the castle that had been created for Sandy's mother – Alec's grandmother – Mimi. Mimi was American and found it hard to adjust to the Scottish weather, more specifically, how grey the days and weeks could be. She identified the wing that held Watson's former office as having the best light, with windows to the south and west, and charmed him into flitting to the library. The apartment had its own private direct entrance through a small side door and up some stairs, as well as an internal entrance off one of the castle hallways, which was where Ally met Susan, already waiting with a tray.

'Oh, thanks Susan, but you could just have let yourself in.'

'Only in emergencies, Ally. It's your space, I don't like to intrude. I said I wasn't even coming in, but I'll set this tray down on the coffee table for you. I'm assuming the kitchen is still completely out of bounds?'

'Come in for five minutes and let's look around together

and see what progress Scott the Builder and his team have made today,' Ally said.

'OK, you twisted my arm. I'm excited for you Ally. It'll all be worth the upheaval in the end,' Susan enthused. 'Kite Room for this tray?'

Ally nodded yes and put her stuff down in the same room. The Kite Room was the only room that wasn't being touched in the renovation that she had seen fit to undertake shortly before finding out she was pregnant. Ironically it was the only room that Mimi hadn't redecorated either, so it would remain intact in its Art Deco resplendence. The rest of apartment was all Mimi's sixties-tastic vision, which was great fun if you were visiting, but Ally felt like she was living in a museum. Some of Mimi's choices seemed like a travesty now, like white-washing the almost floor-to-ceiling oak panelling and window architraves, and tearing out the original eight-foot-tall mantle in favour of a comically small gas fireplace.

Thankfully, redecorating it had been mentioned as soon they took the apartment over, but tearing it all out felt like the end of an era for the family. Ally had had a brainwave: through business contacts, she negotiated the apartment as the setting for a shoot, for a photographer who was as prickly as he was talented, with models who were as sullen as they were skinny. Now Mimi's sunshine yellow Formica kitchen, Hollywood-worthy pink bathroom suite, and sleek wood-laminate electric fireplace surround were immortalised in shots that oozed glamour and would have made Mimi very happy. The remuneration had been a bonus and Sandy insisted Ally use it towards the renovation.

Ally and Susan picked up the corners of polythene sheets in the kitchen to inspect Scott the Builder's work underneath.

'Still no top for the island I see,' Susan commented.

'No, apparently I chose the hardest to source dark maple wood there is,' Ally said. 'If I'd known I'd just have chosen something else. I just need this to be done. I thought I could manage with a toaster and air fryer, but it got old, fast.'

'Nah, stick to what you really wanted. I know it seems like an age now, but as I say, it'll be worth it in the long run,' Susan said.

The biggest room in the apartment was a once-Victorian office, now a mid-century living room. They mulled over the shades of Farrow and Ball green that Scott had painted in patches over the whitewashed oak. Ally would rather have stripped back the panelling to the natural grain but that was a weeks-long and toxic job. The fireplace issue remained on the 'to be decided' list, yet another thing it felt like Ally was running out of time on.

'Right, I've earned some time with my feet up too, so I'll leave you to it,' Susan said.

'I'm sure you have. You'll be glad when the Strawberry Fair is over for another year. I looked at the forecast – clear and sunny for Thursday.'

'It always is,' Susan smiled. Ally walked her to the hall.

With her hand on the doorknob, Susan took a deep breath, considering, then seemed to rethink.

'What?' Ally asked. 'That was a mysterious look.'

'It's just that Sandy told me about what happened with Leslie today,' Susan answered.

'Ugh, yup. Just what I needed,' Ally said.

'Sandy and I feel terrible that Leslie is taking all this out on you. I just wanted to say – don't take any of it personally. I had a couple of weird encounters with him years ago, that I didn't even tell Sandy about.'

Susan hesitated again, but Ally gave her a 'well?' look.

'I caught him a couple of times being a bit of a peeping Tom,' Susan said, matter of factly.

'Eew,' Ally recoiled.

'Exactly. It wasn't long after I moved here and at first I

thought I was imagining it. But I mentioned it to Mimi and she drove straight round to his and told him she'd call the police if he trespassed on Glenberry again.'

'Did that work?' Ally asked. 'He's not someone who'd let a woman tell him what to do.'

'Well, I don't know exactly what Mimi said to him, but yes, it seemed to do the trick. Anyway, don't mention it to Sandy or Alec, but I thought I'd tell you. The "Lady of the Manor", as he likes to put it, that he's really angry with is more likely to be me, or Mimi, than you.'

'He was out of his mind this morning, just spewing all sorts. I'm going to try not to think about it and just get on with getting to the bottom of this claim of his.'

'Good for you. Now, I wrapped that pasta in foil, but it won't stay hot forever. Go and put your feet up and put on a rom com.'

Ally felt a pang of guilt. Susan had just shared an old confidence with her, trusting her not to tell Sandy or Alec about it, but Ally herself was privy to a potentially shattering piece of their history – Elsie Morris's letter – that the family knew nothing of. *Or did they?* How was she to know if anyone else had come upon this letter over the years?

No, she thought, no one who had read this letter would simply replace it and move on: it threatened to uproot the whole Douglas-Lauder family tree, which until now had been very clear-cut. Alexander and Mimi had been late to start a family, by the standards of the time, with Mimi well into her thirties, and Alexander ten years older. Sandy was their only child and sole heir to the estate. In the next generation, Alec was the first born and male, so antiquated patriarchal traditions of succession hadn't required to be challenged. (Though Alec regularly joked about relinquishing his primogeniture rights – one of his sisters just had to say the word.)

It was all very neat and uncomplicated.

But what would happen if an illegitimate child, an older, a half-brother to Sandy, was suddenly part of the story? Ally would Google for the inheritance outcome later, but it would hardly resolve all the moral questions swirling around her brain.

Her purpose in the library that day had been to find historical evidence of who owned a small section of the estate, and she had ended up discovering a threat to the whole blooming lot.

Elsie Morris's letter was dated late in the year, which meant that anything Watson had gone on to record would be filed in subsequent despatch boxes, still shelved high in the gods of the library. She would have to wait for Alec to return from his business trip to retrieve them. If the 1959 case was anything to go by, it would be thorough: orders, bills, correspondence, and Watson's journal, written in his fine, fastidious hand.

Ally tidied her dinner tray, which she would return to Susan's kitchen first thing in the morning – she looked forward to the simple luxury of having her own kitchen sink again. She retrieved Watson's journal and made herself comfortable for what she promised herself would only be a short browse before she retired to bed.

She quickly ascertained that 1959 was, in fact, the year Mimi moved to the castle: early spring, according to Watson's log. In the weeks beforehand, he recorded the anticipation and preparations for the return of the Laird and his new American bride. As she read, Ally was quite shocked at how snobbish and superior he was, to the point of disdain. Poor Mimi. Ally wondered whether his lofty elitism had been apparent to her too. What kind of reception had she received when she arrived?

~

From the desk of Iain Watson, Glenberry
Saturday 4th April, 1959

I find myself banished to my quarters for the second time today.

The big day dawned and tensions were running high. Mr D-L requested that I leave his motorcar at the station, with the keys in the glove compartment, rather than meet them there. This had the consequence, however, that he had no reason to commit to an exact train time down from Glasgow.

I resolved this issue by telephoning the manager of Central Hotel to request that he telephone me back when the D-Ls were checked out and on their way. When I received said call and informed Mrs Law, she snapped at me: as if I'd had any influence over their plans.

I retreated to my office to let her marshal the final flurry of activity without my getting underfoot.

At exactly 3pm, I gathered the staff together in our woefully short reception line of three. Changed days indeed. Bad enough that there was no one but myself to bring in their luggage, but Mr D-L even insisted on relaying some of it up to their quarters himself.

I had, of course, a notion of Mrs D-L's appearance from the wedding photograph that he sent (I knew to expect a bottle blond, for example), but she's quite another thing to behold in ~~garish~~ glorious technicolour. I couldn't be sure if the green suit she was wearing was the same one as her bridal attire, but the American looking tailoring was similar, so it may have been. Definitely the same were the mink pill-box hat (which I quickly discerned was in fact musquash), and her diamanté costume jewellery, being a large brooch and wrist cuff, rather old-fashioned in their Art Deco style.

Mrs D-L came bearing gifts, which was kind. Mine was a fancy packet of ginger snaps, my favourite, so I suspect her husband had a hand in them.

They were no sooner in the door, than Mrs D-L requested some time to freshen up, and Mrs Law made it clear I was not welcome in the kitchen as she prepared their first meal at Glenberry.

[Hattie has informed me the Laird has just appeared from his short absence so I must go for now.]

4

Alexander didn't seem to notice that Mimi had slipped her legs under the satin quilt that topped the bed, in an attempt to warm up her feet. She was sitting up, while Alexander was fully reclined, hands behind his head, clearly elated to be home and have Mimi by his side, proud of his new Lady of the Manor. This, at least, gladdened Mimi.

When she met Alexander, he was a happy gadabout and a reluctant Laird.

'You have a castle in the Scottish countryside, but you're down here living in smoky old London?' she had asked soon after they got together.

'Oh, it's not all it's cracked up to be. There's nothing going on up there, London's where it's at. Or Monaco! Let's go to Monaco next summer!'

They grew close, fell in love, and, as happens, their conversations grew deeper as they tried to find out everything about each other, feeling out what their future may hold. The more Mimi prompted Alexander to tell her about his unworldly-sounding upbringing, the more fondly he began to recall things. As time went on, he'd positively light up when he talked about the castle, his late parents, and the stalwart Iain Watson.

Eventually in his stories, he'd reinstate himself, along with Mimi, into Glenberry's future. Telling her about summers swimming in the loch, he said cheekily, 'Maybe I'll be able to talk you into a skinny dip one day.' After a story about hide-and-seek in the walled gardens he mused, 'I'm sure they'll need attention. I must make sure Watson knows that's a part of the estate I want properly looked after. You'll love wandering them, watching the changing seasons.'

Mimi knew Alexander didn't notice the shift himself. She bided her time and waited for him to make the realisation. She was ready to leave London: it had been a blast, but life in Scotland, with this man she loved and cherished, sounded idyllic, and like the peace Alexander needed.

She smiled now at his happy sighs, as he lay on the bed looking up at the upholstered roof. (Roof? Ceiling? Mimi had never been in a four-poster bed, so she wasn't sure of the terminology.) The gadabout was no more, and instead, lying beside her was a contented, dutiful Laird, ready to get to work.

'I must thank you Mimi. I don't know when I'd have got round to coming back, if I didn't have you by my side. It feels good, you know? I'm a bit late to the game, but I'd like to do my dearly missed parents proud. Hell, all these bloody forebears proud.' He laughed and waved his hand towards a portrait over the fireplace, as if Mimi hadn't noticed ancestral eyes on her from all around the room.

'And Watson? I think there's part of you wants to make him proud too.'

'Yes,' he admitted. I feel guilty about how long I've been absent, taking it for granted that he'll just hang around steadfastly sorting things out here – things I don't yet know need sorting. I'm going to make it up to him. I think he and I will make a dream team. I'm ready to work, you know? What? What are you smiling at?'

'You're quite the change from the man I met in the American Bar at the Savoy, not even two years ago.'

'I know, but it feels right. It's time. I was just waiting for you to come along I suppose – I just didn't know it until you did. Talking of champagne, we absolutely must have a toast to your first night in the castle. I'll go and talk to Watson and Mrs Law and see what plans they have made for dinner.' Alexander sat up on the bed and felt around for the shoes he had kicked off.

Mimi caught another long-dead member of the Douglas-Lauder family staring at her from the forest-green walls. She had been relieved to see any paint at all – thankfully the ubiquitous oak panelling was only over and around the fireplace in this room – but wondered at the decision-making behind such a gloomy colour. The room had plenty of windows, but the heavy drapes veiled about half their width, and what felt like almost all of their light.

A small consolation was that the curtains were plain, and not the same busy brocade fabric of the four-poster bed. She could understand the utility of the bed's design, given how draughty the castle was, but could not imagine ever being tempted to draw its curtains closed. Surely it would feel like sleeping in a cave. What a remarkable feat it would be to actually feel claustrophobic in this huge room. She ran her hand over the base of the post next to her, spotting a turn in the wood that would make an ideal point to have the posts sawn off seamlessly, to modernise the bed. What was it? A hundred years old?

'Honey, will we be able to change the decor, to make it feel a little more homey?' she asked, as Alexander laced his shoes.

'Of course! Anything for you. What do you have in mind?'

'Well, for a start, do you have great affection for any of these people keeping their beady eyes on us while we're sleeping? Or doing more fun things that I'd rather do without an audience?'

Alexander looked around and gave a hearty laugh. 'I've never thought about it that way. You're right, let's rehouse them. What do think instead? We could go shopping around the castle; there's artwork everywhere. Some landscapes maybe?'

'Oh.' Mimi's heart sank, thinking of the 'artwork' she'd seen in the castle already. 'I was actually thinking of those beautiful photographic prints at that gallery in Chelsea. There were a few of the Manhattan skyline and a few of the skyscrapers from interesting angles. Remember?'

'Gosh, it's hard to imagine them in here. I'm so used to art from bygone centuries. But if a taste of home makes you happy, my love, then we'll contact the gallery in the week. I can't wait to see Watson's face – I'm not sure he "does" modern. They will look quite striking against that paint colour, though.'

'Well, about that. Don't you think something lighter would really brighten things up? I wouldn't mind putting on my over-alls and climbing a ladder with a paintbrush.' Mimi tried for a charming smile.

'That won't be necessary, of course, but I believe there's a system for walls. We alternate between washing them and painting them, so we'd need to check with Watson when the next painting year is.'

'Wow. I have a lot to learn. Well, maybe in the meantime we could at least whitewash the oak on the fireplace wall there? The dark wood sucks so much light out of the room.'

'Paint over oak? Are you trying to give Watson heart attack?' Alexander laughed, the question too absurd to be taken seri-ously. 'Talking of whom, let me go and figure out what the rest of our day looks like with him.' He stood, gave his clothes a perfunctory smoothing down, and came round to Mimi's side of the bed.

'You are going to be a breath of fresh air around here

darling, but let's ease gently into things. Get your bearings. It's going to take about a week just to show you around once, and another to take you round again, so you really get to know all the nooks and crannies.' He kissed her and bounded out the room cheerfully.

Mimi's smile dropped as soon as the door closed. Alexander's advice was sensible of course, but she really was going to have to lobby for some changes to the interior of the castle. It had appeared like a dream from the motor car and the butterflies in her stomach had danced with bliss. Then, walking through that door, less than an hour ago, everything changed. In an episode of *I Love Lucy*, it was where the music would change, and there would be a close up of Lucille Ball's exaggerated sad-clown mouth, her false eyelashes blinking back tears.

This wasn't a home; it was a museum. A mausoleum for all she knew, given how much they seem to like to keep their ancestors around, and it certainly was as cold as a morgue.

She thought of Alexander, pleased as punch with himself, and snooty old Watson looking at her, the American hick, no doubt expecting her to be giddy at the honour of calling this dusty – no, filthy – old relic, home. And Mrs Law: Why did they need a cook anyway? What if she just wanted to make herself a grilled cheese and canned tomato soup? Would she have to ask permission?

She couldn't help thinking that there was an expectation that she should be deferential to them, grateful to them for deigning to accept her presence here.

Mimi steamed for a moment or two in her own juices, giving the imagined personas she'd conjured for Watson and Mrs Law a piece of her mind. Sure, she'd never lived in a castle, but there was a lot to be said for her parents' home in New York: less than a decade old, with efficient underfloor heating that warmed the house at a flick of a switch, and a TV in the wall instead of a fireplace. Her flat in London hadn't been too shabby either. For a start, she had treated herself to a continental quilt from Selfridges instead of the scratchy old blankets layered up on this bed.

Mimi sat up, swung her feet onto the floor, and braced herself with her hands pressing down on the mattress. She closed her eyes and took a deep breath, her brows furrowed. Then, as she let it out, her face softened and she gave a small laugh.

Well, that was a relief: the disappointment and adrenaline let-down were making her annoyed and indignant, not upset.

It had been an emotional and tiring few days, so she knew if she cried, it would be hard to stop. Mentally giving her Glenberry housemates a dose of her umbrage was far preferable to becoming a sobbing mess.

She should stop before her ire turned on poor Hattie too.

Deep down, she knew that everything would work out fine. She wouldn't have come here otherwise. Contrary to some common first impressions about her, born of how much she'd made of life already, Mimi was adventurous but not flighty; brave, not foolhardy; considered, not impulsive. She had married Alexander and agreed to come to Scotland with her head firmly screwed on, knowing it would be a long learning and settling-in curve. Her nerves had simply got the better of her for a moment.

Alexander adored her and would do anything for her, and she knew together they could find a way to turn Glenberry into their home, hopefully for their children too.

With a little shake of her head and a roll of her shoulders to reset, she stood up.

'Right, let's see what we've got here,' she said out loud.

She may as well take the opportunity, while she was alone, to scout the room for a secure spot for her cherished possessions. With the verging-on-haunted air of the place, she wouldn't have been surprised if pulling one of the heavy tassels around the bed would reveal a clever sliding panel in the wall, and she could easily imagine one of the scary portraits concealing an old safe. Running her fingers along the apparently sacred oak mantel, she noted the ornate woodwork, prime for disguising a hidden compartment. Or the window seat would have plenty of space if it was hollow. She checked and was correct: it was hinged. She lifted it to find it filled with more scratchy blankets.

That was the problem. Any of these movie-worthy hiding spots she was imagining, if they existed, would be known to others, almost definitely Watson, with his intimate knowledge of all things Glenberry.

Mimi would have to come up with a completely new hiding place. Instead of stumbling upon a disused compartment underneath a trap door, she would have make one herself, maybe by loosening a floorboard under a rug, as she had in her London flat. Finding the perfect place would take time. She had to get to know the rhythms of the house, who came and went, which rooms were truly private, which corridors saw more traffic than their dusty corners suggested. Alexander had said it would take a full week to show her all the nooks and crannies, so she would wait, learn, and in time choose somewhere *properly* safe. Until then, her current ploy of hiding her secrets in plain sight would do.

Mimi's feet were cold again. Why on earth had she remained in stocking soles when she got up from the bed? She ought to go and find her fellow castle-dwellers. Smoothing her skirt, she put on her shoes and a smile. She wondered how long it would take her to find where Alexander was, in her sprawling new digs. Not too arduous a problem for a wee lassie from Long Island to have, all things considered.

5
———

Ally was just getting to the interesting bit, Mimi's arrival at the castle, when she heard the door open.

Then, 'Ally? It's Louise. Mum sent me up to pick up your dishes.'

Oh no. Alec's youngest sister. There was no way Ally was going to get away with a quick hand-off at the door. Louise was sweet and of the three sisters, had most embraced Ally as another older sister, but she was...a lot.

'Hi Louise, how are you? I was just thinking about heading to bed,' Ally said.

'Already? It's so early!' Louise had a hair dryer in one hand and a glass of wine in the other, which she raised, saying, 'Good job I didn't bring the bottle then! I was going to, but thought that would be a bit off, since you can't indulge. How have you been today? Dad was telling us all about your morning, and my big brother getting himself in quite a state about it. I'll just put your hairdryer back in your bedroom – long story – and then can I check on the kitchen progress? How is it coming along?'

Ally didn't get up as Louise breezed through. Her inspection of the kitchen was cursory, and she returned and flopped on the couch, lifting her glass in a little 'cheers' before taking a generous slug.

'Where's Jack?' Ally asked. Jack was technically Louise's wire-haired Jack Russell, but he mostly lived at the castle, preferring Susan and Sandy's company to being alone in Louise's flat in Glasgow all day while she was at work.

'He's in my bad books – part of the long story. Gosh, all of a sudden you're quite big, aren't you?' Louise said, pointing at Ally's bump.

'Thanks Louise!' Ally replied, wide-eyed.

'Sorry, but what can you expect with twins I suppose,' Louise said.

Alec's sisters were all very good looking. Blond hair and blue eyes ran through each side of the family, so they were all bound to inherit both. Louise was a primary school teacher and taught the P1s, and Ally could only imagine how gaga the wee ones must be about her, so pretty and bright. When the school year ended, she said some of them cried when she had to explain that she wasn't going to be their teacher next year. Louise and Jack usually spent a chunk of the summer holidays at Glenberry.

Ally's favourite book was *Little Women*, specifically her prized copy of a 1950s British edition which stayed true to the original publication, *Little Women, Part 1*. (The one that ends happily at Christmas, Father safely home from war, and, crucially, Beth doesn't die.) She couldn't help compare the Douglas-Lauder sisters to the March sisters, and Louise was pure Amy. Louisa May Alcott seemed to have a good take on birth order theory before it was popular: Louise, like Amy, lived up to every youngest-child stereotype. The other siblings teased her for 'getting away with murder' in her more lenient upbringing as the fourth child. She wasn't attention-seeking, but she certainly thrived in the spotlight. People flocked to Louise's charm and brightness, so she had a large circle of friends, who also seemed fun and interesting.

There hadn't been any boyfriends since Ally came on the scene, Louise just seemed to be enjoying the tail end of her twenties, in no rush to meet someone. The older two sisters weren't married yet, but they had serious partners, and unbeknownst to them, there was a family book running on when the engagements would happen, the prize a speech at the wedding. There was no family book on Louise settling down, but Ally wouldn't be betting on soon if there was. Footloose and fancy-free suited Louise.

Something was up with her sister-in-law this evening. 'What you got brewing away there Louise? You've got ants in your pants, even for you. What's up?'

'Is it that obvious? OK, I have to tell you – I'm in love.'

Well, that took a turn. 'What? When did this happen? With whom?' Ally asked.

'Oh God, you must have noticed him too. Scott? Your builder? Bloody hell Ally, he's a dream. The dark hair, the tartan shirts, the muscles, the pencil behind his ear...the tool-belt?! He's out of central casting!'

Ally laughed. Scott was indeed very attractive.

'I'm in bits when I see him,' Louise went on. 'You know me, I'm never lost for words, but I'm tongue-tied around him.'

'You've only been back at the castle for a couple of days! How many times have you come across him?'

'Three. And all of them have been mortifying. Mortifying for me, not him. One of them involved your hairdryer – and Jack.'

'Right, well, this is fascinating. Do tell.' Ally made herself comfortable.

'OK, so the first time was the morning after I arrived,' Louise began. 'You know my crazy friend Poppy?'

'A bit hippy dippy, but lovely all the same? Yes, I remember her,' Ally replied.

'Well, she's got me into grounding. It's where you connect with the earth's surface to absorb its negative charge. It's supposed to help you sleep, reduce inflammation, and all sorts of things like that. Poppy swears by it, so I thought I'd give it a go over the summer – I was too self-conscious to do out in the little back garden of my flat with all the neighbours looking on. So I made a wee resolution to do it first thing every morning while I'm here.'

'Uh oh,' Ally said.

'Yes exactly, "uh oh". But usually no one's out and about here at half past seven in the morning, so I thought I'd be safe.'

'Oh dear, Scott likes to start early so he can finish and get out my way promptly in the evenings,' Ally noted.

'So I discovered! I was barely awake, but I got up, put on my ratty pink towelling dressing gown and my Ugg slippers.' She paused and held up a *'wait'* finger, because Ally could see where this was going and was cringing, but laughing, already. 'I *left my retainer in*, and, to multi-task, donned some gold under-eye masks.'

'So you were quite the picture then,' Ally laughed.

'Yup! I decided the Great Lawn would be good for a wee pad around, so wore my Uggs to get over the gravel, then left them at the top of the slope down to the grass.'

'And that's the first glimpse that hunky Scott got of you? Tramping around like that?' Ally was properly laughing now. Louise was trying not to, but failing.

'No Ally, if you can believe it, it gets even worse,' she whined.

'Oh no, Louise, I can't! How can it have got worse?' Ally laughed.

'I remembered that old wives' tale about washing your face in the morning dew.'

'Isn't that just on the first of May?'

Louise shot Ally a 'hardly-the-point' look, and continued.

'So I was bending over and scooping droplets and smoothing them across my face, carefully avoiding the eye pads, when I heard a van on the gravel. I was smack bang in the centre of the Great Lawn, so I couldn't even quickly scurry inside. I stood back up and started walking back as if this must look perfectly normal to whomever was in the van, and of course, then he appeared. A vision. As handsome as a TV makeover show host.'

'Oh Louise, this could only happen to you!'

'That's what I was thinking! He waved and said good morning and flashed me a smile, but of course I could only wave back –'

'Because you'd left your retainer in!' Ally finished for her. 'Well, it's an amusing meet-cute story, maybe?'

'Not for me!' Louise said, wide-eyed.

'True. OK, what's the next one then? The second encounter with him?' Ally asked.

'Well, it was nice and sunny yesterday, right? So my mum and I were sitting having a cup of tea on the back patio, and I kind of turned my back to her to face the sun. I was sitting there with my eyes closed and my hair was hanging over the back of the chair and my mum just started braiding it.'

Ally could picture it. She'd seen Susan absentmindedly play with Louise's hair before.

'It's nice and relaxing. But Scott and his workmate appeared with their own cuppas just as mum was finishing. I had a French braid on one side of my head, and a regular one on the other side.'

'That's not so bad, surely,' Ally said, trying to console her.

'Ally, I must look like the "special" sister!' She made the air quotes. 'He probably imagines I'm mostly confined to the attic, like Mr Rochester's poor wife. The sight that greeted him in the morning, then someone in their late twenties having her mum do her hair?'

Ally bit her lip, trying to conceal a laugh.

'See! You know that's a real possibility,' Louise said.

'OK, my cheeks hurt from laughing, the babies must wonder what on earth is going on,' Ally said smoothing her dress over her belly. 'But there's a third time? One that involves my hairdryer?'

'Yes. So...I wanted to make sure the next time I saw him I was looking my best. I did my hair and make-up – not too much, just easy, breezy, glowy, the way I go to work, as opposed to a night out. I put on jeans and a graphic t-shirt and, to my regret now, thought that bringing Jack along would add some meet-cute magic.

'I knew you were in the library, so I just came in. Jack and I were looking all adorable and walked through, but it was just the other guy in the kitchen. He started to tell me where Scott was, but I got flustered and said I wasn't looking for Scott, I was just here to borrow a hairdryer and headed to your bedroom. While I was unplugging your hairdryer, Jack nosed the bathroom door open –'

'Oh no. Oh no, please no,' Ally said, with her head in her hands, bracing for what was coming next.

'Oh yes. Oh yes, I'm afraid so. I suppose Scott shut the door from the hallway, but didn't realise the other one from your bedroom wasn't quite closed tight.'

'Was he sitting or standing?' Ally asked, hands now either side of her face in horror.

'Oh God, standing. He'd just...well, he'd just finished, and was, well, zipping up. But we both just stood there like rabbits caught in headlights, while Jack ran back to me, the wee troublemaking coward.'

'Did you say anything?' Ally asked.

'I think I spluttered an apology while I gathered up Jack and the hairdryer. Oh my God Ally. Can you believe it?' Louise asked, with a helpless chuckle.

'Not really, no. It explains why he didn't drop me a text at the end of the day. He usually does, and sometimes I'll pop along so that he can talk me through where they're at. He's probably too mortified about flashing you.'

'Don't make it worse than it is – he most definitely did not flash me. Thank God.'

They dissolved into a few more breathless laughs – and expletives – to round off Louise's tale.

'Well, that was my day, how was the rest of yours? Bet you can't top that,' Louise asked.

'I certainly cannot. Very dull and unremarkable compared to that,' Ally fibbed. They chatted a little longer as Louise finished her wine, Ally yawning more and more.

'Right missus, I need to let you get to bed. We can discuss our plan of attack for recovering from my series of unfortunate events with Scott another day,' Louise said, getting up and blowing Ally a kiss.

As Ally gathered the energy to get off the couch and go to bed, she rolled her eyes. The tray Louise was sent to retrieve was still on the coffee table, alongside Louise's fingerprinted wine glass.

∼

From the desk of Iain Watson, Glenberry
Saturday 4th April, 1959 (contd.)

The day has been long and exacting, yet it is a relief to be fully occupied once more.

I have mentioned in previous entries Mrs Law's prolonged deliberations, and consultations, over the choice of a wedding gift for Mrs D-L. The big moment arrived before dinner. To say it was well-received is a quite the understatement: Mrs D-L was reduced to tears!

I was quite ill at ease and made myself scarce, and when I returned, it transpired that the D-Ls would dine in the kitchen. So much for the perfectly laid out dining room I had painstakingly coached Hattie through.

The Laird looks well, though his hair is a little too long, so I shall put in a call to the barber first thing tomorrow. Marriage, and hopefully a gentler lifestyle, suit him well. He looks rested and happy, which in itself is plenty reason for all to give Mrs D-L our full respect. ~~and try not to judge a book by its cover.~~

Postscript: Incidentally, there was a considerable period of hat-wearing indoors before it was finally doffed.

6

———————

Mimi found Alexander in the kitchen, sitting at the long pine table with Watson, while Mrs Law busied preparing dinner. Hattie was in an adjoining room, which was lined with cabinetry, assembling tableware. The two men stood as Mimi entered.

'Oh please, sit, no need to stand to attention for me,' Mimi said.

'You can't teach an old dog new tricks I'm afraid, eh, Watson? I'm afraid you'll have to put up with his impeccable manners and faultless chivalry. You should have seen the cajoling it took to be allowed into the kitchen and have him sit down at the kitchen table with me.'

'Well, is it OK if we all sit now?' Mimi asked.

Both men gestured *after you*, waiting until Mimi sat before they did.

'What are we talking about?' she asked.

'The important business of dinner. Can you fill my wife in on the feast you have in store for us please Mrs Law?' Alexander requested.

'I certainly can. We have Cullen Skink soup to start, which

I'm afraid is what you can smell. It does tend to overwhelm the kitchen, but your husband insisted on sitting in here and getting under my feet, so I apologise on his behalf,' Mrs Law said.

'You know you're going to love me being back, Mrs Law,' Alexander said with a cheeky smile. 'And for the main?'

'Steak pie and potatoes. I hope it is still your favourite and that your head hasn't been turned on your travels abroad,' she replied.

'I haven't had steak pie since the last time you made me it. I didn't want to be unfaithful to you,' Alexander said.

'And for dessert, rice pudding. I'd have loved to make you cranachan, but, of course, it's a little too early for the raspberries.' Mrs Law explained this directly to Mimi, who was touched that she assumed she would know, a) whatever dish she had just named, and b) when the raspberry season fell in the Southwest of Scotland.

Mimi replied with a polite smile. 'Well, I'd love to say it all sounds delicious, but I have to be completely honest, I've already forgotten the name of the first course you mentioned. I'm so sorry. I'm quickly realising I have a lot to learn about Scotland, even the diet.'

'All you need to know is that Mrs Law is an excellent cook, and you're going to devour it all with relish,' Alexander said. 'And I happen to remember she's a handy seamstress too, if you need her to let out your clothes after a few weeks of her irresistible fare. My goodness, Mrs Law, when summer comes, never mind the Cranachan, I'll have your rhubarb crumble and custard for breakfast, lunch, and dinner please! Wait until you see our rhubarb patch Mimi – you're so dainty, you'll be able to hide under just one of the leaves.'

Mimi was enjoying seeing Alexander in his element. In person, she could see what she had never quite grasped from his descriptions alone. She would happily admit to having the

American Dream upbringing: her parents owned their own home, with a white picket fence in a neat post-war development, and her dad wore a white collar to work. But their echelon did not involve staff, unless the cheerful milkman counted. For Alexander, however, it was ingrained. He talked about Mrs Law, Watson, and other members of staff now gone, as often as he talked about his parents.

'They are a bit like family,' he had tried to explain.

'Family who literally serve you?' she had laughed.

The blatant inequities made it hard for her to understand how the relationship could ever be less than formal, never mind verging on cozy, and she had suspected Alexander might be romanticising things. Now though, she could see he hadn't exaggerated. Mrs Law had a maternal role which she was happy to play, as Alexander teased her with excessive praise. She and her husband lived in a small house in the village of Berry, owned by the Douglas-Lauders, and with their children grown, her stipend had allowed her to avoid other work during Alexander's absence. Mimi could see she was delighted to be back at the castle; this was her element too.

If Mrs Law was the mom figure, what did that make Watson? A stern older brother perhaps.

Alexander had tried to explain that too: 'Watson has worked for us, well, forever. I've no idea exactly how long. He never married, and I've never been aware of any romantic relationship. He always has a look of mild disapproval on his face. Mind you, perhaps that's only because I've done so many things worthy of that disapproval over the years,' Alexander had chuckled. 'He's certainly very strait-laced, but he has a heart of gold, as they say. And if anyone can crack his veneer, it's you, my peppy little Yankee bride.'

Mimi wasn't so sure. Watson seemed like a tough nut to crack.

She caught him eyeing her hat, still firmly on her head. She had in fact defrosted a little in the warmth of Mrs Law's kitchen. It wasn't just the heat from the stove: the wood tones here were softer, the sturdy old pine table they sat around was welcoming, and the mantle over the range was comforting instead of austere.

'Gee, I hadn't realised I'm still wearing my hat, how ridiculous,' she said, taking it off and gently patting her hair back into place. 'Actually, maybe I'll take it upstairs.' She hated to think how long the pungency of that soup, whatever it was called, would linger in the musquash.

'Don't get up darling, I'll hang it on the hat stand on my way to get the champagne. Watson has it chilling in the drawing room, but I'd rather have a toast in here,' Alexander said, rising. 'Just this once Watson,' he added, correctly predicting that Watson was getting ready to protest the inappropriateness.

When he left, Mimi spoke up before a silence could settle.

'I must say again how nice it is to meet you all. Alexander has spoken so highly of you. It was very kind of you to meet us at the door.'

'Our pleasure Mrs Douglas-Lauder,' Watson replied. 'I hope you found everything satisfactory in your quarters. As you know, Hattie is new at Glenberry, and relatively new to housekeeping, so please do let us know if there's anything we could be doing better.'

Hattie was close enough to have heard her name, so Mimi replied deliberately in a volume that would carry to the little side room. 'Everything was perfect, thank you so much. I could have bounced a dime off the bed it was so well made. And my new slippers you laid out by the bed look divine. Whatever made you think of that?'

'You'll find them useful for trips to the amenities, especially during the night. We also placed an electric torch by your bed, for the same convenience. When the castle was electrified, the decision around the number of sconces required in hallways erred on scant.'

Alexander had warned Mimi of the proud Scottish tradition, some might say affliction, of frugality. He tried to explain that 'enough' was, by definition, excessive.

'The flashlight? I wondered what that was for.' This was a fib. She had figured out the flashlight's purpose as soon as Alexander had said, 'You will not be disappointed in our bathroom, it's just along here.' Which turned out to be quite a trek from their bedroom and past the rogues' gallery that was spooky enough in daylight.

Alexander clinked back into the room with a champagne bucket and glasses. 'Hattie, please leave your labours for now and join us for a toast,' he said, as he passed the entranceway to where she'd been quietly sequestered.

Mimi saw Watson flinching, which again Alexander seemed to anticipate.

'As I say, this is a special occasion. I won't make a habit of getting in your way, Mrs Law, nor of forcing any levity upon you, Watson. However, let's acknowledge that this household is a long way from the olden days of 'Upstairs/Downstairs'. The five of us can't rattle around the castle, avoiding eye-contact, pretending it's 1909, not 1959.'

Alexander had been filling glasses as he spoke, and now he distributed them. 'Tonight, I'd like you to welcome my beautiful bride to her new home.'

He raised his glass in Mimi's direction, then continued. 'Hattie we're glad to have you in the Glenberry nest, and Mrs Law, I'm eternally grateful that you agreed to return to it. Finally, an overdue but heartfelt thanks to my friend and rock, Iain Watson, for being here when I was not. But I'm back now, an amazing woman by my side, ready to achieve great things together. Cheers!'

Mrs Law and Hattie didn't linger for long. Hattie looked mortified to have been included in the first place and Mrs Law had to get back to her post at her stove. The conversation was mostly between the men, which didn't offend Mimi, it was only to be expected, so she sat quietly, taking things in.

Eventually, the conclusion of dinner preparation was signalled by Mrs Law removing the tea towel that had been hanging over her shoulder and folding it into perfect quarters.

'Mrs Douglas-Lauder? Could I trouble you to join me in the butler's pantry?' she asked.

Mimi was caught off guard and didn't even know which offshoot of the kitchen was the butler's pantry, until Mrs Law dismissed Hattie from it.

Like everything else in the castle, the butler's pantry was substantial. Her parents' whole kitchen, her mother's gleaming pride-and-joy, could fit inside it. A long, high table centred the room, and Mimi supposed it was a landing station for items taken down from the surrounding cabinets. At present, however, it housed a very large package.

'Mrs Douglas-Lauder, the staff, former staff, and many of Glenberry's local purveyors, wanted to let you know how happy we are to have you here, and that we hope you and Mr Douglas-Lauder enjoy many years of health and happiness together.' She gestured at the giant oblong box, wrapped roughly in flimsy silver paper covered in bells and horseshoes.

'You're kidding? You got me a gift? Why?' Mimi was shocked.

'It's a wedding present.'

'But we didn't even have a proper wedding.'

'That's no reason for us not to buy you a gift.'

'Really? I'm so confused. Of course I'm very touched, but confused. Who did you say it's from?' Mimi felt Alexander's hand on her shoulder.

'Mrs Law, what have you done? This is too kind,' he said.

'I was just explaining that it's from all of us, and people from the villages, who wish you well. There's a card – you'll recognise the names, even if you are a little rusty on who's who.'

'Well, I can always ask you to jog my memory if I'm stuck. How kind of everyone.'

Alexander kept repeating how kind it was, but he didn't seem surprised, or rather astonished, as Mimi was. She'd never received a gift so large. Maybe it was some Scottish tradition and there was a giant haggis in there or something.

'Aren't you going to open it, dear?' Alexander gently nudged her in its direction.

Mimi pulled back the paper and lifted the lid of the box.

'I took the liberty of unwrapping a few items from their brown paper and laying them on top, so you'd get the gist. There are more pieces underneath obviously,' Mrs Law explained.

Mimi stared. A coffee pot sat flanked by a milk jug and sugar bowl on one side, and two cups and saucers on the other, and there were apparently, 'more pieces underneath'. It seemed she had just been given a bone china coffee service by the very people who were employed by her husband.

'I'm speechless. It's beautiful.' Her emotions made it hard to get even those words out.

'Oh I'm so glad you like it. We looked through a lot of catalogues to decide. The thing is, there are dozens of china sets in this house, but we thought you might find them a bit old-fashioned. It's called Melrose, one of Wedgwood's latest designs. The tea services only have teapots, as you'd expect, but we thought that our new American mistress might prefer coffee. So we bought you a coffee service instead.'

So, not only was it the largest box Mimi had ever opened, but there had been much thought and care had gone into choosing it too.

Unable to stop herself, she took Mrs Law by surprise by throwing her arms around her. As she'd suspected earlier that day, once the tears came, they didn't stop.

7

———

Ally heard Scott the Builder and his guys letting themselves in to the direct entrance into the apartment. She was up, of course – a fairly sleepless night saw to that – but nowhere near awake enough for a morning catch-up with Scott, so she snuck out through the castle instead. The main door looked down on to the dew-covered Great Lawn and she wondered if Louise had kept her daily 'grounding' ritual or decided not to risk another mortifying encounter with Scott. To save getting damp shoes, she took the path around the massive lawn instead.

She and Alec had been married there, and one day, when the twins were older, the space would easily hold a football match on one side and a game of rounders on the other, or whatever sports they took up.

Yesterday's dabbling in the past, though, had left her stuck there. She left the path and moved through the chilly morning shade of the giant rhododendrons and picked her way over their gnarled roots. That was how her brain felt: tangled, tripping from one problem to the next – Derek Leslie, Elsie Morris – making progress on neither.

All of it churned beneath a worry of her own, that she'd kept mostly to herself – she hadn't been entirely honest with Alec how emphatic her doctor had been that she needed to slow down. Bed rest was a real possibility, he'd warned. A gentle morning walk was fine, but beyond that he wanted her taking it easy, easing off work, and above all, avoiding stress.

She'd assured him she was just tying up a few loose ends on the GMF, ready to hand over the heavy lifting, literally and figuratively, to Susan and Sandy when the Strawberry Fair was behind them. After that, her working day would shrink to running Glenberry's social media: pleasant research, easy posts, casual interactions with followers on Instagram.

To avoid yesterday's route, she took a right along the burn today instead. The loop would lead her past the comically huge rhubarb plants, which always made her smile because she felt like... what? *Alice in Wonderland? Gulliver?*

OK. Focus, Ally. With some deep breaths of lovely Glenberry air, she could clear her head and strategise. What were the priorities? The boundary issue was most pressing. Without clarity on that, GMF might not be able to go ahead. She would just have to keep plodding on through Watson's journal entries, some of which were very dry, bogged down in the minutiae of estate business. But it was some peculiar old agreement she was looking for, so having a pedant like Watson was hopefully a good thing. Perhaps the human-interest element would pick up now that Mimi was on the scene to keep him on his toes.

Her pace quickened as she straightened out the plan in her head. The sooner she got on with it, the closer she'd be to a solution. She was perfectly aware that her logic was inherently flawed: press ahead with all the stressful things, before the doctor ordered her to bed for being too stressed. But she'd be keeping that little contradiction to herself as well.

Ally took the direct route into the apartment, and on the way up the stairs heard Sandy chatting to Scott the Builder.

'Morning Ally,' Sandy greeted her. 'Nice walk this morning? Less eventful than yesterday's, I hope. Was it quite fresh out there so early?'

'A little. I was glad I was wearing this giant, and particularly fetching, fleece of Alec's. I'm sharing his wardrobe more and more these days.'

The men acknowledged her dismay with a small laugh.

'I brought the guys real coffees from my fancy machine as a wee change from that builder's tea they're addicted to. Scott's being catching me up on progress,' Sandy said.

'Good good,' Ally replied looking around at the dusty, half-finished kitchen. She kept doing that, and it kept not changing much.

'Susan's out all day today on Strawberry Fair business, then she's taking the girls from the gift shop out to dinner as a thank you for all their hard work,' Sandy said, explaining why he was loitering around, looking for company, procrastinating his chores. 'What have you got today, then?'

'Just more of the same. Just trying to get to the bottom of this Leslie thing.'

Sandy turned to Scott and asked, 'Ever dealt with Derek Leslie? My esteemed neighbour to the north?'

'Not directly, but I know who you mean,' Scott replied.

'He's trying to claim that a tract of land – that we've tended to for the last fifty years, mind you – belongs to him. It's all B.S. It's purely because he wants to put a stop to GMF. He thinks it's going to turn into Scotland's Glastonbury.'

'I loved GMF last year,' Scott said. 'Surely it was a huge boon for the whole of Mid-June, not just Glenberry?'

'Exactly, Scott. Ally did an amazing job. We are so proud of her. And then that wee weasel comes up with this, out of thin air,' Sandy said, annoyed. 'Och, anyway, I'd best get on. When the Strawberry Fair is over, Susan will be able to tell how hard

I've worked, or otherwise, while she's been tied up. She has eagle eyes, that one. See you two later. I'll grab your plate from last night on my way past Ally.'

Ally thanked him, and Scott returned his 'See you later.'

There was an awkward silence.

They both spoke at once. 'Right, I'd best get on, too...' Ally began, just as Scott said, 'Ally, did you see your sister-in-law last night...?'

Ally paused just a little too long to lie. 'I did.'

'Did she tell you what happened? That her wee dog...'

Ally tried not to laugh, because she could swear Scott had actually turned white he was so horrified.

'She did. She told me. She's absolutely mortified.'

'She's mortified? When The Laird appeared in your kitchen I thought he was coming in for a piece of me, because he'd heard I flashed his daughter,' Scott said, wide-eyed.

'Oh Scott, sorry, I shouldn't laugh. Louise told me the story because she was so embarrassed, but I couldn't help but see the funny side, and we ended up having a laugh about it. Besides, she said there was no flashing?' Ally asked with a cheeky quizzical frown.

'Oh good, well as long as she knows I was...decent.'

'I'll never mention it again. Or at least I'll try,' Ally teased, as Scott huffed. 'No really Scott, I won't mention it. Please don't given it another thought.'

'Thanks Ally. I get a hard enough time from friends that I'm working up here with the hottest, most eligible girl in Mid-June, in residence...'

'Eligible? I'm married and pregnant, Scott, how dare you,' Ally joked. 'Look Scott, there's more to Louise than just her looks and castle. She's really sweet. You should say hi. Properly this time – with your trousers fully done up.'

'Ally,' Scott groaned.

'I know, I know. Sorry, couldn't resist. That was the last time, promise. I'd better get to work. And so should you. The twins won't be waiting around for any building delays.'

~

From the desk of Iain Watson, Glenberry
Sunday 5th April, 1959

We managed to get some time this morning to reacquaint Mr D-L with the grounds. It was shorter than I'd have wished because it took much longer for Mrs D-L to surface than one would have expected, and because we were cut short by rain.

(Mrs D-L's accent is pleasant. I was relieved to learn that not all New Yorkers speak with the 'colourful' accents portrayed in ~~Guys and Dolls~~ *12 Angry Men.* Or perhaps she managed to temper it in London.)

Mr D-L and I spent a fruitful afternoon alone, going over the estate accounts and such. It was a relief that he was happy to dig in on his first day: I had feared the distractions of showing his wife around might mean a long settling in period. I'm just as pleasantly surprised that he is not daunted by the areas needing attention, of which there are more than a few. He repeatedly assures me that he is ready to 'roll up his sleeves and get to work.'

He would like to surprise his wife with new artwork for their bedroom and has asked me to track down the number for a gallery in Chelsea, London. It appears she favours photographic prints of the Manhattan skyline.

We shall be removing oils by somewhat eminent Scottish portrait artists in favour of photographic prints. Of skyscrapers. In Glenberry.

I did not opine, simply took down as many details I could about the gallery I am to try to contact. I don't suppose that the new mistress of the house can be expected to appreciate the quieter dignity of ancestral interiors in her first week. ~~In time, perhaps, she may come to appreciate what a fortunate position she is has landed in, especially for someone from such humble beginnings.~~ In time, I hope she that she will see that Glenberry's walls are more suited more to local landscapes, than foreign cityscapes.

There will be other nudging in Glenberry ways required: it's simply not appropriate that any main meal be served at Mrs Law's kitchen table. I admit that some of the blame lies with Mr D-L on that particular issue, after his insistence that we drink champagne together in the kitchen, nonetheless, it must be established that meals are taken by the D-Ls in the dining room.

8

On her first morning at Glenberry, Mimi slept late and only wakened when Alexander came into the room with a tray of coffee and toast. When he pulled back the curtains, he betrayed the dustiness of the room as the specks danced in the shaft of sunlight. Mimi barely noticed as she was more struck by how much brighter the room was this morning than it had been yesterday afternoon. She wondered if she had already got used to the low levels of light, or if the room was east facing, and hoped it was the latter.

'Oh, honey, you look like you've been up for ages. What time is it?'

'Just after ten, my dear,' Alexander said, kissing her on her head, before setting about finding the optimal position for the tray.

'After ten? Oh no! Why didn't you wake me? Did you have breakfast already? They must all think me such a lazy-head!'

'These muckle great curtains don't let a lick of light in, so it's easy to sleep in.'

'Muckle?'

'Just means big, or hefty,' Alexander explained.

'There were quite a few words Mrs Law used that I wanted to ask about, but it felt a bit rude,' Mimi said.

'Mrs Law wouldn't mind, just ask her the next time.'

'Yes, I will. I was just a wee bit intimidated yesterday. I know I shouldn't be. Just look at this coffee pot they gave me, isn't it snazzy? I still can't believe it.'

'Nice use of "wee bit" – we're getting to you already,' Alexander laughed. 'It's very nice, yes. And your emotion about it is still written all over your face, I'm afraid.' Alexander picked up the antique hand mirror from the dresser and handed it to her.

'Yikes! My eyes! I look like I've been in the ring with Sugar Ray Robinson. I'm sorry I couldn't stop sobbing last night. It was just such a neat gesture by people who've never even met me. There I was, with my pristinely packaged cookies –'

'Biscuits,' Alexander corrected.

'Thank you, biscuits. I'm embarrassed about them now. They seem quite pathetic in comparison.'

'Oh please don't be, Mrs Law said she and her husband scoffed the lot last night. I probably warned you too much about Scottish frugality and not enough about our generosity. If you think the wedding present was a lot, wait until there's a baby born. If it wasn't bad luck, Mrs Law would already be knitting hats and bootees. Anyway, after your coffee a splash of cold water will do the trick: there's no shortage of that, icy-cold, straight out the tap. You'll love it, it's bracing!'

MIMI DID her best in their bathroom along the hall, not surprised to find that closest thing to a shower was a handheld sprayer attached to the tub. She was glad of her new sheepskin slippers for the walk back to the bedroom, where she found Alexander on the bed looking at the morning papers. On the dressing table were her make up bag and other bits and pieces, which was strange – she hadn't unpacked anything apart from her nightgown and toilet bag last night. She looked to the corner where she had left her overnight case, and her heart sank.

'Alexander. Where's my suitcase?'

His head darted up from his newspaper at her clipped tone. 'What's that, darling?'

She tried to soften her voice. 'I take it you unpacked my things from the suitcase that was there in the corner, which was nice of you, but where did the case go?'

'Oh sorry, I should have explained. We have a dressing room next door, so Mrs Law and I took those things out –' he gestured to the mysterious 'women's things' on the table, 'and she took the suitcase next door to press and hang your things for you. She's already made a start on the bigger suitcases and trunks that Watson and I plonked down there yesterday.'

Mimi forced a smile, though her pulse had begun to hammer. 'Well, that smaller case I'd prefer to sort myself. It's got...personal things in there.' She thought fast. 'For a start, my lingerie is in there.'

Alexander folded his newspaper at once and swung his legs off the bed. 'Darling, I'm sorry. I should have checked with you. Mrs Law was halfway through before I realised she'd swooped in. She meant well. Let me go and fetch it.'

He had barely left before he returned. 'There we are, no harm done. It was unfastened, but Mrs Law seems to have gone back to kitchen duties for now, so I doubt she had time to open it. I'll put it back where you left it.'

He held both her hands and met her eyes. 'I'm sorry, I didn't think. I should have stopped Mrs Law.'

Yes, you should have, Mimi thought, but said only, 'It's fine, really. Look, you go downstairs and let me get ready. I won't be long, promise. Did you say Watson's going to show us around outside?'

'Yes, the forecast is for rain later in the day, so we thought we should make the most of the dry weather first.'

'OK, I'll dress warmly.'

Alexander pulled her in for a hug. All she wanted to do was push him away and check her case, but she bided her time.

'Right. With apologies again, I'll get out of your hair,' he said, kissing the top of her head and slipping out.

Mimi listened at the door until his footsteps along the creaky floors faded. Then she darted to her case. She set it on the bed, dropped to her knees, and opened it with shaking hands. It took a heart-stopping moment, feeling around inside the lining, to find the familiar hard edge of a small oblong box. Beside it, a second, squarer and taller. And then, most important of all, two envelopes, rigid enough to recognise by touch alone.

Her entire upper body went limp, flooded with relief. The boxes would certainly raise questions if Alexander ever came across them, but if he opened the envelope marked 'My Dearest Mimi,' his trust would be shattered and their marriage changed forever.

She smoothed the lining back into place, fingers still trembling. It felt like a narrow escape. She needed to get a grip on this place and find somewhere safer than an overnight case to hide those two empty boxes and the very much not-empty envelope. First step: today's tour with Watson.

The construction company who built Mimi's parents' spanking, modern home on Long Island boasted that each new house took just sixteen minutes to build. Or rather assemble. Even at the time, Mimi thought that a strange thing to admit to, never mind brag about, but her father proudly considered it cutting edge. So when Alexander and Watson stood before the castle's vast facade, debating which parts of it belonged to which century, she thought it best to keep the 'sixteen minutes' anecdote to herself.

As they tramped around the grounds, the two men discussed the foresting of Scots pines, the 'juniors' of which were fifty years old, the elders, close to three hundred. In her parents' neighbourhood, the only trees were twin sycamore saplings in each front yard, planted with pinpoint symmetry. Everything was so meticulously prescribed, that to prevent things from looking too regimented, the streets were curved, to give different-angled views of the nearly identical homes and landscaping. Glenberry, in contrast, stretched around her in natural storeys of tangled, beautiful wildness.

The skies opened up when they were inconveniently a ten-minute march from the house. They sloshed back into Mrs Law's kitchen soaked and spattered with mud, but it meant Alexander was able to persuade her into letting them eat lunch there, around her pine table.

When they finished, Alexander sat back with an exaggerated satiated sigh to please the cook. 'I'm about to shock you Watson. Since the rain has curtailed our survey of the grounds, perhaps we should get straight into business. There's no time like the present after all.'

Watson raised a duly surprised but approving eyebrow.

'And Mrs Law,' Alexander added, 'perhaps, you could give my wife time to change into dry clothes and then make a start on showing her around inside? The interiors feel like more of a woman-to-woman thing to me anyway. You'll remember your way around, and certainly the names of the rooms, far better than I do.'

THE FIRST ROOM on Mrs Law's tour was the dining room, up just a few steps from the kitchen. She led Mimi inside with a proud little flourish.

'That's the family coat of arms, of course,' she said gesturing above a graciously long sideboard. Between pairs of crossed swords – they did like their weaponry – was the crest Mimi knew fondly from Alexander's early love letters: two Scottish birds of prey, called red kites, flying over an oak tree, with the family motto underneath: *Fortitudo et Gratia* – Courage and Grace.

'When we set the table for two, we'll put you both at this end, because the bell is just behind your seat there,' Mrs Law explained.

A bell. Mimi was going to have a bell to ring for service. She doubted she'd use it, but still. The grandfather clock in the corner chimed and she could almost hear the clinks of bone china and crystal glasses from elegant dinner parties held here decades, even centuries, before.

Soon into the tour, Mimi understood what Alexander meant about being Mrs Law being well-versed in the terminology used to distinguish the myriad rooms. It was a struggle to keep track. The Drawing Room, which she thought sounded office-like, was in fact an inviting, feminine space, where the ladies withdrew to after dinner. The Cigar Room, confusingly, contained a billiards table, so could also be referred to as the Billiards Room. There was the Morning Room (east facing), the Music Room (piano in the corner), the Parlour (furniture as old-fashioned as its name), the Fencing Room (fortunately only due to the wall-decor – yet more swords), the Stag Room (unfortunately due to the wall-decor), and the Oak Room (how that differed from any of the other rooms drowning in oak was beyond her).

When they reached the 'Kite Room', Mrs Law said, 'I think you'll like this one,' and let Mimi step in first. 'Mrs Douglas-Lauder – your late mother-in-law, I mean – had this done up maybe twenty years ago. Top to bottom. I think it feels like a wee oasis. She had an eye for beautiful things when she was left to her own devices.'

Mimi took in the exquisite oasis, as Mrs Law had aptly put it. The wallpaper was turquoise, patterned with stylised Art Nouveau birds – kites, supposedly, though Mrs Law suspected they were simply hawks. The room was perfectly symmetrical: teal velvet sofas faced each other across a mahogany coffee table that displayed treasures from Alexander's parents' travels, like a peacock paperweight from India and an ashtray with pink galahs from Australia. Matching dressers flanked the fireplace, with chinoiserie lamps casting the warmest, softest light. It felt like being wrapped in a mink throw, or how Mimi imagined that might feel. And blessedly, the only oak in the room was the miniature tree on the small coat of arms above the mantle.

Upstairs, Mimi lost track of the number of bedrooms. Mrs Law breezed past several with only a brisk, 'Another one,' not even bothering with the doors. The modest houses back on Long Island had attics engineered for future conversion, a luxury her parents had never taken advantage of, but Mimi had grown up believing that extra space was an unimaginable treat. Here, she couldn't even hazard a guess: twenty bedrooms? Thirty? It was complicated because some had anterooms the size of main bedrooms, others had separate chambers just for beds. Imagining showing her parents around, she thought of President Roosevelt's observation: comparison is the thief of joy.

Mrs Law eventually deposited Mimi back at the office, just opposite the Kite Room, where Alexander and Watson were poring over ledgers. Mimi had expected a cramped study. Instead, it was vast: soaring ceilings, tall windows on two sides, and, unsurprisingly, oak panelling climbing to the picture rail.

'All done, Mrs Law?' Alexander asked.

'No, just ran out of time. I've got to get the dinner on,' Mrs
Law replied.

There was more?

'We didn't manage either of the towers. I'll leave those to
you, Mr Douglas-Lauder.'

'Oh, happily. Take my new bride to those creepy old turrets
so she'll cling to me for dear life? Don't mind if I do.'

9

———

'I'm not sure about you taking the Vespa to the Gillie's Rest, Louise,' Sandy said.

Ally had had dinner with Sandy and Louise in the castle's main kitchen and now Louise was heading out to join friends at the pub.

'Dad, I'll be fine. I'm only driving there – my friend is going to drive us all home. And look – it's July, in Mid-June – it's still broad daylight outside,' Louise pointed out. 'I'll take it easy, I promise. How about I text you when I get there?'

'Please do. And make sure you take that lift back.'

'Of course, Dad,' she said, getting up and kissing him on the top of his head. 'Right, I'm off, have fun you two.'

'Let's go and get a comfy seat in the sitting room,' Sandy said. I might treat myself to a wee whisky and you can treat yourself to Susan's winged back chair with the footstool and put your feet up.'

Ally nodded, 'OK - you had me at *feet up*. I'll take you up on that.'

The large coffee table always had the same short stack of three art books, topped with a vase of fresh flowers from the garden. Ally knew that it was a deliberate policy by her mother-in-law, hoping a permanent aesthetic would prevent clutter. But apparently with the cat away, the mouse was taking the opportunity to play. The usual books-and-vase centrepiece had been moved to a sideboard, and the coffee table was strewn with old photographs.

Sandy came in to find Ally with her hand on her hip, and a what's-going-on-here look.

'I know, I know! I'll clear it all away before Susan gets back. I got a little waylaid this afternoon – you know what it's like when you get looking at old pictures – it's a time-suck.'

'It sure is. What made you get them out?'

'Och, I'm feeling bad about this whole Derek Leslie business and that it's been dumped on you. I know you're taking on Watson's despatch boxes, but when we were clearing out my mum's apartment for you and Alec to move in, there were all these old shoes boxes of stuff. I just wanted to make sure there weren't any rogue papers in there too. I'm afraid it's just old photos though. She never put them in albums – she liked that she would just open a box and jump from year to year, even decade to decade, in moments. She said it was like a box of Liquorice Allsorts for memories.'

'That makes this chaos sound appealing, I suppose,' Ally mused.

'I've been quite enjoying bouncing around in time like *Doctor Who*.'

He sat down in his usual chair and picked up a photo from just in front of him. 'Look at her here – isn't she beautiful? And guess what? Turn it over – it says it was taken at her first Strawberry Fair.'

'Wow,' Ally gasped, taking the picture. Mimi was in cat-eye sunglasses, a checked top and pedal pushers, looking like a bombshell from an Elvis film. It was in black and white, but Ally would have loved to know what colour the top was. It could be red – Mimi had a strong lip going on, so maybe it was red lipstick and red gingham. Just under the shirt collar, she could see the sparkle of a brooch. Was it the same one that Watson had disparaged? She glanced at Alexander and Mimi's wedding photograph on the sideboard to confirm.

'Same brooch as her wedding day,' she showed Sandy. 'Does Susan have that now?'

'Nah, I don't know what happened to it. I don't remember her wearing it when I was growing up. I think she probably just outgrew it – my dad was known to buy her the odd bauble in real diamonds.'

'I've been looking through Watson's papers from that year. There is a journal entry of your mother arriving here,' Ally said.

'Oh really, I'd love to see that. Though knowing Watson, it's probably all a bit dry.'

'Well, a lot is, but a lot is quite surprising.'

'Oh yeah, how so? You uncovering some dark secrets?'

Ally nearly choked on her sip of water. 'No, no. I mean... well...everyone speaks so fondly of Watson, but he comes across as quite snobbish in his writing. Quite the superiority complex.'

Sandy laughed. 'I could see that. There was a strong sense of right and wrong about him. Or rather proper and improper. He was old-school. Much more than my parents. And my mother landing here with her new-fangled American ways must have had him in a tizzy. But those two ended up being as thick as thieves.'

'Well, I'll look forward to him being a bit nicer about her in his journals. He was definitely very wary, to put it nicely.'

Sandy laughed louder this time. 'Oh, that's brilliant. And you know who would have found it even funnier? Mimi!'

Sandy wasn't grasping quite how cutting Watson had been

about his mother. Ally wasn't convinced she was going to warm to him any time soon.

'Talking of the Strawberry Fair, everything in hand?' Ally asked.

'I'm sure Susan will have it running like clockwork. For my part, today BBC Scotland ran the piece I recorded last week – my annual explanation and justification of its roots.'

The Strawberry Fair at Glenberry Castle was a tradition dating back many centuries, perhaps even to medieval times. It was as renowned throughout Scotland as Lanimer Day in Lanark, or the Ba' Games between the Uppies and the Doonies in the Border towns. On the second Thursday in July, residents from all over Mid-June and beyond came to Glenberry and headed out into the grounds in droves to pick berries. People kept as many berries as they want and gave the rest back to the estate. To end the day, there was a huge picnic on the Great Lawn. Legend had it that it had never rained on the day of the Strawberry Fair.

Every year Sandy was asked the same pointed question: wasn't this just free labour dressed up as a festival? He'd have to explain, again, that it was visionary not exploitative, because in the days when this began, it was more common that labourers only had access to leftovers after the landowners had harvested, a process known as gleaning. At the Strawberry Fair they got the pick of the crop.

'There's great buzz on Instagram about it, by the way. People sharing memories from all through the years –' Ally was getting her phone out to read Sandy a few of the comments, but he interrupted her.

'Oh, Instagram – I nearly forgot. I found a couple of other pictures taken at the Strawberry Fair, that would make a great post.' He looked around the coffee table. 'Here.' He handed them to Ally.

The top one was of four women and eight children. She turned it over.

In Mimi's neat handwriting was: *Sadie, Geri, Flora and Mimi, with all the weans. Strawberry Fair, 1962.*

Ally laughed, '"All the weans". Mimi was giving the Scottish vernacular a go.'

'That was my playgroup. That woman there, Geri, she spoke in broad Scots, so my mum would have picked up a few words from her. The younger woman there on the left, Sadie, was from Skye and had that beautiful Skye lilt to her accent.'

'You remember them?' Ally asked.

'As I say, it was my playgroup, they all used to come up to the castle all the time. I think they met when they were pregnant. It was great, because I had no siblings, obviously, and they all loved coming up to play here.' Sandy was smiling fondly. 'Those two lived on the farm. In fact, the one that's my age runs the farm now, and his mum Flora is still on the go. As sharp as a tack. She must be in her late eighties now I suppose.'

'That's amazing. Do you think they'll be at the Strawberry Fair? And we could take an up-to-date picture? The Instagram algorithm loves a "then and now". And I'd love to meet Flora.'

'Oh they'll definitely be there – I'll introduce you,' Sandy said.

'I'll keep hold of these for now but we'd better tidy all this up, or you'll be in trouble.' Ally started to pull photos together into rough piles, trying to avoid getting pulled in as Sandy had. It was tempting though, with photos from toddler Sandy in his pram with a messy ice-cream cone to elegant group shots at the Christmas Ball catching her eye. She tapped her last stack on the table to neaten it like deck of cards then reached for the last few strewn stragglers.

There was one of the young family in front of the castle in the snow. The couple were trying to pose for the camera, but the boy was caught mid-turn, eager to get to the expanse of pristine snow on the Great Lawn behind them. He strained towards the snow, one hand clenched around the sledge rope, the other in Alexander's. It looked like Alexander only just managed to hold him fast for a fraction of a second for the photograph to be taken, before he sprung free. Mimi was laughing at the scuffle going on beside her, as always impeccably just-right in her winter coat.

But then Ally saw it: the way she was standing, one hand resting lightly across her middle, a protective gesture so instinctive that it's unconscious. But universal and unmistakable.

Ally looked more closely. There was no doubt Mimi was gently protecting a small bump under that soft wool coat.

Which meant, of course, that the young boy was not Sandy. She could see it now, even though his face was only just in profile.

She turned the picture over. It was blank.

'Who's this wee boy, Sandy?'

Sandy reached for his readers and looked at the boy closely. 'No idea,' he said simply.

They both nearly jumped out their skin at a sudden thunderous noise.

The ancient brass knocker against the front door.

'What the hell?' Sandy shot to his feet. 'You stay here Ally.'

The urgent crashing of the knocker was ominous, especially because the castle had had a perfectly acceptable doorbell with a pleasant chime, for decades.

Ally's heart sank. They hadn't checked if Louise had texted, as she'd promised she would when she got to the Gillie's Rest. She did now and there were two:

> Louise: Hey folks, made it safe and
> sound. It's going to be a quiet night here I
> think, won't be late. xx.
> Louise: On my way home now.

Relief came briefly, but vanished as voices echoed from the Grand Hall. Sandy's was sharp and commanding, with another male voice slurred and furious. She couldn't make out words, only the anger in them. Phone still in hand, she hurried toward the noise.

Sandy was trying to shove Derek Leslie back out through the open door. Leslie was wild, his face blotched red, his rants tumbling out in drunken, venomous bursts.

'You...you fucker...my land...my father assured me...suits you to ignore me...that damned music festival...it'll ruin Mid-June –'

He caught sight of Ally. 'Oh there she is. Little Miss Fucking Fauntleroy, Queen of the Castle.'

Ally was shaking, but managed to keep her voice steady. 'I beg your pardon?'

Sandy snapped, 'Who the hell do you think you are? Don't you *dare* come in here, calling my family names!'

'You're just like the rest of them. All of you women who swan in here, thinking all of a sudden you own the place, looking down on the rest of us. Married in, that's all. You're nothing special. And this family's a piece of shit anyway.'

Sandy managed to wrestle Leslie out of the door, probably because Leslie was incapacitated: his unhinged vehemence was fuelled by drink, but his co-ordination and strength weakened by it. Ally stood at the threshold, ready to slam the door if he lunged back in. Sandy heaved him toward his still-running car and Leslie stumbled against the seat. To escape Sandy's shoves, now dangerously close to becoming punches, he kicked out blindly, slung himself into the driver's side, slammed the door, and tore off across the gravel.

'He shouldn't be driving!' Ally yelled to Sandy, who stood chest heaving, watching the car fishtail toward the gates.

'I wasn't sure what to –'

He didn't finish.

A screech of brakes split the air, followed by the sickening skid of tyres – and then a scream.

~

From the desk of Iain Watson, Glenberry
Friday 17th April, 1959

Well, we are at the fortnight mark of Mr and Mrs D-L back in residence at Glenberry. The household is gradually getting to know their needs and habits. Mrs D-L has developed a liking for spending time in the Kite Room, so we make sure to light the fire in there by lunchtime every day. I noted the domestic periodicals and fashion magazines she left behind there and put in the appropriate order with the newsagents to add them to our deliveries. Mrs D-L expressed an interest in writing, so we set up a handsome desk and elegant writing set in their quarters.

I needn't have worried that Mrs D-L would ~~lower the tone~~ bring more casual American attire habits to Glenberry for she is always very well dressed, to the extent that her diamanté pieces, to which she seems very attached, are considered daywear. Mr D-L's appearance is less formal looking: the barber duly came, but his hair length did not seem to change. Mrs D-L said she had instructed him just to 'shape it' whatever that means. As for her own coiffure needs, the barber opined that only a Glasgow hair salon could do her hairstyle justice, so she has requested a copy of the train timetable. I shall ask that she keeps me informed of those appointments: I wouldn't care to bump into her when I'm on a jaunt to the city myself. For the theatre or what-not.

Mr D-L is at an appointment at the bank today, so I have taken the opportunity to invite Mrs D-L to my the office for a meeting, regarding my thoughts that there may be benefit in having a social debut of sorts. I have compiled a list of people who would be suitable weekend guests, either on their own, or if we gather a few at the same time, we could host a small party. Smaller than days gone by, but a starting off point, springboard if you will, for Mrs D-L.

Building up a picture of her life in America, it was rather provincial. The country is being sold on the 'American dream' of motor cars and 'the suburbs' and her parents, I gather, have embraced it. It sounds to me like neither one thing nor the other, neither city nor country-life: the worst of both worlds. As I was reading the newspaper the other day, I drew comparisons with our New Towns Act, which is merely the building of over-spill social housing in fields around Glasgow and Edinburgh, devoid of history and character, and even proper amenities.

However, Mrs D-L presents quite well for coming from such a background.

The old guard of society, the generation above, would be stuffy and unaccepting of an American, so I have limited my list to the D-Ls' own age-group. Like Mr D-L, many of them are settling down now, but also like him, enjoyed the post-War giddiness of London for a long spell before they did. Although Mrs D-L is the first female to visit Glenberry, I do believe Mr D-L is not short of prior attachments. For one, I'm fairly sure there was a dalliance with Mrs Margaret Campbell, the Duchess of Argyll, between her marriages, so who knows what other land-mines there are.

10

———

'Watson has come up with quite the writing nook here, my dear, I'm rather envious,' Alexander said.

A Queen Anne ladies' writing desk had miraculously appeared in front of one of the windows in their bedroom, liberated from somewhere else in the house. On it was a leather writing case monogrammed with Mimi's Sunday-best initials: *AD-L.* On one side was weighty cream notepaper, also marked, as well as a pad of Airmail-weight ruled paper and the other side held envelopes, regular and Airmail, and postage stamps of varying amounts.

'I'm very grateful but still a little bemused. Tell me again what he said to you about it.'

'He reminded me that on one of our little jaunts together, the three of us, you said you'd like to take up writing.'

'Hmm, I don't recall that, but I'm happy to have such a swell little corner all of my own.'

With some neat little drawers that locked, too. Unfortunately, they were just a little too small for her red boxes and the telling envelopes that were still stowed in her overnight bag lining.

'You can take your swanky new notepad along with you today, for your big meeting with Watson'

'I guess so,' Mimi smiled. 'Should I be nervous? Is he going to chide me for all the misdemeanours I've committed in my first couple of weeks?'

'Of course not. I suspect it will be to talk you through budgets, or menus, or such, now that you're settled in,' Alexander said distractedly, looking for his cufflinks. He had a meeting at the bank. He was hoping they'd be as understanding as Watson about his years *in absentia*.

'He can be so stern,' Mimi said.

'Ah, you'll be fine, just bat your lashes at him.'

'I don't think that will work.'

'Of course it will, how can he resist you? Right, quick kiss and wish me luck. I'd switch places with you if I could,' Alexander said.

'Good luck, honey, you'll do great. See you at dinner.'

IF SHE WAS HONEST, Mimi was more curious than she was nervous, but any progress she could make in chipping away at Watson's armour, took her closer to broaching the subject of the renovation she had in mind.

She had fallen in love with the Kite Room and would retreat there with her copies of *Ideal Home* and *The Studio* whenever she needed some time alone. It was there, reading an article called 'Lofty Ideas in Manhattan', on disused industrial spaces in SoHo being converted into artists' studios, that inspiration struck.

The piece described how creatives were drawn to the generous light of such spaces, and Mimi, thinking back to the office's vast south- and west-facing windows, realised that even on gloomy days that room felt relatively bright. The office lay directly opposite the Kite Room and she wandered between them, cogs turning. That wing of the house that had been added most recently, in Victorian times, when people entertained, grandly and often, so extra sculleries, cold storage, and staff bedrooms had been added. It was an ambitious proposition, but not impossible: to convert that part of the castle into a separate apartment.

Mimi made her way to the office now. It was technically the Laird's office, but Alexander was happy to concede that it was more Watson's domain than his. Getting Watson to agree to move, when she didn't have the same faith in her feminine charms as her husband did, might be a challenge.

The door was open, but she knocked on it to get his attention. 'Hi there, how are you today, Mr Watson?'

'Good afternoon,' was the reply as he double-checked with his watch that his greeting was correct. 'I am well, thank you. Thank you for agreeing to talk with me.'

'Of course, I've been looking forward to it. May I sit?'

Watson gestured, 'Of course, please. I took the liberty of having tea and coffee ready. Which would you care for?'

'You know, you guys are kinda winning me over on tea, so I'll join you in one of those.' As he poured, she set up her side of the desk. 'I bought this beautiful notepad from my desk. Thank you so much for organising all of that.'

'You're most welcome. I hope it encourages you in your new undertaking.'

Right – this new writing hobby he thought she had.

'So, what we got? What's going on in Glenberry Land that you need the Lady of the Manor to take a look at?' Mimi asked.

'Just some things for you to think about really, nothing we need to plan in detail today.

'I'm aware that you are far from home, and from your erstwhile adopted home of London. I thought you might want to become acquainted with some of the families in Scotland that the Douglas-Lauders have traditionally socialised with. With your husband away for several years, Glenberry dropped off the circuit, and I wondered if between us we might be able to rectify that.'

Watson paused for her reaction.

'Well, being *on* the circuit sure sounds like more fun than being off it. What do you have in mind?'

'It would be up to you: one idea would be to invite small parties for an overnight, which usually involves a formal meal and some planned activities such as fishing or shooting for the men, and croquet, bridge or just wandering around the grounds for the ladies.'

'OK...' Mimi had only just got here. Surely this would be a subject better covered with Alexander here.

'If we hosted a couple of weekends over the summer, it would mean that we could perhaps put an autumn or winter event back on the calendar. Your late parents-in-law had an annual event on the last weekend of November, just after the tree had gone up. It was the first festive event of the season.'

He'd certainly thought this all through for her.

'If I may, I have prepared a list of families that we might write to, introducing you, and informing them you and the Laird are back in residence.'

Mimi smiled at the flourish with which Watson presented her with his paper, in perfect slanted cursive script.

'You can have a short peruse, then I can help you get your bearings among the names and the titles.' Watson sat back and waited.

Mimi scanned down the list. She could put faces to a lot of the names and lifted her pen to mark the ones she'd need help with. Watson put out a hand to stop her, and she realised he wanted the master copy of his own Scottish Who's Who left in pristine condition. She tucked her pen behind her ear, signalling she'd got the message.

'Right, well starting at the top, Ian and Margaret Campbell, aka the Duke and Duchess of Argyll. First off, I should let you know that Alexander and Margaret had a fling –'

Watson spluttered his tea.

'Oh – are you OK?' Mimi asked.

He waved a hand that he was fine, using his handkerchief to dab his mouth.

She continued. 'It's nothing to worry about it, Margaret and I have had a good laugh about it. She teases Alexander about it too. Anyway, that's not really the issue – it's more that Ian and Margaret are most definitely on the skids. Their company has been toxic for a while. My heart used to sink whenever I heard that he was in town. She is great fun on her own, but she changes with him around. Margaret says it was the war. He never recovered from his ordeals as a POW, and he takes it out on her. I've seen him be downright cruel.'

Mimi wondered if she had overstepped, because Watson was silent. Everyone knew the Campbells were on the verge of divorce, surely he wasn't annoyed at her for being indiscreet? 'Mr Watson?'

'Yes, quite. So, you've spent time in the company of the Duke and Duchess?'

'Oh yes, lots. And she's been to Glenberry a few times, hasn't she?' Mimi asked.

'When she was much younger, a child. Her maternal grandparents lived this side of Glasgow and were friends with the elder Mr and Mrs Douglas-Lauder. But not since then,' Watson replied.

'That's one of the things she likes to make fun of – that they used to swim together wearing only their underpants as children, and then, well, you know. Sorry, I didn't mean to embarrass you. Margaret has no filter, so I guess I forgot her stories are usually quite inappropriate.'

'Well, I had heard that perhaps the Duke and Duchess's union was not long for this world, but I added her anyway, due to the aforementioned connection with Glenberry –' Watson stuttered. 'I mean – the house, not the Laird.'

Mimi laughed. 'Of course, that's OK. So, who's next? Ah, William and Pamela Murray. Pamela is a darling, such a bundle of energy.'

Watson cleared his throat and asked, frowning quizzically, 'So your husband introduced you to Lord Scone and his wife also?' Watson had pushed his tea to the side.

'Oh gee, did he? Let me think,' Mimi pursed her lips, trying to recall. 'London really is a whirl...No, I remember now – I introduced Alexander to them. They're a little younger than me, so although the families knew each other, those two had never met – Alexander is practically half a generation older than William. Pamela is so charismatic and kind, that they were an easy couple for me to seek out if I was at an event on my own. Then when I started seeing Alexander, the four of us had dinner a couple of times. They have a baby boy now though, so they're not out and about so much.'

Mimi looked at Watson. He had slid his list back to his side of the desk and was looking at it, a little despondent. It dawned on Mimi that he hadn't expected her to know anything about these people, far less have met them. This afternoon had been his moment to shine, and to come to her rescue, as the poor little Yank who knew little of the ways of Scottish society. In a way it was sweet. In his own pompous way, but sweet, none-theless.

'Maybe it's best if you mark this up, after all, and I can advise on those whom you haven't met. If there are any, that is,' he said.

She felt bad. He sounded put out. How to handle this? Mimi placed a bet with herself that Watson wasn't above a little gossip. Surely that was what the whole upstairs/downstairs thing was all about.

'Why don't we keep going down the whole list: you can tell

me what you know, and I'll tell you what I know?' Mimi wasn't shy with the mischievous tone in her voice, and she saw the corners of Watson's mouth twitch. Aww, he was cute when he smiled. Well, nearly smiled.

'OK, pass your paper back here, this is going to be fun. Going back to the Duchess first though, I'm sure you've heard rumours of numerous affairs?'

Watson just raised his eyebrows, giving nothing away. He had resumed drinking his tea, so Mimi took that as a sign that he wasn't appalled at the turn the conversation had taken.

'OK, you don't need to answer that, but I know you must have. Isn't it interesting that we see more in the press about her extra-marital activities than his? But here's the thing, and this speaks to her character, because she remains graciously silent: she's only covering for lots of the men she's seen with, her reported paramours. They're actually homosexual friends of hers.'

For a second time, Watson choked on his tea, this time spilling some onto his jacket.

Mimi delighted in watching Watson desperately trying not to let his composure slip as they made it through his rogues' gallery. He'd offer up an occasional observation, like, 'the apple doesn't fall far from the tree' or 'they never were regarded as having much class.' She'd throw in anecdotes she thought might tickle him and judge her success by the width of his eyes and animation of his eyebrows. The Mitford sisters and Noel Coward were top of the list for a while, but she had an ace up her sleeve.

'The Ramseys? I'd never invite them to Glenberry. Their entitlement and boorish behaviour is the worst I've ever seen. Except for –' *drum roll,* she thought, 'the night I sat two seats down from Princess Margaret and watched her make the French ambassador get on his knees to blot wine off her dress.'

Watson's eyes almost popped out of his head.

. . .

THEY ACHIEVED nothing on Watson's agenda, but Mimi thought the afternoon a success and felt some bonding had occurred. Watson gathered up a few files of papers and mentioned that they were stored in the library.

'Why is there no storage in here?' Mimi asked.

'I've never been sure. Perhaps it was only intended for meetings, or more likely, the addition had already cost too much and resources were needed elsewhere.'

'That seems very inconvenient for you having to work between here and the library,' Mimi noted deliberately. 'One last thing – I cannot remember for the life of me what my grand writing plans were. Can you remind me of when I mentioned it?'

'Certainly. It was the day we were touring the old coach house and stables.'

Mimi threw her head back laughing, realising the confusion. 'And I said, maybe I'll take up riding! Well, that got lost in translation! I guess with my accent, riding and writing sound the same.'

Watson chuckled too. He was handsome when he laughed. Well, chuckled.

From the desk of Iain Watson, Glenberry
Friday 17th April, 1959 (contd.)

Well, my meeting with Mrs D-L was illuminating to say the least. It seems that she was ensconced in London's social hubbub in her own right, not because of her union with the Laird. I have to admit to having been quite dumbfounded. Not only had she met most of the people I had intended to present her to, but she was also friends with a few and knew quite intimate details about their lives. To list them all here would be to imply that she was name-dropping, but Mrs D-L seemed to have taken these people at face value upon meeting them, with no heed to their standing or title. It was quite refreshing if I'm honest.

The tales she told! The rumours about Ian and Margaret Campbell are true, though apparently several of the Duchess's 'companions' are ~~homosexuals whom she provides cover for~~ just platonic. I suppose as I mull our conversation over, most of her revelations, some of which were thoroughly scurrilous and shocking, were not a surprise: the families whom I've encountered and regard as upstanding, remain so, and those with a history of gambling and womanising, similarly remain so.

Mrs D-L also had stories about individuals whose reputation I only know from the newspapers: the Mitford sisters, Noel Coward (for heavens sakes!), and the jewel in the crown, so to speak, Princess Margaret. Just one dinner with the Princess and Mrs D-L had enough stories to fill a chapter of a royal biography. Her appalling manners and sharp put-downs of everyone were so prolific and relentless, that Mrs D-L compared it to a nervous twitch.

I'm not sure if we reached any conclusions, but I have to confess to having been quite captivated. The feeling I have this evening is as if I've spent an afternoon at the cinema, immersed in another world.

11

____

In hindsight it should have consoled them that the scream was followed by more screams as opposed to silence, but that requires rational thinking that wasn't possible in the flood of adrenaline.

'It's Louise! She just texted that she was coming home,' Ally said, heading to the gate, but Sandy already knew, and was sprinting towards his daughter's cries for help.

Louise was lying in the ditch on the last bend of the driveway into Glenberry, the Vespa on top of her. 'I'm OK, I think, I just can't get this bike off me.'

Ally instinctively bent down to help Sandy, but he held up his hand to halt her.

'Stand back, Ally' he said. 'Louise, are you hurt?'

'Well – nothing broken, I don't think. I could probably push the bike upwards towards you with my legs.'

'That would help, if you're sure. It's just a deadweight at the moment, but if you give me the start, I'll be able to lift it with the momentum.'

'OK. Hang on.' Louise grunted as she managed to change

position a fraction to make this work. 'On the count of three? Ready one…two…*three.*'

Adrenaline worked in their favour and Sandy dumped the bike unceremoniously to the side then carefully climbed down to crouch by Louise.

'Oh my God,' he said, his voice shaking. 'Oh my God, are you OK?' He gently touched her shoulder and looked into her eyes, then scanned her for signs of injury.

'I think so. I landed on my shoulder, but I can –' She gave a little gasp as she lifted her elbow. 'It's sore, but I can move it, look. Help me sit up.'

Sandy gently supported her back as she sat, grimacing in pain. She tried to take a deep breath, but it caught in starts on the way in and turned into sobs on the way out.

'Oh, darling shh,' Sandy said softly and cradled her head.

'Oh Louise,' Ally said quietly from her position on the road above them.

After some gentle sobbing Louise lifted her head from Sandy's hands and asked, 'Who was that?'

'It was Derek Leslie. He just came storming in, ranting and raving, smelling of booze. God Ally, we should phone the police. I was too concerned about Louise to think, but he shouldn't be out there on the roads,' Sandy said.

'I did think of that for a moment,' Ally answered, holding up the phone in her hand. 'But he'll be home by now, or at least he would be by the time the police got to him. Did he hit you, Louise?'

'No, I don't think so. Actually, I know he didn't. I swerved to avoid him, hit the side of the road and ended up down here.'

'God, he's a piece of work,' Sandy muttered through his teeth.

'That's putting it nicely,' Ally said. 'Right, how do we get you out of there Louise?'

With some grunting and groaning, wincing in pain, they got

Louise back into the castle to assess the damage. Thankfully, she'd had the presence of mind to keep her head from hitting the ground as she fell, as evidenced by pain in her neck, which would no doubt turn into a nasty case of whiplash overnight. Similarly, the whole left side of her body, which took the brunt of the fall, had some grim scrapes, ripe to bloom through the spectrum of the bruise rainbow over the next several days.

Once they got her cleaned up and handed her a stiff drink – for medicinal reasons that Sandy justified too for his own shock – she was in remarkably good spirits. Sandy too.

Ally though, was thoroughly exhausted and a wide yawn caught her unawares.

'Oh Ally, I'm sorry. Please feel free to turn in. I'm fine, honestly,' Louise said.

'Are you sure? I'd offer up a sleepover with me, but Alec's due home sometime in the middle of the night.'

'I'm sure. As we three self-appointed A&E doctors have diagnosed, I'm not concussed, thank goodness. Not even a scratch on this moneymaker.' Louise circled her palm in front of her face. 'Thank goodness for that too, because I saw Scott the Builder at the Gillie's and he mentioned I could "pop in and see him any time",' she said with a deliberately suggestive tone.

'Oh did he now?' Well your dad has been stopping by and bringing him coffee too, so that's all I need, *more* distractions for my builders. These poor homeless babies,' she said, looking down at her tummy, patting it.

'Scott? Your builder? What have I missed?' Sandy asked.

'Don't ask,' Ally and Louise said in unison. Then, 'Jinx!'

'Right, I'm off to bed. I think we'll all sleep well tonight,' Ally said, picking up a small pile of Sandy's photos. 'I'll just grab a few of these for Instagram.'

Going back to the apartment, she couldn't help but replay the evening's events. She had to sort out this issue with Leslie once and for all. Her encounter with him on her walk was bad enough, but she was completely horrified by his manic behaviour tonight. He was positively possessed with rage.

What had he called her? Queen of the Castle? What had she done to deserve quite such vitriol? Susan must be right; there was an old grudge that had a fresh outlet.

She put the photos on her bedside table and when she got into bed, she studied the one of the boy with the sledge. She held it under her bedside lamp, willing clues to come off the page. Its corners were bent and worn, the paper was shiny from being handled, as if it had been looked at often. Yet Sandy didn't know who the boy was. And Mimi hadn't diligently notated the picture on the back as she always did.

If Elsie Morris had followed through with a visit to the castle soon after her December letter, the season and the age of the boy made sense. He might be Elsie's – and Alexander's – son, Charles.

Ugh. Ally wished she could put this out of her mind, at least until she'd sorted things out with Derek Leslie and the GMF, but she'd have had more success trying not to think about the proverbial elephant.

12

Every day, the sun got a little bit higher in the sky, and Glenberry bustled back to life. The permanent staff of only three mortified Watson more than it did the Douglas-Lauders, but suppliers of good and services traced their previously well-worn path back to the castle regularly now.

Daily, there was something going on that excited, troubled, or simply occupied, Alexander. Much as she loved the pants off him, Mimi was ready for the honeymoon period to be over and knew it would be good for them both to find routine in their new life together. She took a long brisk walk every morning, Mrs Law's cooking living up to Alexander's predictions, and she never had to take the same path twice, so her exercise was always an exploration too. On one of her walks she had a very pleasant chat with an adjoining landowner and his son, the Leslies, but usually it was just her and layers of birdsong, unlike anything she'd known in London or New York.

Watson's writing desk misunderstanding had made Mimi a diligent correspondent, mostly to her parents. She talked Mrs Law into kitchen privileges in the daytime, which she also enjoyed. Her job, and the very basic amenities at her London apartment, meant she was far from experienced cook, but it was nice to be able to make herself a snack, or to learn from watching Mrs Law. When she began to receive return mail from her mom, she requested some of her classic everyday recipes, and she and Mrs Law tried making them together: brownies (a success all round); candied vegetables with brown sugar and cinnamon (none of the Scots were convinced); meat loaf (they'd stick to haggis, thanks); and devilled eggs (Mrs Law had made them before, but was bemused to learn they were widespread and served at parties. 'Aren't they a bit pungent for company?').

ON HER FIRST trip to Glasgow alone, her housemates were like clucking hens, especially Watson, whom she thought she had successfully convinced that she wasn't some hick from the sticks. The break from their unusual – vast, yet very small – world, was welcome. A city trip every time her roots needed re-blonding was probably a little too often, so she decided that a home peroxide treatment, alternated with a salon trip to Glasgow for cut, colour and set, would work.

The salon owner was attentive and prepared: he had looked up Mimi and Alexander's wedding announcement picture in *Scottish Field*, and had correctly deduced that where Mimi was concerned, there was no such thing as too blond. He recommended a stroll around the perfume department of House of Fraser, a delight of a store all round, an ogle at the jewels in the Argyll Arcade, and a sly stroke of the furs in Arnott Simpsons.

Not wanting her delicious time alone to end, she found her way back to Rogano for oysters, and the Central Hotel, for a final glass of champagne. When she got on the train home, she was already looking forward to her next trip back. Watson might yearn for the days when Glenberry's household was sufficient to attend the Douglas-Lauder round the clock, but

Mimi relished every second of being *un*-attended and footloose.

AS SUMMER APPROACHED, Mimi was grateful for the heavy drapes that had almost made her cry on her first day at the castle.

'You should see what it's like further north,' Alexander said. 'If you were at Iain and Margaret Campbell's place in Inveraray, the sun hardly goes down before it's coming back up.'

On the secret subject of a separate apartment, Mimi went from dreaming, to mulling, to stealth measuring and sketching. One afternoon, she was going over her sketches on her favourite Chesterfield in the library when she heard Watson clearing his throat to get her attention.

'Oh, I'm sorry, do you need to be in here?' she asked. She was all too aware that Watson was back and forth between the office and here frequently. It made no sense at all, which she hoped could work in her favour.

'No, I was hoping to find you. I'm afraid I have an apology to make.' He was delicately holding an envelope between the thumbs and forefingers of both hands, address side down. It had been opened cleanly with a paperknife, not by hand.

'In opening the morning post, I failed to notice that this is addressed to you: *Mrs* Alexander Douglas-Lauder, as opposed to *Mr* Alexander Douglas-Lauder.'

'Oh gee, don't worry about that,' Mimi said, taking the envelope. 'Let's see what's in here. Oh, it's a cheque!'

'I'm afraid, I noticed that too before I realised my error. Again, I'm terribly sorry.'

'Please stop apologising and don't think any more of it,' Mimi said distractedly, reading the letter. 'Oh, well that's a little bonus! It's my final week's pay, plus a tax adjustment. I'm not sure what the last part means, but I'll take it.' She smiled up at Watson. 'It's all good.'

Then her shoulders slumped as realisation hit her: 'Ah, but they've been very clever and addressed it to my married name. That's not so good.'

'How so?' Watson asked.

'My bank account is still under Amelia Johnson,' Mimi explained. Oh well, in the scheme of things, this wasn't a large amount of money, she was sure it could be lodged into her husband's account. She was certain, in fact, that it was the easier route.

'I'm sure if we just write, or perhaps even call them on the telephone to explain?' Watson said.

'You have no idea the hoops they made me jump through to get that account,' Mimi said.

'How so?' Watson asked again.

'Well, think about it – I was a single gal, fresh off the boat from across the pond. Where was I going to find a man to co-sign a bank account for me? No husband, no father around. I'd nailed the interview for this job, had what I thought was a great offer, feeling like I was doing great in my bold new life – Miss Independent. Then I had to go back to the Stock Brokerage, with my tail between my legs, and ask if there was a male employee who was willing to come to the bank with me to open an account.'

Mimi searched Watson's face for the 'gotcha, I'm with you' expression, but if anything, he looked more confused. Surely he had to know all this? Mind you, as a man, why would he?

She may as well ask: 'You know that women can't open a bank account on their own, don't you?'

'No! But that's appalling.'

He looked genuinely aghast.

'I'm quite aghast.'

She was right.

'Mr Watson, won't you sit down? Take a load off.'

He obeyed her request.

'I'm sorry, this is really news to you? You thought that women could get bank accounts just like that? Without a male co-sign?'

'Why shouldn't they?' he asked simply.

'Yup, good question I suppose,' Mimi laughed.

'It's 1959. It's more than –' He stopped to do the arithmetic. 'It's more than forty years since women were granted suffrage. I'd expect them not to have to ask a male colleague a favour to open an account.'

Well, how about that – Watson was a feminist. 'I hear ya! And, not to nitpick, but when you mention forty years ago, let's not forget that at first it was only women over thirty years old. It was another ten years – 1928 – before there was true voting equality.'

'Yes, my mistake, I do recall that. Very knowledgeable of you Mrs Douglas-Lauder,' Watson said, nodding.

'My mom was in the Suffrage movement, thanks to the women she worked for who educated her about it. In New York, it was the wealthy women who had the time to be very involved.'

'Yes, I believe it was the same here in the UK. I'm dismayed to learn that modern-day discriminations like this exist, after all their hard work.'

If only Watson knew. The Seneca Falls Convention had been more than a century ago. Twelve demands had been set out, and so far, only one had been fully granted: the vote. In many states women still couldn't serve on juries, and in some they weren't permitted to work in bars, to protect men's morals.

But Mimi knew that no matter how sympathetic an ear you thought you had on this subject, your time ran out fast. It was better just to stick to the headlines and not be perceived to be going on a rant – heaven forbid.

'Anyway, wanna know the kicker? About my bank account? I'm pretty sure the guy they sent with me earned less than me, but he had to vouch for me.'

They both shook their heads.

It wasn't so much that Mimi was cracking Watson's veneer, as Alexander had assured her she would, more that she was getting to know him better, the man behind the role.

She should strike while the iron was hot – or while the estate manager was softened up. It was time to raise the subject that had been keeping her awake at night with excitement: the possibility of their own apartment.

'There's something I've been meaning to talk to you about. I'm not going to pretend that it's not a bit of a doozie. I haven't even mentioned it to Alexander yet, but I'd love to run it by you and see what you think.'

~

From the desk of Iain Watson, Glenberry
Monday 1st June, 1959

I had another very interesting talk with Mrs D-L today, in the library.

By mistake, I had opened an item of post addressed to her. (Which in itself was quite revealing: Mrs D-L's salary before she married was quite respectable for a woman, by which I mean, a woman in a male-led area of work. Jolly good for her!)

I was terribly embarrassed, but she was very understanding. In our conversation on how best to deal with the cheque (it is addressed to her married name, but her bank account is in her maiden name), I learned that her mother was active in the Suffrage movement, and Mrs D-L revealed herself to be well-versed and principled herself.

As regards the next topic of conversation, I rather wonder if Mrs D-L took advantage of my being on the back foot regarding my error. If so, I doff my hat to her deftness, for she presented a thorough and sensible argument for a fairly substantial rejig of the upper West wing of the castle (complete with some sketches) and managed to get me onboard.

My The current office will be relocated, to the ante room of the library, which makes sense: all the records and filing cabinets are there and I can't complain about its ambience either. The office will become the D-L's new living room (her plans for which are terribly up-to-date). I have been aware, and concerned, that the main hindrance to Mrs D-L-s enjoyment of Glenberry is the unpredictable (to put it patriotically) amount of sunlight. It was evident, as she laid out her well-considered plans, that the abundance of south and west facing windows will bring her joy, and that alone was reason to make every effort to take her side. A small scullery will become her modern 'fitted' kitchen and they will have a bedroom with an 'en suite' bathroom, which Mrs D-L assures me is about to be 'all the rage'. The Kite Room, her favourite retreat, can conveniently become part of the apartment too. Its decor will remain untouched and will act as the couple's formal reception room, should they have guests.

It is entirely reasonable that a new mistress is allocated some capital budget to make the place feel like home, and Mrs D-L has astounding vision. There will be efficiencies in the household running costs, for example heating, in that we are moving all habitations closer together. We could possibly even shutter some of the east wing for the winter altogether.

I have the feeling she was quite trepidatious in broaching the plan with me, but as the staff has been anxious to see her happy, and her enthusiasm was infectious. To be honest, I have a spring in my step to be embarking on something so fresh and new, breathing life into the old pile, rather than making the same old rounds of repairs and maintenance. We leafed through some of her magazines on interior furnishings and department store catalogues together, and I found it quite exhilarating!

Postscript: As regards the aforementioned cheque, Mrs D-L was happy for it to be lodged into the couple's account. However, after doing so, I am going to write a cheque from the account for an equivalent amount and send it to her personal bank account in London. That only seems appropriate for pre-marital earnings.

13

———

Ally felt a little guilty at missing the parade of the berry pickers into the castle grounds, but Alec's offer of missing it, in favour of a morning to herself in a quiet apartment with no builders around was too good to refuse. Louise had also been left to sleep in, for obvious reasons.

Traditionally, the family stood on either side of the main gates, thanking people for coming and shaking as many hands as they could. Last year Ally had been taken aback that it made her a little emotional. People were well-meaning, but today she was happy to miss a literal procession of enquiries about her health and comments on her appearance. Her plan was to join a little later as the giant picnic began to gather on the Great Lawn, when Sandy would introduce her to Flora Sinclair.

She leafed through her props once again. There were a few innocuous photos of Mimi, the playgroup, and the staff, and then the loaded one: Mimi pregnant and the boy with the sledge. Mimi and Flora had met during their pregnancies, so it was worth a shot.

. . .

ALEC AND SANDY had wheeled round the teak patio furniture for Ally's and Flora's comfort, and Ally arrived to a welcoming circle of chairs around a table of lemonade, iced tea, scones, and of course, berries in abundance. Flora sprung to her feet effortlessly to hug her. 'Spry' was an understatement, Ally thought.

'My dear, I've just been catching up with your handsome husband. Twins! Lucky you! How are you feeling?'

'Och, fine thanks. Glad that I'm being treated to a proper armchair. I wasn't relishing getting in and out of a low deckchair,' Ally said, sitting.

'I know, what a lovely set up the boys have made for us. My lot are still out picking. My son and his family I mean. Can I pour you a drink? Lemonade?' Ally felt looked after and liked Flora already.

'Talking of hard work – Dad, I think you and I should get back to it. I'm not happy with the visual of us sitting around on vintage furniture, sipping tea with the ladies,' Alec said.

'Agreed,' Sandy said. 'Ladies, enjoy getting acquainted and we'll join you a bit later when the picnic is in full swing.'

Ally lifted her head to Alec for a goodbye kiss.

'He was the apple of his grandmother's eye, that boy,' Flora said, smiling, as Alec left. 'Now, he tells me you've been renovating the apartment. About time too, I'm sure. I became friends with Mimi when she was ripping it apart and making it modern the first time, but that was about sixty years ago now. It looked so progressive to us then, but I'm sure you found it awfully dated, did you?'

'Well, it was quite hard to say goodbye to Mimi's vision, but it did feel a bit like living in a time capsule, and lots of things just weren't practical anymore. I thought you might be interested to see this though,' Ally said. At the last minute, she had thought to bring the slim coffee table book which contained the beautifully artistic shots immortalising Mimi's apartment in all its mid-century glory.

Flora gasped and then gave a small gasp again at each turn of the page.

'Gosh, this is quite something, isn't it?' Flora said. 'Mimi was a bit of a glamour-puss herself, so she'd have loved it. Well done you, Ally.'

Ally was touched that the older lady praised her so genuinely. 'That's what the family said too, that Mimi would have loved it. Talking of glamour-puss, Sandy and I found these pictures of Mimi's first Strawberry Fair.'

Ally handed Flora three photographs, Mimi in her cat-eye glasses on top.

'I remember that day!' Flora said, chuckling. 'Everyone was so curious to see Alexander's new wife, and my goodness, she did not disappoint. And there I was, feeling particularly frumpy, as a relatively new mum to my first son. I didn't even go over and introduce myself, she was so dazzling. We laughed about that later, when we became such good friends.

'It was hard to believe, but she said she was anxious that day, trying really hard to please. And she had set her sights on making friends with – well, making some friends.'

Flora stopped there and turned to the next picture which included the staff.

'Ah, Mr Watson, he was a good sport,' she said fondly. 'And Mrs Law's baking was to die for!'

'You say that about Mr Watson, but I've found some of his journals and he can sound like a right old fuddy duddy in them, yet everyone seems to have loved him,' Ally said.

'You're reading Watson's journals?' Flora gave a small frown.

'Yes, Sandy suggested it might help with a mission I'm on to sort out a land dispute,' Ally said.

'I see. Well, Mimi ended up bringing out the best in Mr Watson. Gosh, the capers we used to get up to. Some tried his patience and some we just out-and-out did behind his back. We women must have some secrets we keep to ourselves don't we Ally?' She winked at Ally and turned to the third picture.

'Oh!' She was taken aback.

'It says on the back that the other lady is – Peggy,' Ally said, taking the photo back and turning it over. 'No surname, just Peggy.'

'Oh, her name is on it, is it?' Flora seemed surprised, then appeared to choose her words carefully. 'Well...then...in actual fact, it was Peggy that she was trying to impress and make friends with that day.'

'And did they become friends?' Ally asked.

'Oh yes, Peggy helped Mimi form our playgroup actually. But she moved away...'

Flora trailed off.

Ally was confused. This just a decoy photo, intended to loosen Flora up, but she seemed to have hit on something with it. Who was this Peggy?

'Why did she have to move away?' Ally asked.

'I didn't say she *had* to move away, did I? I just said she moved away. It's allowed, Ally. Sometimes people just relocate. Now, what are the other photos you have there?'

'I believe this is your playgroup?' Ally said, passing two pictures, the playgroup on top.

'Ah, look at that!' Flora's face lit up in delight. 'I must get a copy of this. Look at us. We were quite early on in our friend-ship, but we'd already been through so much together.'

'You had?' Ally asked.

'Well, of course. Four babies born for one thing. Mimi intro-duced us to the NCT. You know, the National Childbirth Trust? It was very new at the time. Now that was a story: the time we got Watson involved in a childbirth class with a local midwife. I doubt that made it into his journals. He was mortified, poor man!'

Flora was still giggling as she looked at the last picture, the all-important one: the boy with the sledge. Ally was ready to watch her carefully, for signs of recognition, but she hardly got a chance. Flora barely glanced at it before she immediately scooped up all of the pictures, shuffled them into a neat stack, and tucked them into the coffee table book.

She stood up. 'Come my dear, let me show you a secret place and tell you all about the caper behind it.'

Ally took longer to get out of her seat than her elderly new friend.

What had just happened?

Flora had definitely registered the photo, but she was either completely ignoring it, or this tour she was taking Ally on was related to it and was going to reveal everything.

Ally suspected the former.

FLORA WAS as steady on her feet as anyone a generation below and led Ally through a jumble of roots and ferns towards the loch, in the dappled shade of soaring trees. They walked in silence, concentrating on their footing, until Flora stopped at a slight clearing. They had only been walking through the woods for a few minutes but there was not a sound, which was remarkable given that there were currently hundreds of people rambling through the castle grounds. Ally looked around and saw four large tree stumps, for all the word like outdoor armchairs, and on the other side of the clearing, a huge fallen tree trunk looked like a couch. At Flora's invitation, they sat down on two of the woodland chairs.

'This the playgroup's secret place. The kids were absolutely mad about Arthur Ransom's books, and they'd play at *Swallows and Amazons* day in, day out. Mimi and I helped them make maps putting their own Great Lake and Wildcat Island right here in Glenberry.

'Then it was decided there simply must be a camp out. Poor old Watson was enlisted in the set-up, though he couldn't believe us four women didn't just want to leave it to our husbands. But we'd become so invested in the adventure ourselves, we were actually looking forward to it.

'Watson was paranoid about us lighting a fire, but Alexander persuaded him we'd be fine and dug us a shallow pit, surrounded by stone, so there was no danger at all of the fire getting out of control.'

Ally's eye caught the bark of some trees on the other side of the clearing which appeared to be blackened. Surely that couldn't be from some campfire gone wrong fifty-odd years ago?

Flora went on. 'We assured Watson that we wouldn't go to sleep with the fire still lit, so when the children were persuaded to turn in, us four mums sat – right here – talking quietly, watching the fire slowly die.

'But Mimi always had a trick up her sleeve, and she had brought a wee single-burner gas stove to make us coffees. Irish coffees, of course. She set it up in that far corner –' Flora pointed, 'so that the whistling wouldn't waken the children.

'And thank goodness, because she turned back to whisper something to us, knocked the stove, and there was a sudden flare as it caught on some dry reeds. It shot to that clump of trees and licked away at the bottom of them.

'It was far enough away from the children and moving in the opposite direction, that Mimi's scream was, "Oh my Gawd, Watson's gonna kill me"'.

The older lady's impersonation of an American accent made Ally laugh.

'Oh, the commotion! Mimi hopped around stamping on the ground, not doing any good at all, while Sadie was rooted to the spot in fright. Geri and I had to spring to action with our blankets and smother it on the trees there. Come and see.'

Both women got up and walked over to the tree that still bore the scar of the Mimi's desire for a sneaky nightcap. On the other side of it, faded but still clearly legible, were four carved sets of initials: SD-L, PS, RM, MK.

'How on earth did you explain the fire to the children?' Ally asked. 'Not to mention scary old Watson?'

Flora had a mischievous twinkle in her eye.

'We told the children that we'd heard pirates trying to creep up on our camp but chased them off with fiery torches made from sticks we lit in the fire. In the chase, one of the torches fell, but the mums put the fire quickly and safely. Most important of all, we told them, we should never tell the dads and Mr Watson. They'd be so worried about us ever coming across pirates again, that they might say we shouldn't go on any more *Swallows and Amazons* adventures.'

Ally laughed and nodded a *nicely done* nod.

'As I said, Ally, sometimes, when it comes to the men in our lives, what they don't know can't hurt them.'

Ally smiled all the way back to their spot at the now loud and bustling picnic. She smiled because of the delightfully charming story, and because of the delightfully charming way it had been used as a foil, to draw Ally's attention away from any questions Flora didn't want to answer.

14

———————

July 1959

Mimi was kicking around the construction zone that was to be the new apartment, in her designated site-uniform: cotton shirt, denim pedal pushers, sneakers and a headscarf. She was channelling Rosie the Riveter, but even cuter.

Watson had been able to make things happen fast. He'd practically set the wheels in motion before she'd fully convinced Alexander, which was funny because she had thought Watson would be the tougher sell. In fact, he seemed to be getting a kick out of the whole thing, and she was enjoying the time they got to spend together as joint site inspectors. Alexander had taken a back seat, saying, 'Mimi, if you're happy, I'm happy'.

Local tradesmen were glad of the work and enjoyed seeing Glenberry come back to life – a proper home once again. Watson explained to Mimi that many estates had gone into decline, and the hyper-local economies they supported along with them. There was even a growing trend to remove the roofs from grand houses, rendering them uninhabitable and neatly exploiting a loophole in the law. A story of Margaret Campbell's now made more sense to Mimi: she had told, with scandalous relish, of her neighbours in Argyll, the Malcolms, who had finally admitted defeat and taken the roof off their estate house, because they couldn't afford the rates. After Alexander's parents passed, and while he was off sowing his wild oats, there had been collective concern that similar fates might befall Glenberry and its environs.

'There was a lot more at stake than I knew, when I agreed to be Mrs Douglas-Lauder,' Mimi observed.

'Quite,' Watson said. 'When your husband telegraphed us that he had wed at the registry office, I went straight to Mrs Law's house with the news. She, of course, saw to it that the word went around the villages post haste.'

'Of course. Whatever "post haste" means,' Mimi nodded.

'Then there was great scrutiny of the wedding photo for clues as to your personality, and supposition as to what it meant for Glenberry that you were American.'

'What did *you* think of that?' Mimi asked.

Watson eyed her, lips pursed.

'C'mon. Surely we've been through enough by now, old pal!' Mimi elbowed him, winking.

'I wondered if perhaps the Laird had followed in the steps of many of the gentry in Victorian times, and, well, I don't wish to be crass –'

'You hoped he'd married a rich Yank?' Mimi laughed. 'I'm sorry that wasn't the case.'

'Well, the main thing you need to know is that there was practically rejoicing throughout the land, as they say in fairy-tales, when news got around that the newlyweds had decided to return to the ancestral seat to set up home.'

'You're funny, Mr Watson. "Rejoicing throughout the land" indeed.'

'In all seriousness, your presence was critical...and has turned out to be a pleasure too.'

'Gee, Watson, you're getting me verklempt,' Mimi said.

'I'm sorry. Whatever "verklempt" means,' Watson smiled.

THIS MORNING, Watson was too busy setting up for tomorrow's Strawberry Fair, so Mimi checked on the team in the kitchen first, then came to the large empty office that would be their living room.

She was musing. An enormous oak fireplace dominated one whole wall. Mimi imagined their new nest being a haven of modernity, with wall-to-wall carpeting, streamline seating and cool lamps. This monstrosity was hard to see past – she longed to replace it with a long low mantle.

Obviously she was stuck with the oak panelled walls, but looking at the fireplace more closely now, she thought it was perhaps a separate piece of carpentry. She felt around it and examined the seams up close, then stood back and looked at it from across the room, then repeated the process. It seemed very likely to her that this work-of-art, which she had to admit it was even though it was too ornate and old-fashioned for her taste, had been crafted in a workshop and then put in situ as a complete piece. So it should be fairly easy to lift out, one would think.

Lift out. That's how she'd put it to the foreman. She could see him rolling his eyes and saying, 'Aye, sure, we'll just *lift it out* – easy as that!'

Mimi couldn't resist a further poke around. She tracked down a chisel and chose a corner of the moulding around the bottom and to get to work. Sure enough, she was able to lever it enough to see that it would be able to be removed without damaging the panelling. Not by her, and not today, but she'd done enough reconnoitre work to present her case to Watson and the foreman.

Before she put the section back into place, just enough light got into the space behind it to reflect on something shiny. Treasure! She laughed to herself. She squinted and could make out writing and illustrations. An old cookie tin. Sorry, biscuit tin. She could just reach it, and wiggled it free. Empty. No treasure here. It was probably just the carpenter's lunch box.

But maybe Mimi's lucky discoveries today weren't limited to her quest for a new fireplace. Maybe her search for the perfect hiding spot for her two little red boxes was over.

THE STRAWBERRY FAIR was going to be Mimi's first official event as the Laird's wife, which was putting Mrs Law into a spin, because she expected a teeming crowd, all wanting to be there at the first opportunity to see the new Mrs Douglas-Lauder in the flesh.

'Marilyn Monroe could show up and she wouldn't get second look, compared to you,' she assured Mimi. 'Just you wait and see.'

Alexander and the staff had explained the Strawberry Fair to Mimi, and it sounded adorable, verging on too good to be true: people picked berries all day, keeping as many as they wanted, but also helped Glenberry amass a pile of produce which it then exported to the rest of Scotland. It was an important income stream for the estate.

'I can't decide if it's communism or slave labour,' Mimi quipped. 'What's in it for them?'

'Well, in the afternoon we have a huge picnic on the Great Lawn, and people bring along the jams and preserves that they made with the berries they collected the year before, that we taste, then exchange jars and recipes.'

'That sounds like a nice "thank you". Do we provide the picnic?'

'Good Lord no!' Mrs Law fanned herself at the thought. 'I provide basic sustenance throughout the day, and that's plenty work, thank you.'

'I don't think you're appreciating the scale of the event, my dear,' Alexander said. 'This is going to be the best take you'll get on how many people live here. They'll almost all be here, from babes in arms, to the elders of the villages.'

'I'm just not understanding why they are happy to work for nothing, to profit, well, us.'

'Deep roots in tradition I suppose, and an understanding that we are all in this together.'

This afternoon, Mimi was to meet some coordinators of the Fair. Alexander and Watson wanted to stay true to the tradition of it seeming like a rambling, foraging affair, but behind the scenes there was some structure, for which they needed help. She was excited – to take part, to feel like she was contributing (even if it was just by being the centre of attention), and, most of all, to meet people. It was time for her to make a few friends, and she daydreamed up a few imaginary ones that she could have round for coffee mornings in the new apartment: they were her age, warm, funny, kind – stylish would be a bonus, but not required – and with the beautiful soft accent from this part of the world that she was falling in love with. A gal could dream.

The plan was to walk the grounds and allocate each person an area they would subtly 'shepherd' people through, hopefully without it feeling in any way regimented. Mimi inspected her pedal pushers and decided with a dust down they were actually perfect for the agenda, but she'd ditch the head scarf in favour of a silk neck scarf, and make her hair and make up a little more presentable.

A fold up table served as Watson's desk to greet the group at the front door. The weather was glorious and the forecast in the newspaper for tomorrow even better. Mimi was glad she'd added her cat-eye sunglasses to her ensemble at the last minute. It was easy to forget them, as they weren't in daily use in her newly adopted country. Watson had a team of six, two of whom were gardeners who had already completed a morning shift on the grounds, and were sitting to the side, awaiting instruction. He expected that the others would be arriving on the local bus, which usually stopped at the end of the driveway, but most likely an agreement would be made where the driver brought them all the way up to the gates. He was correct and their four remaining volunteers arrived together. They walked across the gravel driveway towards them: three men, perhaps of retirement age, and one woman, who had a child with her, a nervous-looking young boy holding her hand.

Watson made a noise, and Mimi turned and frowned at him, quickly saying under her breath, 'That's perfectly fine, it's not as if we're covering rough terrain.'

Watson greeted the men with warm handshakes and greetings, which made Mimi think their working lives had been at Glenberry. She felt obliged to be the one to welcome the woman.

'How do you do? I'm Mimi Douglas-Lauder. Thank you so much for coming today.'

'I'm Peggy McPherson, it's a pleasure to meet you Mrs Douglas-Lauder. I hope you don't mind that I brought my son. It was very last minute, I thought my husband...Well anyway, tomorrow he will be able to join his friend's family for the picking. And he's going to be on his best behaviour today, aren't you Jim?'

'Hi Jim, it's very lovely to meet you. You're going to have a great time today. And tomorrow. There's lots to explore here. Oh wait, have you been here before?' The child nodded, shyly. Mimi thought he was about five.

'He's been coming since he was born. I've been coming since I was a wee one too – I'm Kilmour born and bred.'

'Oh well, you two will know more about the place than I do! I only just moved here and I'm still finding my way around. OK Jim, I'm counting on you to help us find our way back if I get us lost,' Mimi said, crouching down to his eye level. 'Gosh, do you know you have the same light blue eyes as your mom? Sorry, your *mum*. How lucky you are to have inherited them. You must think your mum is very pretty, don't you? So do I.'

Introductions were made among the whole ensemble and as Watson gave his opening remarks, Mimi stole a sideways glance at Peggy, wondering if it was too soon to hope they might be friends.

From the desk of Iain Watson, Glenberry
Wednesday 8th July, 1959

Work is well underway in the apartment. It's somewhat ironic that through her unconventional renovation, that is raising eyebrows all around, Mrs D-L has made the castle feel like the good old days: a hive of activity, and hustle and bustle. Mrs Law is in her element, running cups of tea up to the builders and hosting them in her kitchen for lunch of hearty soup, with bread delivered by Mr Rowan the baker, who is delighted to be making a daily visit once again. The tradesmen are similarly glad to be back at Glenberry and are very keen to please Mrs D-L, which is wonderful in terms of quality of work and timelines, though I have to keep an eye on them agreeing to some of her more radical ideas.

Mrs D-L has shown me numerous magazine pages of the vision for their new living room. I agree with her that the existing oak walls are not entirely in keeping with it, to say the least, but there is simply nothing we can do: it would be a travesty to rip out such beautiful timber and expert craftsmanship. Luckily the foreman not only agreed, but convinced Mrs D-L it was, in his words, a 'mud job', which would put her moving-in date back by several weeks, into months. Hopefully the furnishings she has ordered, and a new fitted carpet (we have never had a wall-to-wall carpet in the castle before, so we are bringing in a specialist from Glasgow), will satisfy the aesthetic she has in mind.

Tomorrow the Strawberry Fair is upon us and we expect it to be the busiest in several years, with perfect weather forecast, and the D-Ls in attendance. We had a walk through with the volunteer supervisors today, and Mrs D-L chatted the whole way with a Mrs Peggy McPherson, who was here with her son Jim. They seemed to get along very well, which was nice. Nowadays I don't suppose there would be any harm in a friendship with someone her own age from the villages.

Postscript: Mrs D-L has a hint of a suntan and appeared today in cat-eye glasses, looking like a film star. I can imagine the local ladies tomorrow being captivated by her modern looks and style, and I know, by the reaction of the gardeners today, when she emerged into the sunshine like it was a spotlight, that the men will be ~~ogling~~ charmed.

Postscript: Just as I was finishing today's missive, the foreman tracked me down. It seems that prior to the Strawberry Fair meeting this afternoon, Mrs D-L had already had quite the busy morning. She took it upon herself to take a chisel and attempt to prise apart the fireplace and the skirting board in her new living room. This was to justify to the foreman that the fireplace surround could be 'lifted right out', easily and intact. When I asked him if he believed that to be the case, he laughed, saying, 'easily' was a little unrealistic, but 'intact' he could probably manage. I suspect his professional pride is at stake. And I further suspect that he is as captivated by Mrs D-L as the aforementioned gardeners.

Now I suppose it's down to muggins here to figure out where to store the bally thing. It's too beautiful to scrap, but too big to be passed on and used in any ordinary sized house. I suppose we'll find space in a barn or a boathouse, and I shall secretly hope that it's not its permanent resting place.

15

One of the biggest renovation dilemmas Ally faced was the 1950's, imitation wood surround, electric fireplace, so her eyes nearly popped out of her head when she read about its installation in Watson's journal. No doubt it had been the height of mod cons at the time, but no matter how eclectic a vision one had, today it was just an eyesore. According to Watson's journal, the original fire surround might still be somewhere on the estate. Now, that would be a find.

There was a knock at the door: Scott the Builder. He hadn't caught her earlier this morning, after her walk, so would be doing his check in now.

'Hey Ally, how's it going?'

'Fine thanks, you?'

'Yeah good, just saying hello, nothing new to report really, he replied. 'We were a wee bit later to get started, but we've hit the ground running. I said I'd give them an extra half hour sleep in, after two nights on the trot at the Gillie's.'

'Fair enough, lucky them. As long as their work doesn't suffer,' she joked.

'I bumped into your sister-in-law there two nights ago but

didn't see her at the Strawberry Fair yesterday…' Scott let his pause ask the question.

Ally's heart sank to have to tell him the story.

'Actually, there was an accident, Scott. She's fine, but we all got quite a fright. She came off her Vespa into a ditch. Not her fault at all. Our *charming* neighbour, Derek Leslie, careened out of here in a rage, and she had to swerve to avoid him.'

'Oh no, poor Louise,' he said seriously. 'But you say she's OK?'

'She slept most of yesterday – the shock caught up with her I suppose. She's a bit tender, but no broken bones or anything.'

'Well, when you do see her, tell her I'm asking for her. I thought it was a shame her night out was cut short, and then all that. Poor her.'

'I will do. Thanks Scott, she'll appreciate it.'

She'll be wetting herself, Ally thought.

'While I have you here, I've just learned something very interesting,' she said.

'Oh yeah?' Scott asked.

'Yes, extremely interesting. You know how much we've been struggling to find a replacement fireplace?'

He nodded. They had gone over their quandary a few times. Any ready-made replicas were too small and a bit cheap looking, but a custom one, made to the standard they'd like, would be cost-prohibitive. If they had all the time in the world, they could pick through the architectural salvage yards in Glasgow, but that was a hit and miss, and Ally wasn't exactly in a position to do that.

'Well, what if I told you the original might have been put into storage at the time? Somewhere here on the estate?'

'I'd say that would be jackpot,' Scott said, smiling.

'You know I've been looking through these old papers? It turns out I'm living vicariously through the 1959 re-do, as well as this one,' Ally explained.

'Oh wow, what were the chances? 1959 you say? We'd guessed early sixties, so I guess the Laird's mother was ahead of her time,' Scott said.

'Seems so, and I don't think the estate manager was totally on board with all her modern ideas, the new fire being one of them. There's an entry about when he found out about it, and it seems to have been a fait accompli between Mimi and her builder by the time he did.'

Scott laughed. 'And he wasn't happy about it? He could have saved us some work if he'd managed to stand his ground.'

'I know, but here's the thing: he mentions that he doesn't want to just dump the old surround and – here – 'Ally said, pointing to the entry, 'he's wondering where he can store it.'

'Does he land on an answer?' Scott asked.

'No, he just says in one of the barns or boat sheds,' Ally replied. 'Problem is, there are quite a few of them. I don't even know where they all are, and the couple that I've peeked into are packed to the gunnels with all sorts – literally centuries worth of hoarding.'

'Well, it would certainly be worth a look. As I say, that would be jackpot. Are you going to send Alec on the search?'

'He's really busy with work and couldn't be trusted not to get waylaid and come back with "interesting" junk,' Ally said.

'Could the Laird show me around, maybe?' Scott asked.

'He's worse. You should have seen the rabbit hole he went down the other night, just looking through old pictures.'

Ally had a serendipitous idea. 'What about Louise? She knows this place just as well as her dad and Alec, but she won't get caught up in dusty old artifacts. She could be your tour guide around all the possible sites, and with your expert eye, you can be the treasure hunter. A dream team.'

Louise would be bursting with glee if she was here. Ally tried to keep a straight face.

Scott might be trying to mask a cheesy smile too. 'Well, that sounds like a plan when she's feeling up to it,' he said.

'Oh, I'm sure she'll bounce back quickly.'

Louise bounced back, that afternoon in fact, with the news she'd be exploring dark corners of secluded outbuildings with Scott the Builder. She showed up towards the end of his shift, looking adorable as always, in the perfect OOTD for their mission: a simple navy crew neck, dark jeans and cool new red trainers. Ally nudged her and nodded at the shoes, knowing that red was her lucky colour.

'Well, duh,' Louise whispered, smiling.

They were gone for about an hour, during which Ally gave in to a late afternoon nap. She woke to hear them laughing, coming back into her half-built kitchen. She had a quick spruce and brushed her teeth, then joined them. Scott's team had cleaned up and packed up, and were presumably waiting for him outside, so it was just the two of them.

'Any luck?' Ally interrupted their chit chat.

'Not today, but I know where we've been, and where we've still to cover, so we can resume the hunt tomorrow afternoon,' Louise answered.

'I'm glad you can keep track,' Scott said. 'I'd be going round in circles, I think. So many old huts in random spots. I would have kept going, but my guys and I all came in the same van today, and I didn't want to hold them back. I'll come back tomorrow and continue the search.'

'On a Saturday? Are you sure?'

'It's no problem, I'm hoping as much as you are that we find it.'

All the while he was talking, Louise, slightly behind him and out of his range of sight, was grinning from ear to ear at Ally.

'Sounds like a plan,' Ally said, as business-like as she could, trying to ignore her delighted sister-in-law. 'Are you heading out now then?'

'Yup.' Scott gave a nod, though his feet stayed planted to the spot.

Ally took the hint, turned to leave and said brightly, 'Bye then, see you tomorrow.' She shut the door behind her, knowing that the noisy latch would punctuate her departure, and let Louise and Scott say their goodbyes for the day alone.

Not with much intent, she picked up Watson's journals. When she reached Watson's entry about the fireplace she'd got sidetracked, making plans of attack with Louise and Scott, then lost on Pinterest, dreaming of the beautiful fireplace restored to its rightful place.

She leafed distractedly to Watson's next entry. Her heart sank at his ominous first attempts.

~~I am enraged, yet numb with helplessness.~~
~~There are no words~~
~~I am at a loss.~~
I am bereft.

Yesterday's Strawberry Fair began auspiciously and ended devastatingly. I will be brief as Mrs D-L has been emphatic in her wish that we try to remember the day only as a happy success.

Louise burst through the door with an excited, 'Eeeh!' and threw herself on the couch beside Ally.

The sixty-year-old journal entry would have to wait.

16

—————

'I don't recall my mother putting so much thought into her attire for the Strawberry Fair,' Alexander teased.

Mimi had decided to stick with her denim pedal pushers, but there was a pile of discarded blouses on the bed, as she chose between options Alexander wouldn't understand even if she tried to explain: short and boxy or nipped-in at the waist; linen or cotton; plain or gingham; V-neck or Peter Pan.

Red gingham, with a nipped-in waist was the final choice.

There was still a curler in the front of her hair, as she finished applying her lipstick – 'Berry Red' – but Alexander wouldn't get the cleverness of that either. 'I just want to make the best impression I can,' she said, thinking she might even be feeling the sting of beads of nervous sweat under her arms.

'I'd say everyone is going to love you, but I know the opinion you most care about is your new friend Peggy McPherson's. You really are quite taken with her, aren't you? I never saw you this twitchy before any of the dinners and events we attended in London, no matter who was going to be there. You've been at a dinner with Princess Margaret, but Peggy McPherson from Kilmour has got you all a flutter.'

'I know you think it's silly, but she was so sweet, and it would be lovely to have a pal here. We had such interesting conversations. She seems intelligent and up on things I'd like a friend to be up on. She mentioned doing "clerical work" in the war – and you know what that means.'

'That she was a spy? You think everyone was a spy!' Alexander laughed.

'Well, there must have been a great many spies who helped us win the war, so there's a high chance we've come across a few. I've heard the vague "clerical work" too many times. Anyway, it was lovely to be around her. And her son too. I told her to arrive a little early today – will you come down and let me introduce you to her? I know you'll like her too.'

'Of course, I'd love to,' Alexander said, kissing his wife on the cheek. 'Now I'm ready to go down as soon as you take that curler out of your hair.'

MIMI MET PEGGY FIRST, and Alexander arrived shortly afterwards with three glasses of ginger beer. Mimi was delighted with this charming initiative, and she saw that Peggy was taken aback (in a good way) at receiving a personal welcome from the Laird. *Nice touch, Alexander!*

'I'm so pleased to meet you,' he said, 'and I'm sure Watson has done so already, but let me thank you again for being one of our team today. We couldn't pull this off without you.'

'Not at all, it's my pleasure to help,' Peggy replied.

'Mimi tells me that you've been coming to the Strawberry Fair since you were a child. I'm excited for her to experience her first one,' Alexander said.

Another nice touch. Letting Peggy know they'd spoken about her. Mimi was impressed again: she'd opened up, and he'd really listened.

They chatted and laughed easily, until they were called off on their respective official duties.

The couple's first role was to walk along the long driveway away from the castle, as everyone else was coming in, to greet them and thank them for coming.

'Ready?' Alexander asked, as he took Mimi's hand. 'Knock 'em dead, as they say. They're going to love you.'

The rhododendrons around the gates were so abundant they obscured the view of the driveway beyond, and the hum of the approaching crowd was muffled by the woodland flanking their path in. Passing through the gates, the sound gathered and sharpened, and the full sight on the other side stopped Mimi in her tracks.

Throngs of people were moving towards her, carrying berry-picking buckets, picnic baskets and blankets. Vehicles lined the road – mostly vans and small farm tractors hauling hay trailers – from which yet more people spilled to join the pilgrimage. It felt like a curious crossover between a Fall hayride and Grand Central Terminal at rush hour.

The emotion hit Mimi, in the chest first, taking her breath away. It quickly sprang to her eyes as tears.

'Oh,' was all she could manage.

Alexander let go of her hand and slipped his arm around her shoulders as they kept walking.

'It's quite something isn't it?' he said.

A couple of deep sobs caught her breath. She had joked that this whole Strawberry Fair thing seemed too good to be true, and it turned out it was even more extraordinary than she could have imagined.

The jovial battalion marched towards them along the narrow canyon formed by the tall pines on either side. Adults laughed and chatted among themselves, their daughters skipping neatly beside them, while their sons gambolled in and out of the woods, leaping onto every rock and tree stump, stretching the journey to twice the length it needed to be. The front rows began to wave, and Mimi and Alexander waved back.

Mimi felt an overwhelming mix of celebration and gratitude. Something about it felt familiar, though she couldn't yet place why.

As the first people came into earshot, she heard their warm greetings. 'Welcome to Scotland Mrs Douglas-Lauder... Welcome to Glenberry, hen.'

But it was their well-wishes to her husband that struck her like a bell. 'Welcome home, young man,' took her right back: the whole scene had the same collective, triumphant pride as the ticker-tape parades down Fifth Avenue for soldiers returning from the war.

Well now, that wasn't going to help with her emotional composure.

They walked against the tide, shaking hands where they could, and Mimi tried to take in all the well-wishes, even as she was still tuning her ear to the accent:

Are you settling in all right, love? I hope he's looking after you OK (with a mock-chiding frown in Alexander's direction) Are you getting used to the weather here? Did you like your new coffee set? I used to work in the kitchen with Mrs Law and helped pick it out – it's a bonnie design.

A group of young girls curtseyed and presented her with bunches of daisies and dandelions picked en route, telling her, 'You're really pretty,' and, 'I like your blouse'.

When they reached the end of the procession, they fell in with the group bringing up the rear: a few elderly gentlemen, former estate workers, moving at a gentler pace, with no ambition to join the berry-picking. Mimi enjoyed listening to their stories of their time at Glenberry just as much as they enjoyed telling them. She was almost dismayed when the castle loomed close and she knew she'd have to bid adieu for now. Mimi said she hoped they might come round for a whisky sometime and tell her a few of the stories Watson seemed to keep to himself.

One of them chuckled. 'Oh, hen,' he said, 'he doesnae know the half of it.'

When they returned to the same point where he'd had to give her a reassuring squeeze on their way out, Alexander held her back and did so again. He grinned at her, 'What do you think? Isn't it *swell*? To use the vernacular of your homeland.'

'Oh, it sure is! I'm just blown away. I really am. I want to write and tell my parents about it, but you really have to see it to believe it. Look at all this activity, everyone just knows what to do. They're like soldier ants heading out on their missions.'

'Yes, and I should join them. I'm a mere foot soldier today too, so I'll find Watson and get my marching orders. You're just going to stay and mingle on the lawn, aren't you? There will be plenty of mums and babies, and older guys like your new friends there, who won't be going out picking, so you'll have plenty to keep you busy.'

'Sounds good to me. And I have a little surprise for you later, or a wee one, to use my new homeland's vernacular. Watson helped me with an extra treat. I hope you'll like it.'

'I'm intrigued, can't wait. Right give me a kiss and I'd better be off.'

MIMI HAD WORKED with a certain type of male Londoners at the stockbrokers, who didn't pull their punches about her moving to Scotland: 'Ever heard of Hadrian's Wall – they're Barbarians up there... Did you hear about the Scotsman who dropped a shilling? It hit him on the back of the head on its way down... Get ready for porridge and whisky for breakfast.'

Her friends made kinder jokes around the Scots being a bit rough around the edges, frugal, and liking a drink. But they also assured Mimi the Scots were above all, friendly, kind and chatty. If Mimi was asked to describe Great Lawn that day in three words, those were the three she would choose.

A group of young women surrounded by prams called her over as soon as she walked down the small slope to the flat expanse of grass. They introduced themselves, invited her to coo at their babies and presented her with an empty basket. 'We took all of our stuff out of this one, and we'll make do with sharing on the way back home.'

Mimi thanked them, very hesitantly.

They laughed. 'A lot of people will have wee gifts for you; you're going to need this to put them in.'

'Gifts for me? It's all so kind. Why would people do that?' Mimi asked, genuinely.

'Och, just wee mindings to welcome you and say thank you for having us today. We'll start you off. Last year we picked some lavender, so instead of jam – you're going to get a lot of jam – we made you some lavender bags for your knicker drawers.'

Mimi took the hand embroidered linen pouches, with lilac ribbon, and gulped. Her voice only just managed a thank you and she looked at the women with glassy eyes.

'Och, don't be greetin, you've got a lot of rounds to do! Look over there. That group of old dears is bursting to say hello – you'd better get moving!' And the woman gently pushed her in their direction.

'Hello there hen, come in, come in,' one of the older ladies said, gesturing to an empty folding chair. A warm powwow ensued, and once again Mimi was with a group of people whose company she could have kept all day, but she sensed the pull of her next audience.

'Wait a minute, pet. We have wedding present for you. Something that's a very old Scottish tradition.' The woman's tone was serious, but Mimi saw a twinkle in her eye and heard mischievous giggling all around.

'It's very important that this tradition is passed from generation to generation, so we are honoured to be the elders who bestow it upon you,' she said reaching into a bag beside her chair to increasing cackles from her co-conspirators.

With a theatrical flourish, she pulled out a gleaming silver baton which flashed blazes of light as it caught the sunlight. It was as if she was triumphantly wielding Excalibur.

The women were enjoying this immensely, and the commotion caught the attention of their husbands sitting a few feet away.

'Oy, what you got there?' He squinted and realised what it was. 'Oh Mary, why are you poisoning Love's Young Dream with your jadedness, ya old bag?'

'What is it?' his friend asked.

'It's a bloody rolling pin,' he replied.

The women laughed even louder at his disdain.

Mary confirmed, 'Aye, it's a rolling pin, to keep the Laird in line if he gives you any trouble – just gie him a bash o'er the heid with it!'

Mimi couldn't help but join in the laughter, and accepted the wooden implement, wrapped in foil and decorated with ribbons and dried flowers at each end. She gave both groups a bow of thanks and punched the air with the rolling pin as she walked away, raising cheers from the women and head-shaking mutters from their husbands.

MIMI HAD to request an overspill crate because by the end of the afternoon her basket had been filled several times over. There were jars and bottles of all variety of potions made from last year's harvest and batches of homemade shortbread and oatcakes. The poke of tablet was accompanied by an explanation that a 'poke' means a bag or a pouch, and 'tablet' is a sweet made by boiling sugar and condensed milk (the giver quite smug that Mrs Law hadn't already introduced it to Mimi). There were dried bunches of heather, embroidered handkerchiefs, and lucky horseshoes beautifully decorated with ribbon and flowers.

It all made Mimi wish the small gesture she had organised wasn't quite so small, but she was glad that she had acted upon her instinct to do *something*.

Alexander was lying on a blanket, soaking in the afternoon sun – like everyone else, his belly full and body tired. It was the right time for Mimi to find Watson and distribute the mindings they had arranged for the children. He'd most likely be in the kitchen with Mrs Law, so snuck off towards the side of the castle, rather than go through the castle, turning her back on what was now a quiet hum of subdued chatter on the lawn. She hadn't taken part in the manual labour, but she had that pleasant, contented, end-of-a-full-day feeling: her cheeks hurt from smiling and laughing, and there was a slight sting of sunburn on her arms. Was replete the correct word, she wondered.

Someone appeared at her shoulder.

'Good afternoon, Mrs Douglas-Lauder.'

'Oh!' She was startled by the deep voice, that little bit closer than was polite. She stopped and said, 'Hi, um –'

'Derek Leslie, I met you a few weeks ago, out walking the property line with my dad,' he smiled.

He was standing with his back to the sun, so Mimi was having to squint up at him.

He manoeuvred himself to shade her. 'Sorry – remember me now?'

She did, but it didn't make her feel any more comfortable. 'Yes – yes I do. Have you been working hard today, Derek?'

'Oh yes, I picked quite the crop,' he boasted.

'Good for you, thank you for coming –'

'It's my pleasure. Especially to see you looking so beautiful today.'

'That's nice of you to say, but I really must be getting –'

'I love that shirt.'

Mimi turned away and started walking again. She'd been around the block enough times to not hang around listening to this kid talking about her top. While he stared at it too. 'I've got business to attend to inside, it was nice seeing you.'

'I'll walk with you.'

'There's no need, Mr Watson is waiting to help me inside.'

Surely mentioning Watson would deter this jerk? Nope – he kept step with her round the side of the castle.

They were now out of sight of the lawn.

'It's a clever design, isn't it? Your shirt? Completely covered up and yet very provocative?'

Mimi glared at the hand he'd put on her shoulder, then shoved it off.

'Oh come on now, m'lady. Don't pretend you're not loving being Queen of the Castle. And all the attention. Surely you expected a wee bit extra-special attention too?'

He shoved her against the wall, the impact knocking the breath from her lungs.

The rough stone cut into her back in several different places, one of them directly on her spine, so sharp she felt like she was skewered.

Holding her in place with his body and one arm, he grabbed at her breast with the other hand.

She shoved at him, managing to knock his hand away, but he caught her wrist and slammed it back against the wall, pinning it there.

'Get off me,' she growled.

He answered by forcing his knee between her legs, pushing them apart, his shoulder grinding her back into the stone. His free hand clawed at her over the denim of her pedal pushers. Pain pulsed through her back with every movement. She twisted, tried to pull free, but he drove her into the wall again, harder this time. His violence was sharp and vicious.

Her energy was wasted fighting back, she had to muster a cry for help, but he shoved his face to hers, pushed his mouth against hers, blocking any chance to take a breath.

His bottom lip protruded into her mouth.

She bit down hard.

As he drew back in fright and pain, a metal spade struck him hard in the middle of his back and he fell to the ground.

Peggy dropped the spade and opened her arms to Mimi, at the same time as Watson appeared from around the back. There was a break in the frantic action for a few seconds as he looked from the women to Derek Leslie, quickly assessed the situation, and yanked the man from the ground and pinned him against the spot on the wall Mimi had just escaped.

'Mrs McPherson, may I trouble you to go and fetch Mr Douglas-Lauder please?'

'No Watson, please let's not do that,' Mimi said. She was shaking uncontrollably, but there were no tears.

'I beg your pardon?' Watson asked, not letting his glare or grip weaken.

'I said, let's not do that. Please.'

'But –'

'Let the bastard go. I have something more important you have to do for me.'

Mimi felt bad knowing Watson wouldn't understand, but Peggy nodded and squeezed her arm in agreement. She got it. Women got it.

Watson banged Leslie against the wall five times, in time to 'Get. Out. Of. My. Sight.' and let him go.

'Watson, Peggy and I are going to go inside, and she's going to help me get cleaned up. Could you please take my boxes of sherbet lollipops to my husband and ask him to pass them around the children. Just tell him I couldn't wait to show Peggy the changes I'm making to the apartment. As you know, he'll find that entirely believable.'

Watson said nothing but asked her everything with his silence. She held his gaze and sought his understanding with her eyes.

'It's just what we do Watson,' she finally said, quietly.

❧

From the desk of Iain Watson, Glenberry
Thursday 9th July, 1959

I ~~am enraged, yet numb with helplessness.~~
~~There are no words~~
~~I am at a loss.~~
I am bereft.

Yesterday's Strawberry Fair began auspiciously and ended devastatingly. I will be brief as Mrs D-L has been emphatic in her wish that we try to remember the day only as a happy success.

The mood of the crowd as they arrived was positively jubilant. Word has spread that Mrs D-L is making her mark in the castle, and that the couple is likely to stay at Glenberry, rather than flit back to London having given it a go, as was a concern (including of yours truly). The couple's joy was apparent: Mrs D-L could be compared to a wide-eyed child at Christmas as the denizens arrived, and her husband revelled in her delight, and in how she charmed one and all. We had bumper crops of both strawberries and early raspberries to boot.

Mrs Law and I had a short respite in the kitchen nearing the end of the day. It was then that I heard a commotion from outside. I rushed out to find the neighbour's son writhing on the ground, apparently having been whacked on the back with a spade by Mrs D-L's new ~~acquaintance~~ friend, Mrs Peggy McPherson. She had her arm around Mrs D-L, who was trembling and looked straight at me. There was no doubt what had happened, one didn't have to have witnessed it: Derek Leslie had attacked Mrs D-L, and not in any way that could be misunderstood.

I immediately arrested the young man and asked for Mr D-L to be summoned. Mrs D-L, however, quickly objected and forbade that I do so. I was instructed to release him, which I did so reluctantly and not before I had given him several sharp dunts against the wall. To my utter dismay, I had to let the despicable villain go upon his way.

Quickly and quietly, the ladies retired to 'clean up', which I assume meant attend to Mrs D-L's injuries. (I'm not ashamed to admit that tears sting my eyes as I write that).

Complying with Mrs D-L's wishes, Mr D-L and I dispensed the sherbet lollipops she and I had arranged in secret. This was a thoughtful surprise for him, as well as the delighted children. He was appropriately proud of her. I could only think of her, upstairs, being tended by Mrs McPherson.

I am no innocent, nor a stranger to discrimination, and I hope I endeavour to see the world from others' points of view where I can. For instance, I persuaded a friend to see *Room at the Top* earlier this year (a departure from the frippery they prefer to see at the films), and I felt informed, somewhat, on the plight of some women even in our modern world. However, but Mrs D-L continues to educate me.

We had quite a long conversation this morning and I confessed to her that I am struggling to understand <u>our</u> cover-up of a crime, an assault, <u>against her</u>. Surely, I said, the law is on her side, not Derek Leslie's.

I'm afraid she made me see that, although the law is on the side of the victim, the process and the biases are not. She asked me to imagine the effect on the household and the community, if she were to report this crime. While we lived in No Man's Land waiting for a trial, the hearing, a verdict, there would be gossip and finger-pointing: how had she come to be alone with him in the first place; wasn't it strange the only witness was a female friend; imagine ruining a young man's life over a miscommunication and few bruises. She asked if I wanted to be the one to photograph those bruises as evidence, or should she go to the police station and strip for whoever was on duty there.

Mrs D-L assured me the incident was over in a flash, almost dismissing it as sort of a lucky escape, rather than the violent assault it was. It was upsetting too, how casually she mentioned times when she was 'pawed' in her place of work, or at (elegant) social events, even if none of those had led violence. It's quite sickening.

In the end, whatever twists and turns our conversation took, she is determined that she will not be reporting this to officials, nor to her husband. I feel crushed by the injustice, but now understand her position better.

What Mrs D-L doesn't know is that Derek Leslie's father has been trying to persuade the estate to concede a small strip of land between our properties. He claims there is dubiety over the positioning of an historic stone wall. It would be nothing to us to let him have the benefit of the doubt, and would save him a lot of trouble over the diverting of a stream that is causing problems. Mr D-L had been inclined to concede, but in the absence of equitable justice by measure of the law, I shall be dispensing my own. As Mr D-L would say, the Leslies can whistle for it!

17

———————

Ally only realised she was crying when an escaped tear fell onto Watson's journal on her lap. She scanned back over his words, letting them sink in. Derek Leslie, who had burst into the castle just a couple of night before, ranting, raving and calling her names, had sexually assaulted Mimi at her first Strawberry Fair.

She reached for the photo of Mimi taken on that day. She took in the sunlight on her face, a picture of composure and radiance – a cherished new wife, her future safe and assured. Ally couldn't look away. It was like pressing on a bruise to test how much more it could hurt. It gave her an eery, sickening sense of prescience, knowing what Mimi didn't, what lay waiting just hours ahead.

And Watson – Ally's erstwhile nemesis from a different age. She looked at his photo from the same day, and her eyes welled up anew. His words made plain how bereft he was, how useless he felt, unable to protect his new mistress. Against the odds, Mimi and Watson had been becoming friends, and now they had become confidants in the grimmest of circumstances.

Poor Watson referred to 1959 as the 'modern world' and

lamented what women had to put up with in it. How sad he would be to know that such battles were far from over, sixty years on. Ally had only recently read the disturbing statistics herself: how much went unreported, how long cases dragged on, how often women withdrew, not from guilt or doubt, but because the process itself exacted its own toll.

It occurred to Ally she was turning these facts over as if preparing for a conversation she wished she could have with Watson. Perhaps to comfort him that his helplessness was almost inevitable. It was highly unlikely he'd ever have been able to talk Mimi into going to the police, but he did a good thing in just listening and understanding, rather than trying to sway her.

'Derek. Fucking. Leslie.'

Ally said it out loud to the empty room, through gritted teeth.

She went back to what Watson had written about dispensing his own justice, and about not giving the Leslies the land.

There must be more. Please, Watson – give me something more to go on.

She skimmed the next two entries. Mention of Mimi taking a trip to Glasgow, but uneventful. On the third, however, Watson came up trumps.

I finally managed to get an appointment to visit Leslie Snr. Perhaps it was for the best that there was a delay, because Lord knows my heart was pumping out of my chest even as it was.

I presented Leslie with my envelope, where-within was an agreement I had crafted, sorting out the ambiguity he claims exists over the positioning of the stone wall. The agreement was firmly in Glenberry's favour.

Leslie knows that this hardly matters a jot to us for any intents or purpose, and given Mr D-L's benign demeanour, I suppose he expected us to be complying with his request. My heart thumped even louder in my chest, taking my breath away, as I saw his face gradually fall upon reading it.

The anticipation rose, as I wondered if I'd be bold enough to deliver any of the speeches that had been swimming around in my head. I'm proud to say that I was. When he angrily questioned what he considered to be a change of mind, I suggested he ask his son what might have given rise to it. Of course he looked puzzled, so I appraised him of the events of the Strawberry Fair, and of my firm belief that had Mrs D-L's friend not saved the day, things would have been catastrophic. If he didn't believe me, I was sure his son would have quite the black and blue lower back, from where she whacked him. (And perhaps also from being pounded against the wall by Yours Truly.)

I received no argument in return, which speaks to his own opinion of his son, I think. He signed my missive and handed it back to me silently, his face grave. I explained that my signature on behalf of Glenberry was sufficient, as my mistress had decided to keep the incident private. I was considering the matter closed and did not want Mr D-L to be troubled with it again. He simply nodded his concurrence and gestured towards the door, signalling my exit.

It took me the drive back to Glenberry before my breathing returned to normal.

Ally gave a small fist pump of solidarity at Watson's mettle. *Good for you Watson!*

But where did he put the contract?

She returned to his journal, feeling guilty that she was skimming through Watson's expressions of mixed emotions.

As agreed with Mrs D-L, I have told Mr D-L that the Leslie's have come up with another solution to their problem, and they no longer seek ownership of the strip of land in question. Mrs D-L also requested that she keep possession of the signed document, which she will store under lock and key, along with her private correspondence, 'just in case'. I very much doubt we'll have need of it again: Leslie was resigned, no doubt due to the shocking circumstances.

Wrong, Watson, we do need it, sixty years later.

She pondered for a few seconds, then picked up her phone to text Sandy.

> Ally: Are you around? I need a favour. I might have good news on our Leslie problem.
>
> Sandy: That sounds like a favour worth doing. What do you need?
>
> Ally: Where did Mimi's writing desk end up when we moved it out of the apartment?
>
> Sandy: Hmm, one of the front bedrooms I'm pretty sure. Won't take me long to find it.
>
> Ally: OK, bigger challenge – the side drawers were always locked, but the keys missing. Any good at breaking and entering?

There was a pause. Sandy was thinking.

> Sandy: You probably won't be surprised to know we have another old desk, that has a drawer full of keys. I'll grab a Tupperware and take them with me to track the desk down.
>
> Ally: I'm coming too! I'll meet you and your Tupperware of keys in ten minutes in the front corridor.
>
> Sandy: Roger Wilco.

In a miracle that Ally felt thought she, Watson and Mimi deserved after the week they'd all had, albeit that Watson's and Mimi's was sixty years ago, it took only took ten minutes of methodical and patient shoogling to get Mimi's desk drawers open.

The right-hand one contained just one envelope.

Sandy handed it to Ally. 'You know what it is you're looking for – I haven't a clue.'

She carefully eased the envelope's contents free, unfolded and read, carefully in silence.

'We've found it,' she said with a small smile and handed the paper to Sandy.

'Bloody hell, Ally,' he said, reading. 'How did you know to look for this?'

'Watson mentioned it in his journals. It's a bit of a long story – I'll tell you later.' When she'd figured out what fib to tell him.

It was Derek Leslie's son who answered when she rang the doorbell.

'Mrs Douglas-Lauder, I've been meaning to contact you,' he said, his apologetic tone disarming her. 'I believe my father was round at Glenberry the other evening on one of his rants. Please do come in.'

Sitting in their drawing room, Leslie's son talked as if she was a friend he'd been expecting. He was concerned that his father was in the early stages of dementia. The family was trying to figure out the testing and diagnosis process, and the steps after that. In the meantime, they had organised shifts of people discreetly manning the house most evenings, in part to moderate his drinking. He suspected his father drank to blank out, well, the blanks.

'It's terribly sad, because I think on some level he knows, but he can forget his forgetfulness when he drinks. The problem is, the stress is still there and it often manifests itself as aggression. I'm very sorry that the other night there was a hole in our schedule of friends and family sitting with him, and it ended up in...well, again, I'm very sorry.'

This whole episode from the past had been a roller coaster and it kept on coming. Ally could not have expected to ever feel an ounce of compassion for Derek Leslie, or any of his family, but his son painted such an upsetting picture, even struggling to get the words out at various times. 'I'm sorry to hear all this,' she said. 'It's such a horrible disease.'

'Thank you. I assume his behaviour is the reason for your visit?'

Ally wasn't sure where to start. Tearing into Derek Leslie himself had been plan A, not that she'd really had a firm plan.

'It wasn't just about that, no,' she began. 'It's about this ongoing dispute with your father insisting that there was a transfer of a section of land years ago, over a gentleman's hand-shake. What's your understanding of the history behind that?'

Leslie's son sighed. 'One of the reason's we began to suspect dementia is because of state my father has been getting himself into over that. He just cannot be reasoned with. None of the rest of the family is particularly worried about your music festival. In fact, my children are hoping to attend this year and have some friends down to stay. But Dad has become obsessed.'

He paused. Then: '*However*, I *will say* that I have always understood his story to be true. He would mention it on our walks around the perimeter of the property. Has done for years – while he was still completely astute, I mean. According to him sometime around 1960, when he was a uni student, a deal was done with the former estate manager for Glenberry. I recall his name was Iain Watson?'

'That's right,' Ally nodded.

'He claimed to remember the day it happened. He said

Watson paid a visit and afterwards, his father, my grandfather, told him that everything was sorted.'

Ally had a sinking feeling about what had happened here at the Leslie property after Watson left that day. 'Do you know why your grandfather needed the land?'

'Yes, something about diverting the burn – or damming it or something. But my father said they found another solution in the end.'

He was genuine, telling the truth as he'd been told it. He had no reason at all to suspect that the story had been falsified by his grandfather, to protect his son.

Derek Leslie had never even so much as been confronted by his own father over his assault on Mimi, never mind face the consequence of the law. His father had protected him from his own wrongdoing completely.

This was yet another bitter pill to swallow. The knowledge settled heavily in her chest: that men like Derek Leslie didn't need cleverness or cunning to escape consequence, just someone who thought nothing of looking the other way.

'Right well I'm afraid I have something that casts doubt on all of that.'

Why was she being so nice?

'What I should say is, I have evidence that your father is wrong.'

Ally had two choices now: tell Leslie's son the full story, that the land had not been granted because Watson had witnessed his father sexually assault the Laird's new wife, or collude in the decades-old cover-up protecting a repugnant young man.

She held out the envelope, and Leslie's son read its contents.

'Well, that's fairly clear,' he said, weary from the weight of heavier worries. 'I'm assuming I can trust that this is genuine. How did you find it?'

'With a little sleuthing,' she replied.

'I wonder why on earth my father remembers things so differently.'

Ally had come here on autopilot, fuelled by indignant fury, no question that moral justice would be delivered at Leslie's door. Now ... truth and justice... she felt the choice of truth settle in her body before it reached her mind. Her only comfort was that if anyone would understand, it was Mimi and Watson. Compassion won out, against the will of her ire.

'There must have been some kind of misunderstanding.'

Misunderstanding. Ally felt utter resignation in using the word.

'I brought you a photocopy of it for your records. I hope you can convince your father of its veracity.'

'I will try my very best,' he assured her.

Ally drove home, thinking of Watson, silently apologising to him for letting the insidious cover-up live on.

18

I t was as if Mimi felt the pain of her bruises, which were
yet to even become bruises, before she woke up the next
morning. Perhaps it was the pain itself that woke her up. She
was facing away from Alec but could tell from his stillness
and the regularity of his breathing, that he was still fast
asleep.

Yesterday's events flashed through her mind. They were
bookended by the joyous ticker-tape parade of locals into the
Glenberry grounds in the morning, and Alec's contented
sunburned face in the evening, smiling into his whisky
tumbler. The violent memory of Derek Leslie jarred the reel of
pictures and she felt resentful.

How dare Derek Leslie mar that perfect day. It was one of
many reasons that she made Watson promise to not mention
the incident to anyone else, or for that matter, mention it at all,
ever again. She knew that eventually she'd be able to flood her
memories of the day with only the good ones only, but the
same was not true of her husband. Watson's reaction had been
bad enough. His anger had turned to sorrow, then to indignation, then to determination: he told her about a boundary

agreement the Leslies were seeking and that now 'they could whistle for it.'

Peggy had been amazing, ushering her up to the bedroom with an arm gently around her, hugging her once they were safely out of sight. Then she shifted into pragmatic mode, taking Mimi's blouse along the hall to the bathroom, to wash out the dirt and blood. She made no suggestions that Mimi tell Alexander or anyone else, and there was no disbelief that this had happened.

As they sat on the edge of the bed together, Peggy took in the room and said, 'Well, this is one way to wangle my way into the inner sanctum of Glenberry Castle. My mum would be jealous.'

Mimi gave a small chuckle and replied, 'Yes, welcome to my humble abode. What do you think?'

'Actually, it's probably exactly as I would have imagined when I came to the Strawberry Fair as a wee girl. You've even got a princess bed.' Peggy gestured to the opulent canopy.

'Oh I know. Can you imagine how I felt my first day here? We kinda keep things simple and modern in the States. This was a bit of a shock, I'll tell ya. I'm getting there gradually though. And I've recently brokered a deal with the Omnipotent Watson to make new living apartments. It's very exciting – wanna come see?' She stood up and offered Peggy a hand. 'C'mon, it'll take our minds off that asshole who thought he could get a piece of me.'

'I'd love to,' Peggy said, standing up. Then smiled and said, 'Have you read PG Wodehouse? You saying "the Omnipotent Watson" reminded me…'

'Of the Efficient Baxter from the *Blandings Castle* books?' Mimi finished for her. 'Yes! I've never called him that before, it just came to me there. How funny that you recognised the reference. I read them to prepare me for castle life, not realising quite how silly they are. Maybe we can choose a book to read together next? Peggy, I think this is the beginning of a beautiful friendship.'

'*Casablanca!*' Peggy said, pointing at Mimi and laughing.

MIMI WAS HEARTENED to realise she was smiling into the dark remembering the part of the day that she'd spent with her new friend. She felt Alec stirring, then roll over to give her a squeeze as he did every morning, which made her wince in pain. It was hard to disguise her sharp intake of breath.

'Are you OK?' Alec asked.

'Yes fine, you just startled me. I was just lying here thinking about what a lovely day we had yesterday.'

'It was wonderful. *You* were wonderful. I think we can safely say you were a hit.' He held her tighter, unknowingly finding more pain points.

Mimi knew where this dozy adoration would lead. She couldn't today, and not just because of the physical pain. She needed a little space and some time alone while she became inured to the ugly part of yesterday. She quickly disentangled herself and slid off the bed, turning to smile at him as he groaned in protestation.

'I think I'm gonna head up to Glasgow today. Is that OK?'

'Do you have a hair appointment?'

'No, I just feel like a wander around. Yesterday was lovely, but that was a lot of socialising – it quite took it out of me. I'll enjoy a wee day to myself.' She emphasised the 'wee' to please her husband.

'That sounds nice. I wish I could offer to come with you, but Watson will have me busy with the recap of yesterday and taking inventory of our berry haul.'

Mimi was relieved. She didn't want to reject him for a second time. It wasn't his fault Derek Leslie was causing her to pull away from him and Glenberry for the day.

.   .   .

LEAVING CENTRAL STATION, Mimi started towards Buchanan Street as usual but stopped in front of the ornate Gothic entrance to the subway, or the Underground, as Watson called it. He claimed it was the third oldest underground system in the world, which she doubted – she would get around to fact-checking that in an encyclopaedia in the library one of these days.

She'd asked him where the subway stops were, and he'd replied: 'Oh nowhere you'd be interested in really. And some places you'd rather not go.'

Oh really, Watson? Well, I'll be the judge of that. Mimi smiled to herself and turned towards the station feeling a small thrill of rebellion.

'Where do you suggest I get off?' she asked the man who sold her the ticket.

'Whit?' Was the confused reply. 'Depends whit you're looking for.'

'Some place interesting.'

From behind her, the next person in the ticket line, a young man, said, 'Partick Cross. Get out there. You can walk to the University, the Art Gallery and the Park from there. Turn left out of the station and you can't miss them.'

The train rattled through tiny tunnels and Mimi smiled that the other passengers were completely impassive at being roughly jostled around by the carriage's inelegant movement. Mrs Law would say they were being 'shoogled aboot.'

When she alighted at Partick Cross, she discovered that in the ten minutes she had been under ground, the weather had changed from unremarkable, to as sunny as the day before, and she wished she had her sunglasses. She squinted and walked left as instructed, and in just a few yards a stunning skyline of rust-red domes and towers appeared, crowning the Kelvingrove Art Gallery and the Kelvin Hall across the road.

As she walked on, the hill behind Kelvingrove revealed another presence: the vast bulk of the University of Glasgow, with a breathtaking Gothic spire, not red sandstone this time, but almost black against the blue sky. She studied the sharp points of the soot-stained spire – were they fairytale or foreboding? Both, she decided – like the dark silhouette of the Evil Queen's castle in *Snow White*, its beauty threaded with menace. It stirred the same clashing emotions she'd felt on her first day at Glenberry.

She stood for a while on a bridge, staring down at the river that separated those two proud buildings, mesmerized by its movement and murmur. The heat of the sun on her back was delicious.

Her peace was interrupted by three children, followed by their well-dressed mother, all brandishing bunches of twigs and ferns. They stood at the opposite balustrade and on the count of three, they each dropped a twig down into the river, then rushed to the other side of the bridge to watch for whose floated through first. A winner was declared, the score noted and they went back, chose a new stick and repeated the process.

'What a fun game they've made up,' Mimi said to the mother after several rounds.

'Well, they didn't really make it up – it's called Pooh sticks? You know, from the *Winnie the Pooh* books?' Her accent was polished, very different from the soft accents of Glenberry.

'I don't know those books. I'm American. And don't have children yet.' Mimi offered a couple of reasons for her ignorance and left it to the other woman to decide between them.

'Well, when you do have children of your own, bear them in mind. They are quite charming.'

'Thank you, I will,' Mimi said, but she was interrupted by a loud bell, coming from an approaching van.

'Ice cream!' the youngest child yelled.

'Can we get a cone, Mummy? Please,' the eldest pleaded.

The woman laughed, being pulled away by her children.

'Good luck!' Mimi called to her.

A man walking past, carrying his coat over one arm, caught her eye and said, 'No happier place than Glasgow on a sunny day, eh?'

Mimi thought she'd treat herself to something sweet too, maybe some of the boilings Mrs Law had introduced her to. She figured walking back to the underground stop was probably her best bet of finding a candy store, or rather *sweetie shop*. Now she had her bearings, the walk back to Partick Cross seemed much faster, and she decided to wander past it and see where that took her. Watson had been wrong to dismiss a jaunt on the underground: she was thoroughly enjoying her secret rebellion against his advice.

She soon found herself facing several parallel streets of tenement buildings, four storeys high. The street names were on plaques on the building and meant nothing to her, but they sounded pleasant enough. Watson and Alexander claimed that the layout of Manhattan had been modelled on Glasgow's grid design, something else she found hard to believe, but at least she knew she wouldn't get lost. She could use the same system as Manhattan: if you feel lost just keep making a right and you'll end up back where you started.

She ventured up the widest street, which was on a slight hill and was a hive of activity. The happy din of children playing echoed off the sandstone buildings. There was a chaotic game of football that took up almost the length of the street and involved a large scrap of boys of all heights and ages. A section of road had been claimed by a long, neat line of girls who waited for their turn at jump-rope. Mimi lingered, wondering if she'd recognise the song they jumped in time too: something about bluebells and cockle shells, finding a man and tying him to a lamppost. She didn't know that one.

The street was lined with prams – every close entrance had at least one, and up to half a dozen, parked in the sunshine. Some contained sleeping babies, others toddlers, sitting up and firmly strapped in by their leather harnesses. They wore hand-knitted cardigans in sherbet colours of pink, blue, lemon and white, and some wore matching bonnets. They were all turned out to face the street, to give them a view of the older children running around playing.

An older lady was walking down the hill towards her, pushing a pram. 'You OK hen?'

Mimi had walked less than a mile, but this woman spoke in a completely different dialect from the lady on the bridge.

'I'm great thanks, how are you?' Mimi asked, looking into the pram expecting to see a grandchild, but was face with a bundle of what looked like laundry.

'Aye, fine. Just aff doon the steamie,' and she walked on.

Mimi wasn't entirely sure what she had said, but by her cargo decided she was heading to the laundromat.

As she walked, she looked up and noticed the activity in the windows of the tenements. Women in aprons and headscarves as colourful as their babies' cardigans, were making the most of the sunshine with the windows open. Mimi had the busy housewife version of Jimmy Stewart's view in *Rear Window*: some of the uniformed women were cleaning their windows with newspapers; some were stringing white cloth diapers along makeshift washing lines to dry and bleach in the sun; some were darning or knitting; and plenty of others were just sitting smoking, perhaps on a break, or perhaps they'd clocked off their domestic shift for the day. Mimi tuned into their voices over the hubbub of their children. Their accents were strong, but she caught snippets and worked out that they were talking about their husbands and *weans* (children – she knew that word!), the weather, and what they were making for dinner. Whatever the subject, the aim was always the same – a good laugh – and regular cackles punctuated the conversations across windows and up and down floors. Their conspiratorial camaraderie gave Mimi a pang of envy.

A woman was beating a small rug outside her close, while another, cigarette in hand at the ground floor window, said, 'Can you no dae that oot back? That's nae guid for they weans, all that oose flying aboot!'

It was like a different language.

As Mimi approached, they stopped and looked at her. The woman with the rug said, 'Hello. Ye awright there?'

'Fine thanks. Beautiful day, isn't it?' Mimi replied.

As she passed she heard them say, 'Was that an American accent? She's awfy well-dressed – maybe she's just taking a wee daunder on her way home to Hyndland or somethin'.

A few closes later, another couple of women nudged each other as she approached. Mimi now felt an air of slight suspicion around her presence on the street. She spoke first: 'Hello, it's so nice to see the children out enjoying the weather.'

'Aye, it is that.' The woman's voice was gentle. 'Are you OK, Missus? Do you need directions to somewhere? Can we help you find...anything?'

'No thanks,' Mimi began, then laughed. 'Well unless there's a candy store, I mean, sweetie shop, nearby.'

'Just at the back of the underground station you'll find one,' was the reply.

'Oh thanks, I'm heading back there now, that's great.'

'If you're sure that's all?' the woman asked, gently again.

'Yes, thanks so much. Have a nice day.' Mimi started back down the hill, more self-conscious now, feeling like she was being watched, rather than doing the watching.

Walking back towards the Underground she thought about

how lucky they all were to have that easy female companionship, the constant exchange of talk and laughter. It cast her own life at the castle in a lonelier light. Now that she was properly settled, she ought to do something about that. Perhaps she'd begin by tending her budding friendship with Peggy.

And perhaps, now that the apartment was starting to look like home, the time was right to start trying for a baby.

That warm thought was interrupted as she reached the sweet shop and caught a glimpse of her reflection in the sweet shop window. Her heart sank. No wonder the women had looked at her with concern. The bruise was unmistakable, darkening across her cheekbone and around her eye.

She took a heavy breath and cursed Leslie one more time.

She could take care of the bruise with a compact on the train home. Then she'd tell Alexander her thoughts about a baby. The thought made her smile. He would be giddy.

PART II

From the desk of Iain Watson, Glenberry
Monday 31st August, 1959

Just when I thought the modernization of the D-L's quarters were concluding, I arrived in the new living room this morning to find Mrs D-L on a ladder, rolling white emulsion paint onto the oak panelling. Aghast as I was, the damage was done, and I quickly conceded and told her I'd have the painters finish the job, in order to persuade her off the ladder as quickly as possible.

The thing is, Mrs Law has her suspicions...

Apart from what she describes as obvious 'nesting' in the new apartment, Mrs Law has noticed cravings in Mrs D-L (e.g., Kellogg's Cornflakes and milk as cold as she can get it) and revulsions (e.g., porridge, even the smell of it). I, in turn, remarked upon Mr D-L's request that I add a daily dark stout for his wife to the grocer's instructions, and it was enough to turn her suspicions into a foregone conclusion.

We await confirmation with bated breath.

Monday 7th September, 1959

Mrs D-L has assured me that there will be no more last minute redecorating surprises, so the D-Ls' flit is underway. This involves moving less of the castle's existing furniture than I might have once hoped, but I must admit that the pieces being delivered from Glasgow by Pettigrew's, in Danish teak I believe, are very pleasing in their simplicity.

No other news as yet. Mrs Law explained that the couple's

caution in divulging the news is likely due to Mrs D-L's age, which makes her an elderly primigravida.

Monday 7th September, 1959 (contd.)

Following my earlier missive I tended to the mail, and delivered Mrs D-L a letter from her mother. It seems a friend of theirs has passed away. I left Mrs D-L in privacy to read the newspaper cutting of the obituary that her mother had included. I shall, of course, check in on her later.

19

____

September 1959

Mimi's new pieces of furniture quite literally made her heart flutter, with their sleek understated elegance. Their presence was light and airy, and she couldn't stop running her hands over the smooth teak. Pulling it all together was her favourite part, apart, perhaps, from Watson's reaction to finding her up a ladder with a paint roller in hand. The oak walls just would not have done her new look any justice.

She was happily tinkering away, arranging books, photos and tasteful stoneware on a low-slung sideboard when Watson arrived with the mail.

'Come on in and admire my handiwork, Watson,' she said.

'Oh that's quite lovely isn't it,' he replied, standing back to take it in.

Mimi was distracted as she opened a letter from her mother. She hadn't yet shared her big news with her parents, so she was just expecting her mother's usual chatty update. Even the inclusion of a newspaper cutting wasn't unusual – Alexander often chuckled at the articles for the local newspaper that were deemed worthy of being sent across the Atlantic.

Mimi unfolded it, still eyeing her sideboard display for symmetry. But this clipping was from the New York Herald, not the local rag. The headline bore the news Mimi knew she'd have to receive someday, even of a force of nature like her friend, Red Rose. Her

She sat down with a soft sigh.

'Oh dear, did you receive bad news, Mrs Douglas-Lauder?' Watson asked gently.

'I'm afraid so, Watson. A very special friend has passed away.'

'I'm very sorry to hear that. Would you like some privacy?'

'Yes please, Watson. Sorry.'

The New York Herald, August 31, 1959
Obituary: Red Rose of Fifth Avenue Dies at 89
Champion of Labor and Women's Rights; Rebelled Against
her Privilege

Rose Murray Delacourt, known to admirers and adversaries alike as Red Rose of Fifth Avenue, died peacefully yesterday, at her home on Gramercy Park. She was 89.

Born in Savannah, Georgia, to a prominent family of plantation owners, Mrs. Delacourt was raised amid the trappings of wealth and Southern decorum, but declared herself, that she was 'a handful' from the start: 'My younger brother called me Shush Rose, because that's all he ever heard my mother say.'

At 19, she moved north and married shipping magnate Nathaniel Delacourt. Society deemed it a successful match, until Rose shocked her class by filing for divorce on grounds of adultery, a move considered both scandalous and near treasonous among New York's elite. 'I did not simply leave my husband,' she said, 'they acted like I had left the caste. I did not care: they could keep their frippery and false loyalties.'

She did not remarry, choosing instead to channel her considerable inheritance and divorce settlement into the fight for safe working conditions for women, the eight-hour workday, and most famously, women's suffrage. A fixture at marches, meetings, and on the margins of strikes, Mrs. Delacourt's booming voice was stark contrast to her petite frame. To the horror of high society, she took on the cause of prostitution, arguing for stricter process around the arrests of men involved, and calling for heavy fines, which in turn would be used to set up refuges for the young women.

A close ally and friend of Emmeline Pankhurst, she was arrested three times and denounced from the floor of the New York Stock Exchange in 1912 after climbing onto a balcony and unfurling a banner in red paint: 'YOU GROW RICH ON OUR BLOOD.' The banner had been sewn into her corset.

'She was never afraid to be inconvenient,' fellow suffragist and labour organiser Louise Bowen said of her. 'She believed there was no virtue in comfort, if it came at others' expense.'

She earned the nickname 'Red Rose' after her New York Stock Exchange stunt, and proudly embraced it, adopting the habit of wearing a red rose in her lapel to every protest thereafter. Mrs. Delacourt remained active until her final years.

She is survived by two nieces, five great-nieces and neph-
ews, and countless women who vote, speak, and work
freely because she refused to be shushed.

Mimi read the obituary with a small smile. She thought of
Red Rose every single day.

Sometimes she had imaginary conversations with her, a
recent one being about the quiet justice that she and Watson
had delivered upon Derek Leslie. Rose would have thoroughly
approved, as she wasn't shy of dispensing her own brand of
reckoning.

There had been a boyfriend of a niece, who Rose described
as belonging to the 'bluffing classes'. She could not fathom
what her niece saw in him. He held a phoney role at the State
Department, one Rose was certain had been invented as a
favour to some wealthy relative.

Rose tolerated his presence only as much as one might
endure a bad smell. The staff knew the signs well: the fixed
smile that was more grimace than warmth, the put-downs
delivered so deftly they sailed straight over the dimwit's head.
They tittered behind the scenes as the boyfriend remained
blissfully unaware.

Then one evening, after dinner, and before the ladies withdrew to the drawing room, Rose briefly returned to her
bedroom. She heard sobbing. Inside, she found the young
woman whose job it was to turn down her bed, tear-stained
and shaking.

The awful boyfriend had done an awful thing.

The following morning, Rose made a call to someone at the
State Department.

The cad was promptly despatched on a terribly important
fact-finding mission, way upstate. Rose and her State Department ally were just as capable as coming up with a phoney role
as the next guy.

The maid was sent to Macy's with money to buy a new coat and shoes, and given a day off and the train fare to go and visit her sister in Yonkers.

A ray of sunlight broke through the window and the light danced on the diamonds of Mimi's bracelet. Mimi's other hand was on her heart. That is to say, on the diamond brooch, that today was pinned on the left breast pocket of her shirt.

The clouds had cleared completely and Mimi's new whitewashed walls glowed, reflecting the sunshine pouring in. Her eyes fell to the spot beside the electric fire. Even in this light, the secret panel was invisible.

She crossed the room, knelt down and deftly relieved the hidden cubby of its contents. She placed the old biscuit tin on the coffee table, and reverentially, lifted its lid.

Rose's handwriting was elegant but bold, just like her. 'My Dearest Mimi', the smaller envelope read. The card inside was her signature stationary, a single red rose on a cream background. Mimi always read it fondly, and today it was especially bittersweet.

My Dearest Mimi,

We have discussed at length all the reasons why I am passing my Louis Cartier pieces on to you: of course I adore you, but I intend these more as an insurance policy, than a mere token of my love for you.

This letter therefore serves foremost as a record, should you ever need it, that I, Rose Murray Delacourt, am gifting you, Amelia Johnson, matching Cartier brooch and bracelet, described and certified by Hamilton Jewellers of London herewith.

Ever Yours,
Red Rose

The gifts had come as a shock, of course.

When Mimi expressed her desire to move to London, Rose had jumped into action, relishing the chance of an extended trip to make the appropriate introductions and help get Mimi settled. Rose's regaling of her exploits, opinions and crusades began as soon as they boarded the RMS Queen Mary, and Mimi came to know and admire her, inside out.

As with most things, she had been ahead of her time when she decided to divorce. Her Fifth Avenue and Newport friends bombarded her with visits, beseeching her to stay with her husband. It wasn't forgiveness they urged, but acceptance. What had she expected, they asked, marrying a man as wealthy as Nathaniel? Someone with so many reasons to travel to Europe on business would naturally amuse himself while he was there.

When Rose tried to point out the preposterousness of the whole arrangement, and how neatly it favoured the male role in marriage and suppressed the woman, it fell on deaf ears. What saddened her most was how thoroughly cowed these women had become. Chosen as wives because their intellect and vibrancy allowed them to survive, and even help their husbands thrive, in the highest echelons of New York society, only to shrink themselves once installed there.

Rose believed that bullying her friends out of their marriages was as diminishing as their husbands bullying them to stay, so she learned to hold her bolder counsel. However, she made it quietly clear that no woman should feel trapped in an unhappy marriage simply for lack of financial independence, and that she would always help to remove that obstacle.

Nearing the end of her stay in London, Rose asked Mimi to come to her hotel room. When Mimi arrived, she found two small red boxes placed neatly on the bed.

'I hope you won't be offended,' Rose said lightly.

Mimi was too startled to be offended. When she loosened

the unassuming cloth drawstring bags inside the boxes, she found an ornate brooch and a matching cuff. For a moment, she simply stared at them.

'These are already becoming a little old-fashioned,' Rose said, waving a hand. 'And even when I'd just had them commissioned, some of the Fifth Avenue old guard thought them gaudy.'

Mimi laughed, unsure whether Rose was serious. 'I can't possibly accept these. Apart from anything else, I could be arrested on suspicion of stealing them.'

'Of course you can.' Rose's tone was calm, matter-of-fact. 'There's satisfaction for me in knowing that trinkets bestowed on me to keep me in my place, will mean you never have to be kept in yours. They were ornaments for me, but they are options for you. I have arranged for an up-to-date valuation by Hamiltons and to allay your fears, I'll put my bequest in writing.'

She paused, then added quietly, 'You need never tell your future husband about them. And if they're passed down intact, never having had to be liquidated? Well, that will be success, won't it?'

Mimi safely re-stowed the biscuit tin and its contents.

In her secrecy about her 'insurance policy' Mimi had ended up avoiding mentioning Red Rose much at all. What a shame, given what she meant to her. It was too late to try to call her mother for a chat, but she could sure use one. Maybe she'd risk telling a few stories about her old friend tonight.

～

From the desk of Iain Watson, Glenberry
Monday 7th September, 1959 (contd.)

Mr and Mrs D-L joined us in the kitchen for a spot of afternoon tea. Mrs D-L shared the newspaper article about her friend, Rose Murray Delacourt, from which one could quickly glean she'd had a life well-lived.

But my goodness, the stories she told us. We quickly found out that 'well-lived' would be an understatement!

Mrs D-L's mother had worked for Rose Delacourt, I gather as a secretary of sorts. When Mrs D-L first came to London, it was Mrs Delacourt who accompanied her, to see her settled in. Mr D-L teased his wife about a possible windfall from the will, which she brushed off with a laugh, saying, not to worry, Mrs Delacourt had been generous in her time. She seems to have been quite the spitfire.

She was divorced (shocking in her social circles), a linchpin in the suffrage movement, and a labour rights activist (which earned her the nickname, 'Red Rose').

There was a story about a strike over poor conditions in local factories. Mrs Delacourt funded a soup kitchen to feed the families of striking workers, with makeshift child-care, so they could march in protests. When the factory owners sent their henchmen, Mrs Delacourt had the soup kitchen moved into her own home. Mrs D-L painted the picture of dozens of hungry, tired and sweating men, women and their urchins, lining up for stew, which was then served to them from bone china soup tureens, gilded with real gold leaf. Furniture, like velvet tasselled fainting couches, was requisitioned from all corners of the house and brought to her grand ballroom, lined up like army cot-beds, under massive crystal chandeliers.

A remarkably bold story, that struck me also because it brought to mind castles like Glenberry being turned into convalescence homes for soldiers during The Wars.

I have to admit to knowing little about the suffrage movement across The Pond, so I had a sneak peek into the Encyclopaedia Britannica in the library, to see if Mrs Delacourt was mentioned. She was not: perhaps her passing will prompt an entry in the next edition. However, names of her comrades, who Mrs D-L listed as if we should know them, were there, e.g., Susan B. Anthony and Elizabeth Cady Stanton. I assume that in the US, their names are as well-known as Mrs Pankhurst et al are to us.

Mrs D-L continues to be a well of unexpected acquaintances and stories.

Postscript: Mrs D-L mentioned how well the daily stout is agreeing with her.

20

―――――

August 2019

Ally was on bedrest. And not even in her own bed.

Alec had returned to the apartment one evening to find her motionless on the bed, trying not to move a muscle, because even a turn of her head on the pillow made the excruciating pain of her headache even worse. It felt like her brain had swollen up and her skull was now its tight vice. Alec called for the doctor immediately, who upon checking her blood pressure and other pregnancy vitals, declared the time had come for bedrest.

Ally would have cried in dismay, but she was in too much pain.

The doctor said tentatively, 'If you don't mind me saying, I don't think the paint fumes and carpentry smells can be helping. Is it particularly bad today?'

Alec agreed. He'd noticed it as soon as he walked in. 'The

doc's right Ally, we should move you. It's not like we don't have a spare room or twenty.'

Ally moaned a weak 'nooo'. She couldn't even think of going to the kitchen to get a glass of water, far less flit to new quarters in the castle.

Alec recruited his mother and his sister to help him ready what was deemed to be the best of the said twenty spare rooms. They made the room welcoming and convenient, with everything she needed to hand.

It had one obvious drawback, but Ally was too weak to point it out.

Living in a construction zone seemed to have been a large part of the problem, because Ally felt significantly better after a couple of days. Well enough to be frustrated at still being ordered to stay in bed.

'Anything I could say in consolation is "easy for me to say",' Alec said, 'because I'm not the one growing two humans inside me, and confined to barracks because of the wee rascals. I'm sorry, darling.'

'Thank you,' Ally said, the corners of her mouth turned down into a *poor me* face.

'I'm heading down to do few estate things with Dad. Can I get you anything before I go?'

'Yes!' Ally said with an emphatic nod. 'You said you were going to bring me the rest of Watson's despatch boxes. I do believe you're stalling, my love.'

'Bedrest means you should be taking it easy, not ploughing through old estate matters. You found what we were looking for to sort things out with Leslie. Couldn't you just watch a rom-com or something, and relax?'

Ally knew that the events surrounding the Leslie issue had also played a part in the dip in her health, but surely tackling the next mystery – 'The Case of the Illegitimate Heir' – shouldn't be quite so stressful. Or so she told herself.

'Watson's diaries are a great resource for my posts about Glenberry's history. They're the ones that get the most comments and likes. That's just as relaxing for me, and more fulfilling, than watching crappy rom coms all day. Please?' she pleaded, pulling a face that made him laugh.

'Jeez, you're not pulling your punches with that pathetic wee face, are you? How can I resist? I'll get them later, after our visitors have gone.'

Prior to the bedrest order, her lifelong friend Jill, and their newer friends Inez and Tom, and Inez's niece, Katie, had arranged to come and visit. They had offered to put it off, but though she had to stay in bed, Ally had no intention of staying in her pyjamas all day, every day, so she assured them she'd be perfectly presentable.

Ally told Jill to come earlier, before the others, and before Alec had finished work for the day. She'd decided to tell her about Elsie Morris's letter.

'Wow, Ally, just wow. This is huge,' Jill said, hand to her mouth, holding the letter. 'Have you Googled them?'

'Of course I have. Obsessively. Along with any names that Elsie might be short for and any names that Charles might have been shortened to. Nada. But... I found this.' She passed Jill the photo of the boy with the sledge.

Jill raised her eyebrows. 'And we think this is...?'

'Look at Mimi – you can see that she's pregnant with Sandy. And it's winter. So this was taken around the time of the letter. That might be Charles.'

Jill studied it. And then closer. 'Yup. He looks like a Charles.'

Ally chuckled. 'Jill, any black and white photo of a 1960s boy would probably look like a Charles.'

'I'm telling you – he's a Charles,' Jill said definitively. 'But Mimi looks quite chipper, doesn't she? I don't think I'd be so understanding about an illegitimate child that I'd have them to visit, and think to have a photo taken to mark the occasion.'

'I know. So maybe it's not him,' Ally said, a little deflated.

'Oh no, I still think it's him. And as you say, the timing is too perfect to be a coincidence. I just think that there's something weird going down. Where did they disappear to after this? Or where were they made to disappear to?' Jill wondered.

'Steady on, Jill,' Ally said.

'This is huge, Ally,' Jill said. 'What are you going to do next?'

'I have no idea,' Ally said. 'Look, give me those back, so I can put them away before the others get here.'

'Tom!' Jill said in a brainwave. 'You should ask Tom, if he can still pull any strings down at the police station. Investigate them – Elsie and Charles. Or ask Calum to.'

Tom was a retired police officer and Calum, his former mentee, was still on the force.

'I don't think that's how things work,' Ally began, just as there was a knock at the door.

'I'm telling you, you should ask Tom,' Jill said in a loud whisper, as she got up to open the door. 'Make up some story about why, but it's worth a shot.'

'It's just the two of us,' Inez said as hugged Jill hello. 'Katie is dying to see the work you've done in the apartment, so Alec is showing her around. But I'm not letting Tom get a look at a fancy new kitchen and give him any ideas about changing my marshmallow kitchen, so we came straight up – hope that's OK.'

That infamous day at the spy station, when Ally and Alec first met, forged an enduring bond among all nine members of the motley crew who had been trapped there together. It also sparked a series of romantic liaisons, leading to three – well, two and a half – lasting relationships, and, in due course, the twins who were now on their way.

Strictly speaking, Inez and Tom had rekindled an old flame that day. Inez and Katie had been en route to film a television segment for BBC Scotland, where Katie worked, and Tom had been one of the responding police officers on the scene. It took the best part of the day for Inez and Tom to realise they had shared a brief encounter years before. When the recognition finally came, it gladdened all hearts to see how quickly and easily they slipped into the certainty that they would spend the rest of their lives together.

Then there was the matter of the 'half': Katie and Calum. It wasn't so much an on-again, off-again affair, as a problem of geography. Calum wasn't a man suited to city life – something Katie both knew and loved about him – but BBC Scotland showed no signs of relocating its studios to Mid-June any time soon.

All told, their day at the spy station had been an extraordinary one – a day that, without any literary hyperbole, changed their lives for good. Katie thought it would make a perfect BBC Scotland light drama: three parts, Sunday nights. Or perhaps a charming, feel-good novel. Both, was the obvious answer.

Tom shook his head, smiling, at Inez, then rolled his eyes at Jill and Ally. 'I'm a retired policeman, with literal scars to prove it,' he said, pointing to his cheek, 'and I feel emasculated by my own kitchen!'

'Oh I'm not buying for a minute that you're that insecure.' Ally laughed. 'How are you both?'

'Yup, grand, but more importantly how are you?' Inez asked.

They exchanged updates, Ally enjoying the feeling in her cheeks from laughing. She guessed that Inez had given Tom the memo that they were here to cheer her up, and she was grateful.

Jill cleared her throat. Ally gave her a warning look. It was to no avail.

'Ally was wondering if you could do her a favour, Tom,' Jill said.

'Is it the stripper-gram request again? How many times do I have to tell you ladies, that I know you miss me in uniform, but I just won't do it.'

'Is there some kind of special police database for old records, names, that sort of thing?' Jill asked. 'It's a couple of names – for something that came up when she was researching some historical stuff about the castle.'

'Tom, honestly you don't have to...' Ally said apologetically.

'Well, if they had a criminal record maybe, but honestly, nowadays you can find just about as much on the old Google. But I suppose you've tried that,' Tom replied.

'I have,' Ally said. 'Och, forget I – I mean, Jill – mentioned it. Alec is getting some old files from the library for me later today, I'm hoping they'll shed some light on things.'

'You've got me intrigued, though –'

Tom was interrupted by a scratching-come-scraping-come-knocking sound. All eyes turned, not towards the door they had entered through, but to one set symmetrically on the same wall, disguised as a linen press.

'Jeez, have they moved you to a haunted room, pet?' Inez asked, uneasily holding Tom's forearm.

And there it was: the major drawback of this particular room.

From the desk of Iain Watson, Glenberry
Friday 25th September, 1959

C redit where credit is due, Mrs Law's predictions were correct: Mrs D-L is expecting!

Hattie and I were strictly instructed by Mrs Law that our reaction be one of utter and complete surprise, as it would be in poor taste to let Mrs D-L suspect that we had, well, suspected, and been discussing it behind her back. Hattie and I duly played our parts, while in the meantime, when Mrs D-L challenged, 'I bet you had already guessed,' Mrs Law responded with a (mildly inappropriate) hug, tears, and a full confession that indeed she had divined it.

What happy news! A baby at Glenberry for the first time in forty-something years. The minister was informed and given permission to include it in his intercessory prayers last Sunday; as a result, the D-Ls' lunch had to be served late, they were delayed for so long outside the church by congratulations and well-wishes.

Postscript: As regards succession, it would be somewhat convenient if the baby turns out to be a boy, though I recognise this is not a sentiment one airs aloud.

Postscript: Mrs Peggy McPherson is a frequent guest at Glenberry, and Mrs Law and I are thoroughly approving. I feel somewhat foolish now for having considered Lady Jean Fforde as a companion for Mrs D-L. Mrs McPherson's plain-speaking, practical background is a far better match. She appears to be a valued friend and adviser, and her son is well-behaved and respectful, by no means a burden to have about the place. Mrs Law (and, I dare say, Mrs D-L also) is already forming a picture of him as something of an elder-brother presence to Baby D-L.

Friday 9th October, 1959

Mrs D-L has been reading up on a new organisation called the National Childbirth Trust: she discovered it in a periodical that she has sent up from London and wrote to them requesting further information. Such matters are, and will forever remain, foreign to me, but I detect some cynicism in Mrs Law.

The first step is to gather a group of expectant mothers and Mrs D-L received a list of local women from the doctor. Her friendship with Mrs McPherson is one thing, but a blanket invitation to the women of the villages to Glenberry is quite another.

I have, however, bitten my tongue on the matter.

Thursday, 29th October, 1959

Mrs D-L is quite a-flutter prior to the first meeting of her Ladies' Group.

Of the five women she invited, we heard back from three: Mrs Flora Sinclair, Mrs Sadie Strachan, and Mrs Geraldine Lyons. Of the three, I only know of Mrs Sinclair, who lives in a handsome farmhouse, on a farm that has been in her family for generations. Her husband took it over from his father-in-law shortly after they married. The Sinclairs and D-Ls have mixed in the same social circles over the decades, so I'm confident this is an appropriate match.

~~Judging by the addresses of the other two ladies~~

The other two ladies live in Railway Rows; the small cottages built for the plate-layers when they laid the railway.

Mrs Peggy McPherson, will also be in attendance even though she is not, herself, expecting.

Mrs D-L wants to greet her guests by herself and intended to show them into the new living room in their private apartment. After some to-ing and fro-ing, we compromised and I agreed to the former, but not the latter. These women are strangers and we have several reception rooms perfectly appointed for such occasions as this.

21

———————

October 1959

At the risk of seeming superficial, Mimi had consulted Peggy on which notepaper to use for the invitations to her first Expectant Ladies Group.

Alec had assured Mimi her invitees would be 'here with bells on', just out of nosiness. Mimi hoped that she could convey a genuine offer of empathy and gentle support for each other, and that they'd accept for those reasons, not just out of curiosity as to what lay behind the front door of Glenberry.

Peggy understood her dilemma: the family crest headed paper might seem like a summons from the lady of the manor, whereas plain notepaper might suggest they weren't worthy of a 'proper' invitation. They compromised on her own monogrammed set.

That was the difference between Peggy's female counsel and Mrs Law's. Mimi still felt a flicker of self-consciousness at the thought of asking a really stupid question. It wasn't that she worried about keeping up appearances with Mrs Law, because they had grown quite close, but concerns like notepaper, or her later conversations with Peggy about the nuances of what to serve the ladies, might sound frivolous to someone as pragmatic and hardworking as Mrs Law. That was where Mimi risked seeming like the lady of the manor, with too much time on her hands.

Peggy's answers were thoughtful and patient, aware of the small but important nuances. When Mimi wondered about the delicate etiquette of the church raffle – how many tickets to buy, and what to do if more than one turned out to be a winner – Peggy knew exactly what to say. For the homemade jam, accept it graciously, then send a note effusing about how delicious it was. For the bouquet of flowers, donate it back to the church to serve as that Sunday's pulpit arrangement.

It was a good thing to have a good friend. Mimi felt lucky.

The note itself had been simple:

Dear Mrs X,

I'm hosting an afternoon gathering for local expectant mothers next Thursday, 29th October, at 2 p.m., at Glenberry Castle. It would be lovely if you could join us for tea, conversation, and a chance to meet others. Nothing formal, just a warm welcome and a biscuit or two.

With all good wishes,
Mimi Douglas-Lauder

Although the inspiration had been the National Childbirth Trust, she deliberately did not mention them, or any their terms such as 'ante-natal classes.'

.   .   .

THREE PEOPLE ACCEPTED HER INVITATION, making a group of five, which Mimi thought was perfect. Peggy knew one of them, Geraldine Lyons, who she said was 'a bit rough around the edges, but a real bright spark.'

Sadie Strachan arrived with a single chrysanthemum wrapped in wax paper, and Flora Sinclair an apple crumble, saying, 'I do hope you won't be offended, Mrs Law, but there's such a surfeit of apples at the farm that I'm baking all the time.'

Mrs Law's face had softened in the knowledge that it was a gift made by Mrs Sinclair herself, not one passed from cook to cook, as if she wasn't perfectly capable of making her own apple crumble.

Geraldine Lyons (Geri) brought just a toddler.

She was surprised to see Peggy and gave her a long hug. 'I haven't seen you since back when I was Geri Robertson. When I had a good Scottish name, not the Irish one I got from my man. And you had the good sense to stop at just one Peggy? This is number four for me. I'm getting too old for this.'

Mimi showed them to the reception room that Watson had deemed appropriate. Mrs Law had laid the tea tray, with short-bread and scones already buttered with jam ('No need to set people up for the embarrassment of crumbs and spilled jam,' she had explained).

'I'm pretty new to afternoon tea, but I have to say, I love it. Especially Mrs Law's baking. You must try her shortbread *and* a scone. I don't know about you, but I'm quite enjoying eating for two,' Mimi said pouring the teas.

Geri had already handed her son a shortbread and was putting a scone on a tea-plate for herself. 'Och, I've been preg-nant so many times, I think I just always eat for two now. Not to mention, when you're breastfeeding you're starving, all the time.'

Geri was a tall, strong-looking woman and someone you couldn't imagine was ever lean, even when not pregnant.

'So you breastfed you first three then? Do you intend to with this baby too?' Mimi asked.

'Aye, they went straight from breast to cow's milk. I'm not interested in making up some new-fangled potion with powder and water. And messing around boiling up bottles, or however you have to sanitize them.'

'What about you Flora? Did you breastfeed your first one?'

Flora looked slightly sheepish after Geri's forthrightness. 'I did not. My doctor thinks that formula feeding is better for promoting routine in babies. It worked well for me. But I suppose you have to go with what suits you,' she said tactfully.

'Aye, what suits you and the baby – not the doctor. They've got awfy strong opinions sometimes, for people who'll never give birth themselves,' Geri said, in her own rough-and-ready brand of tact.

'I'm not sure what I'll do yet. Peggy will testify that I've changed my mind a dozen times. Have you given it any thought, Sadie?' Mimi asked, trying to bring the youngest women into the conversation. She was so young – she must only be about twenty.

'I think I'd like to try breastfeeding first,' she said quietly.

'You have such a beautiful accent, Sadie. Where is it from?' Mimi asked.

Sadie blushed. 'I'm from Skye.'

Flora interjected gently when Mimi waited for further explanation, which wasn't forthcoming. 'It's an island off the northwest coast of Scotland. And I agree with you that the accents from there are quite lovely.'

Sadie blushed even more. Her shyness was endearing and Mimi was impressed that she came along despite her nervousness.

They took the spotlight off Sadie, letting her get comfortable with the older women in her own time, and made some introductions about themselves, to break the ice.

Mimi went first, and then Peggy, who talked about her son, and as Mimi had noticed was usual, shared very little of her life before she had him, or about her husband. She had a knack of turning the conversation away from herself.

Flora described herself as a farmer's daughter, though her poise and polish made it apparent that it had not been a down-and-dirty farmyard upbringing. She had met her husband at a Young Farmers Ball, while at university in St Andrews, and they both now ran her family farm. When Mimi mentioned living in London, Flora nodded with familiarity: Mimi had a feeling that due to the mixed backgrounds of the company, Flora was downplaying the more worldly aspects of her past, and up-playing the more down-to-earth ones.

Geri grew up in the same row of houses she lived in now. Her husband was a painter and she did some housecleaning part-time. She also took in 'mending' which both Mimi and Flora expressed an interest in.

'I'm hopeless with a needle and thread,' Flora said. 'My mother never had the patience to teach me. There are a couple of things I can think of already that I'd love you to look at for me.'

'No bother at all. Any knitting you need done too. I just ask for the yarn money. You know – if you need any wee baby bonnets or cardigans, or that.'

'Gosh, I'd love that,' Flora said, 'but I'd pay you for time as well, of course.'

Mimi gently tested if Sadie's nerves had settled yet. 'So you're from Skye, Sadie? How did you meet your husband?'

Sadie cleared her throat and began quietly, 'Bobby's cousin is a joiner on Skye, so he came up and lived with him for a year, working as an apprentice, learning the trade from him. We started courting and then got married just before his year was up, so we could move back down here together. Then I fell pregnant before I'd even managed to get a job, so I don't really know anyone here. I was ever so please to get your invitation, Mrs Douglas-Lauder.'

'Oh Sadie, please, call me Mimi. I just feel sorry that we're all a bit older than you,' she said. 'No offence ladies,' she added to Geri and Flora.

'None taken,' Geri said. Her son had fallen asleep in her lap, but she was managing to reach for another scone nonetheless. 'I think I'm closer in age to your mother-in-law, than you Sadie. How is that old battle-axe? How are you managing living with her?' She winked at Sadie conspiratorially.

Sadie smiled. 'Och, she's fine. Though she didn't believe me when I said I'd received an invitation to Glenberry Castle. She thought it must be a prank. Then I got plenty of lectures on how to behave when I got here. I ended up saying to her, "I'm from Skye, not the moon!"'

Geri gave such a loud 'ha!' that her son startled in his sleep. 'Good for you! You tell her Sadie!'

'Well I hope you can see that though the castle may be grand and a bit scary – I certainly thought so when I first moved here – I'm not. And I don't have many friends either. I'd love to make this a regular thing – for some good company and an excuse to enjoy Mrs Law's baking. Then when the babies are born, we'll have a ready-made little playgroup for them. What do we think?' She smiled at her new friends hopefully.

'I'd like that very much,' Flora said first. 'And I'd be happy for you to come to my house too.'

'Is it rude of me to not invite you to mine?' Geri asked. 'God knows it's a pokey wee place anyway, never mind the mess the three weans and my man make.' She said it entirely unselfconsciously, just as a matter of fact.

'We wouldn't dream of putting more on your plate, Geri. I don't know how you do it all, with three kids and a job. Makes me feel guilty about the afternoon naps I've been having.

Coming to our get-togethers at Glenberry can be a wee break for you.'

'Well, I'll happily take you up on that,' Geri said. 'Right, I'd better figure out how to get this sleeping bairn home.'

'I can drive you both,' Flora said, gathering up the tea things and stacking them back on the tray.

'Oh, leave that,' Mimi said. 'You can drive? Did you come here by car?'

'Oh yes, a consequence of growing up on a farm. We were all taught to drive on tractors – the girls as well as the boys.' Flora replied.

After they saw the others off in Flora's car, Mimi looked to Peggy, with a 'Well?'

'I think it was a great success, don't you?' Peggy replied.

'I do - I like them!' Mimi said enthusiastically, with a touch of surprise. Not surprise that they were likeable, but that she'd got so lucky with her random guest list.

'I do too. Geri is still a hoot – I told you she just says it like it is. She was ever afraid to share her opinions. Flora is so gracious – she reminds me of Deborah Kerr. And wee Sadie – well, she's just so sweet.'

'What a great bunch of gals we've found, Peggy. I'm happy. This was a lovely afternoon.'

'I think you were right not to bombard them with any of your NCT information yet, though. Sadie looked like she wanted the ground to swallow her up just talking about breast-feeding.'

'Oh I know, whereas I think Geri would happily have given us any gory details we asked. I think you're right too – but there's always next time,' Mimi said, winking.

22

———

Several days after Tom and Inez's visit, there was the same random scraping and knocking sound again, which Ally recognised precisely by its randomness.

In landing on a secret knock, they had gone through a whole playlist of Ally's favourite band, Take That, carefully evaluating them for clarity and uniqueness – as if anyone else, apart from Louise, would be coming through the secret passageway into Ally and Alec's temporary bedroom.

They were being housed in a part of the castle that dated to Tudor-Stuart times. There were two hallways, facing each other over a stairwell, which were perfectly symmetrical. Identical doors opposite each other led into the respective, separate, chambers of the master and the mistress of the house. From the hallway, there was only one door into each room, the panelled minstrel's gallery being the main feature on that level. However, behind the back wall of the gallery, a secret corridor connected the husband's and wife's rooms, allowing for conjugal visits, that none of the ever-present servants would know anything about, for their morning gossip.

In their teens, the two large rooms had been the sisters'

domain. How thrilling it must have been to have a secret adjoining passageway. Their sleeping arrangements changed constantly: two here, one there; then a different combination; then all three crammed into one room, with the other serving as their living room. It reminded Ally of a sitcom setup like *Friends*, and with those three, there must have been plenty of similarly madcap moments.

She was living one herself right now. *Let me guess.* 'Louise? Is that you? Come in.'

'I got the knock wrong again, didn't I?' Louise said.

'Yup!' Ally said, in a yup tone.

'What did we settle on again? *Relight my fire*, right? Wasn't that what I did?'

'Not even close,' Ally said, smiling.

'I guess Alec got all the musicality in the family.' Unbothered, she flopped onto Ally's bed. 'What you been up to?'

'Ha-ha. Not much, just stuck here incubating your niece and nephew.'

Ally had also been living a second pregnancy, Mimi's, vicariously, as well as witnessing her win Watson over, hook, line and sinker. His journals were filled with tales of the long walks she was still taking, her burgeoning friendship with Mrs Peggy McPherson, who visited regularly, and she had even set up a faction of the National Childbirth Trust, that met every fortnight at the Castle. The NCT was only a few years old then, so Mimi and her group were pioneers. Ally was impressed.

'What's going on with you? How's Scott?' Ally asked Louise.

'Dreamy!' Louise gave an exaggerated swoon.

'How was your first proper date?'

After a couple of afternoons tramping around cobwebbed storage scattered all over the estate, Louise and Scott had tracked down the fire surround that Mimi had seen fit to rip out. Ally got update photos of the sixties' eyesore being removed, and the original being re-placed, in its former place of honour. It was beautiful. Scott hadn't even wanted to change the original finish, the craftsmanship was so masterful, so a good clean and a buff up was all it needed.

And that wasn't the only win. Somewhere between their dusty searches and coffee breaks, Scott had asked Louise out on a proper first date, for a bar meal at the Gillie's Rest: low-key, local, appropriate.

Louise had only just begun her gushy rundown, when there was a firm knock at the main door.

'Yes?' Ally called.

'Ally, it's Scott. I have a couple of things to run by you and wanted to pass on something I found too.'

Louise was off the bed in a flash, miming a scream and gesturing at her make-up-free face and ratty pyjamas. She held up a hand in a 'wait' signal and made for the door, tiptoeing in exaggerated, cartoon-like steps.

'Just a sec, Scott,' Ally said, waiting for Louise to exit safely through her own secret door. 'OK, you can come on in.'

'How are you feeling today?' he asked.

'Och, the usual. What's going on?'

They covered a few things and scrolled through dozens of pictures of progress on his phone. Then he turned to an old tin he'd put on the dresser when he walked in. 'I was saving this wee time capsule for last. I found it in a cubby built into the skirting board of the old electric fireplace – it was hidden with dust and wear over time, but it was definitely put there on purpose. A wee secret hiding place. And this old biscuit tin was inside.'

'Anything inside the tin? A cache of diamonds maybe?' Ally said, prizing it open.

'A couple of envelopes. I didn't want to pry, or risk ripping them. They've been in there for donkey's years and then I go in and they crumble to dust in my hands? No thanks, I'll leave that to you.'

He started to leave, but at the door said, 'Eh, Ally, I won't actually be here tomorrow, I'm going Up-By for the day. I've given my guys a few jobs to be going on with though.'

'Up-By' meant over The Glass Pass, the road out of Mid-June into the rest of Scotland, though more often than not, it meant Glasgow.

'Oh OK, no problem. Safe travels,' Ally said.

'Eh, yup. Just for the day. I'll see you the day after. OK, take it easy,' he said.

Ally set the ancient biscuit tin on her bedside table and rearranged her pillows, getting comfortable to give the contents of these envelopes her full attention.

The first contained a card with a single red rose on, and the second a piece of paper, which she carefully smoothed out on the lap desk Alec had bought in an effort to keep her in bed.

Her eyes darted from one to the other, unsure where to settle first. It seemed she hadn't been far off with her quip about a cache of diamonds.

The card was written in exquisite handwriting that could only belong to another era, and the official-looking certificate also betrayed its age merely at a glance.

When Ally finally managed to still her mind, and her racing heart, she read the card first. Twice.

My Dearest Mimi,

We have discussed at length all the reasons why I am passing my Louis Cartier pieces on to you: of course I adore you, but I intend these more as an insurance policy, than a mere token of my love for you.

This letter therefore serves foremost as a record, should you ever need it, that I, Rose Murray Delacourt, am gifting you, Amelia Johnson, matching Cartier brooch and bracelet, described and certified by Hamilton Jewellers of London herewith.

Ever Yours,
Red Rose

Cartier.
Louis Cartier.
Pieces.
As in, more than one.
Bloody hell.
Ally put down the letter and picked up the more official looking paper.

Hamilton & Co.
Jewellers of Knightsbridge
Statement of Valuation
(for Insurance and Record Purposes)

17th February 1955

We hereby certify that the following jewels have been examined and appraised at our premises, and that in our professional opinion are authentic works by Cartier, Paris, circa 1910.

ONE PLATINUM AND DIAMOND BROOCH, square, designed in Islamic influence, an early example of Art Deco design. Openwork scrolling edges style, around a cushion cut (modified brilliant cut) diamond weighing approximately 3.5 carats, of fine colour and clarity. Surrounding the centre stone, are one hundred and twenty diamonds, rose-cut and single-cut, set in millegrain platinum, weighing approximately 8.25 carats.

Total diamond weight is estimated at 11.75 carats.

The brooch bears the Cartier maker's mark and appropriate French assay stamp and is housed in its original red leather Cartier fitted case.

We assess the present value of the piece for insurance and record purposes at £10,500 (Ten Thousand Five Hundred Pounds Sterling).

ONE PLATINUM OR DIAMOND BRACELET OR CUFF. Complementing the Islamic influence of the brooch, the cuff is 1.25 inches wide and 7 inches long. There are three panels of scrolling pattern, around three cushion cut diamonds, which weigh approximately 2.5 carats each, and are of fine colour and clarity. The scrolling diamonds number over four hundred, are rose-cut and single-cut, and set in millegrain platinum.

Total diamond weight is estimated at 12.5 carats.

The cuff bears the Cartier maker's mark and appropriate French assay stamp and is housed in its original red leather Cartier fitted case.

We assess the present value of the piece for insurance and record purposes at £13,000 (Thirteen Thousand Pounds Sterling).

James Hamilton
Master Jeweller

Bloody hell, again.
She reached for her iPad and found the photograph of Mimi on her wedding day. She didn't need to count the one hundred and twenty diamonds in the brooch or the four hundred scrolling diamonds in the bracelet: there was no doubt that the jewels, shining as brightly as Mimi and Alexander's beaming smiles, were the Cartiers.

Louis Cartiers, no less.

But what on earth happened to them? Just as Watson had assumed in his journals, Sandy had told her they were just costume jewellery that she'd outgrown.

'Hardly,' Ally thought.

She looked at the certificates again, this time registering the numbers. After a quick Google, she punched the figures into an online converter: just over £300,000 in today's money. She tried a second site. That one came out at more than £400,000.

The name Rose Murray Delacourt was familiar – she'd been mentioned in an entry in Watson's journal.

She Googled again.

Rose Delacourt's Wikipedia page included her obituary. Ally scanned the screen, absorbing the outline of a life she might have read about in school. Rose Murray Delacourt: socialite, activist, suffragist. Born 15 July 1870 in Savannah, Georgia, died 31 August 1959 in New York City. There was a scandalous divorce, a woman who broke the rules of society, and the stunt that earned her nickname, Red Rose.

Ally looked back to Mimi, wearing her small fortune so casually. *How on earth did a girl from the suburbs of Long Island like you, become so close to someone like Red Rose?*

And what happened to your trinkets, Mimi?

Ally grabbed a shoe box of photos she'd been attempting to sort through. She took out a couple of handfuls, and dealt them like cards into two hands: one of photos where Mimi was wearing the jewellery, the other where she wasn't.

She pondered.

The Cartiers didn't show up in any pictures taken after Sandy was born.

It could just be the change in lifestyle, she supposed. Mimi looked polished in even casual snaps, but wasn't in clothes that would warrant that level of over-the-top glamour.

She reached for some more pictures, not sure what she was

hoping to spot. A photo of Mimi with a masked man in a striped top, and a bag marked 'SWAG' lurking in the background?

In the pile was dark-green folded card frame, embossed with 'Philips Fine Photography', and a small compliments card from the Glasgow Central Hotel, dated November 1960, and signed simply, 'Hope to see you soon, JM.'

Ally opened the green folder to a picture of pure joy. It was in bright, bold colour, in contrast to every other in the batch. The background of the photo was a large framed reproduction of the cinema poster for *Singin' in the Rain*, with the three leads in their bright yellow raincoats and umbrellas. In front of the poster, to the left, outshining any Hollywood star, and looking like she'd just stepped out the pages of Vogue, was Mimi. To the right, Alexander, with Sandy, a chunky baby, in his arms.

Mimi dazzled off the page in a cartwheel tilted hat, a bright blue satin boat-necked cocktail dress, with a nipped-in waist and full skirt. Her stilettos and clutch had matching jewel details.

Ally's phone rang.

'I'm on my way up,' Alec said. 'Need anything from the kitchen?'

'No, I'm fine thanks.'

Ally quickly refolded the certificate, put both envelopes back in the biscuit tin and tucked it under her bed.

Alec gave a brief knock before strode in. 'What have you got there?'

He kissed her on the head and managed to perch on the bed beside her.

'Look at this picture. Isn't it gorgeous? Your grandmother was a *movie star!*' Ally said.

'Oh, look at that! That's amazing, isn't it?'

'Yes, and look at how cute Baby Sandy was. Do you know what the occasion was?' she asked.

'I do actually, it's part of family folklore. My grandparents had a *Sliding Doors* moment at the New York premier of *Singin' in the Rain* – he was inside as one of the posh invitees, she was outside as a screaming fan, hoping for a glimpse of Gene Kelly.'

'No way!' Ally said.

'Way,' Alec nodded. 'Years later when they met, they realised they'd been ships that passed in the night. Once they moved back here, they were regulars at the Central Hotel, at the height of its glamour. The hotel had a big renovation and they installed some memorabilia showing off some of their famous guests, one of whom was none other than – Gene Kelly. My grandparents were invited to the Grand Re-Opening and had their picture taken with the poster. It's a good one, isn't it? We should put that in a frame.'

'I think I want an even bigger version of it to hang some-where. It's like art, I love it.'

Alec looked around the folders on the bed and pursed his lips, disapprovingly. 'I'm cutting you off, my love, enough work for the day. Let me tidy this all away and get us dinner. Then we can sit and watch something together?'

'I give in – deal,' Ally replied.

'By the way, you know you said Scott was Up-By again today, and that's why he wasn't here?' Alec asked.

'Yeah?'

'I saw him a couple of times when I was out and about today. Once just outside Kilmour, and another on that straight stretch between Berry and here,' Alec said.

'Hmm, his plans must have changed,' Ally said, still distracted by the photo in the Central Hotel.

'The thing was, there was a woman in his van with him. Quite an attractive one,' Alec added.

'Maybe his next client? Don't tell your sister about his passenger being pretty though,' Ally answered without look-ing up.

She admired and analysed Mimi's outfit from head to toe again. There was one thing for sure: that exquisite outfit, and glamorous event, warranted equally dazzling jewellery. It would have topped off Mimi's resplendence.

If Mimi had been able to wear her Cartier jewellery to that event, she would have.

Ally had narrowed down the date of disappearance in 'The Case of The Missing Cartiers'. The brooch and bracelet had vanished sometime between Mimi's arrival at Glenberry and November 1960.

~

From the desk of Iain Watson, Glenberry
Thursday 10th December, 1959

In the matters of Mrs D-L's Ladies' Group meetings, I have been somewhat redundant. The Laird sensed my consternation and advised from behind his newspaper one day that I stand aside and let the women get on with it: our fairer sex will be running the whole world soon enough, he said. We'd better start getting used to it.

I was, however, called to arms today.

Decorum does not allow me to explain what Mrs Law surmises about this evening's event, but suffice it to say it's being referred to as a 'birthing class'.

The ensemble is to be sitting on cushions and pillows strewn on the floor, that Mr D-L and I sourced and arranged, at the instruction of the young midwife. Bad enough, but she requested a comfortable armchair for herself! The expectant ladies, and gentlemen (including <u>the Laird</u>), will be sprawled on the floor while the youthful woman employed to the direct proceedings will be enthroned above them all.

I'm glad my contribution is complete, save from provision of a jug of water, required because, I quote, 'the breathing can be quite taxing'. Heaven help us all.

I shall retire after that one small task and come the morning, make no further enquiries about the goings-on.

10th December, 1959 (contd.)

~~The indignity~~

~~The mortification~~

~~The profound discomposure~~

I have retired early as planned, but not before I was required, briefly and against my will, to substitute for Mr Lyons at the ante-natal class. The less said about the practicalities, the better. I have changed my mind about committing it to paper: it is not a memory I want to visit now, or in the future.

23

December 1959

The Ladies Group had been going rather well. Well enough, in fact, for Mimi to be nervous about blowing it at the next meeting. Mrs Law was in full agreement. The Thanksgiving-themed gathering had been ambitious enough, she said; this new-fangled idea went far beyond anything she'd expected.

'And you're dragging the husbands into it too?' she added. 'I've never heard the like.'

THE DATE of their third meeting coincided with US Thanksgiving.

'We should do something fun! Perhaps some Thanksgiving food and a little sherry instead of tea?' Mimi suggested.

'I'll not say no to a sherry,' Geri said, 'but I think you've got your dates wrong – Harvest Thanksgiving at the church was few weeks ago.'

'Yes, it's earlier. Alexander thought it was something to do with the Harvest Moon?' Mimi directed the question to Flora, who nodded in agreement.

Mimi's mind was already racing ahead to how she could translate a Thanksgiving feast into finger food, and, more importantly how she could talk Mrs Law into any of it.

And talking of ambitious proposals: 'Let's decorate a Christmas tree together! Not the main one in the Grand Hall, but perhaps a smaller one in our new apartment. None of you have seen that yet, apart from Peggy.'

Flora's face lit up. 'Oh, I must admit, some of the tradesmen we have in common have been telling me it's must-see.'

The apartment tour and tree decorating were resounding successes, but the Thanksgiving experience received more mixed reviews. Against Mrs Law's advice, Mimi served a couple of her mother's Thanksgiving recipes.

'I'll eat my hat – or even that ambrosia thing – if they so much as make a dent in those two dishes,' she warned.

The turkey and stuffing sandwiches, at least, were a hit.

'These are what we have on Boxing Day,' Flora commented. 'With our leftovers from Christmas Day. What do you have at Christmas? Turkey again?'

'No, we generally have ham. Or people might have beef. But turkey is a Thanksgiving thing. Now, pass me your plates and you can try some ambrosia – its sweetness goes so well with the saltiness of the turkey and the stuffing.'

Mrs Law had all but dumped the potion into her best trifle dish, holding her breath because she couldn't quite bring herself to hold her nose. Mimi's friends eyed it suspiciously.

Geri spoke up first and the others visibly relaxed, happy for her frankness at this moment.

'See, here in Scotland, Ambrosia is a make of rice puddin'.

And it's – well – a puddin'. You know, that you have after your dinner.'

'We have rice pudding too, but this is quite different. It's marshmallows, canned fruit, whipped cream, coconut and Jell-O.' Mimi imparted the recipe proudly.

'Yer kidding – I think even ma weans might turn their noses up at that. That'd curl yer teeth!' But then she sighed and said, 'OK, I suppose it would be rude not to. Geez a wee dollop here. A wee one!'

When she tried a tentative spoonful, she pulled a face that suggested her teeth really were curling, and everyone laughed.

They all tried it, each reaction more ridiculous face than the last.

'OK, now you're doing it on purpose!' Mimi said, hands on hips, mock-offended.

Dessert was pecan pie and pumpkin pie. Mrs Law had been wary about both, but certain that the pumpkin pie would be a disaster.

And she had been right again.

The warm pecan pie, served with ice cream, was scoffed to contented mmm's, whereas of the pumpkin pie, Geri said, to renewed fits of giggles, 'So you say this is a Thanksgiving dish? Aye, nae wunner you only have it once a year!'

To avoid Mrs Law's told-you-so's, Mimi covered the dishes with foil, hoping to talk Alexander into having some later, but he turned out to share the Ladies' Group opinion.

Mimi had already broached a few cautious NCT nuggets, and with all the laughter and good-natured teasing, she decided it was time to take the plunge.

'You know I've arranged for the young midwife from the nursing hospital to come to our next meeting, to talk us through breathing exercises?' she said. 'What do you say we invite our husbands?'

·   ·   ·

'WHAT ON EARTH have you got me into?' Alexander asked, as they stood hand-in-hand by the gargantuan, exquisitely decorated Christmas tree that now stood in the Grand Hall, awaiting their fellow participants. The young midwife, Miss Turner, had arrived earlier to instruct Alexander and Watson in the moving of furniture, and placing of blankets and pillows in a circle on the floor.

'It's very old-fashioned of you to think you need only be involved in the initial, fun part of the pregnancy,' Mimi teased.

'Listen, I consider myself a little worldly, but I'm positively Renaissance Man compared to some of the more traditional types round these parts. I've no idea how the three other wives managed to talk their husbands into this.'

'It wasn't easy by all accounts. Flora's husband was the easiest, but I'm afraid to say that it's only because he's birthed so many animals on the farm, and he said, "why not, what's one more?"'

Alexander laughed loudly. 'He really said that? I can't tell if he's brave or stupid to say that to his pregnant wife.'

Right on cue Flora and Fergus arrived. Alexander was still grinning as they shook hands firmly. Sadie and Bobby followed so closely behind that Mimi wondered if they'd been hiding in the rhododendrons by the gate, rather than be first to arrive. Bobby was dressed in his Sunday-best and looked just as young as Sadie, a boy beside her own husband and Fergus.

They admired the tree, and Alexander explained that the red and green glass baubles were handblown in Germany and had been a gift from his grandfather to his grandmother, on their first Christmas. 'So they date away back to when we were a bit friendlier with the Germans,' he added.

'The electric fairy lights are new this year,' Mimi picked up. 'I think they make the baubles glow beautifully – and much safer than real candles.'

'I agree,' Alexander said. 'I didn't resist you on that issue, my dear. Mind you, apparently I find it hard to put up much resistance to any of your ideas, as evidenced by the proceedings this evening.' He rolled his eyes at Fergus and Bobby, causing to Mimi elbow him in the ribs.

Finally, Geri bustled in.

'I'm sorry I'm a wee bit late – oh my Good Lord, now that's a tree! That's bigger than the one in Market Square in Kilmour.'

'I'm sorry, but I don't think ma man will make it tonight. The woman whose hoose he's painting is nippin' his heid about getting it finished by the weekend. Some big fancy party she's having.'

Then she added, 'No offence,' inexplicably nodding at Mimi and Alexander.

Since Peggy wasn't coming tonight, the party was complete and they headed to the prepared reception room.

Somehow, Mimi had known that when husbands were included, Peggy would make her excuses. Mimi had explained it was as much about getting to know each other, and forming friendships, as it was about involving the men in the ante-natal class, but Peggy had declined, giving a different excuse each time Mimi tried to cajole her. The only reason she knew Peggy's husband's name was because her son was named after him. If she thought about it too much – how reluctant Peggy was to talk about him, or rather, how well she managed to avoid the topic at all – it troubled her.

The more perturbed Watson had been by the entire premise and setting up process, the more entertaining Alexander had found it, and Mimi caught him smirking again now. She chided him with her eyes, and he raised his eyebrows in an innocent, '*what?*'

The midwife began by talking them through the origins of the new organisation, the NCT, and what it was advocating: less medical intervention and more control for women, in their own childbirth experiences. 'The NCT believes that childbirth is not a medical event, but a natural process. Pain, while real, can be understood, managed, and lessened, through breathing, relaxation, and the right environment.'

'Has anyone told the babies this?' Geri laughed, not unkindly. 'Or the doctors?'

'We'll talk about your rights in the hospital later, but for now I thought we could relax with some breathing exercises. Gentlemen, if you could sit behind your wives and let them lean back against you. Oh, Mrs Lyons –'

The midwife remembered they were a man short.

'Don't worry, I'll just lean back against this chair. It's probably more use than my man would be,' Geri said, arranging herself.

With perfect comedic timing, Watson entered and placed jug of water on the sideboard, beside the glasses he'd set up earlier.

Alexander took his chance.

'Watson, what perfect timing! We are short a father-to-be. You've done some amateur dramatics in your time – I'm sure this role has nothing on the Major-General in *The Pirates of Penzance*. Come and join Mrs Lyons for breathing practice.'

Watson was frozen to the spot like a rabbit caught in headlights, his smile fixed and his hands hovering uselessly at his sides, as the midwife said earnestly, 'It really would be a tremendous help for this exercise, Mr Watson.'

Geri had a twinkle in her eye. 'That's so kind of you to volunteer, Mr Watson. Where should we go now Nurse, now I have a man?'

The midwife directed: 'Mr Watson if you take that cushion and sit there – that's right – and if you sit with your legs open, Mrs Lyons can lean in against you.'

Watson could be quite stiff and formal at the best of times, but he positively looked like he had a broom up his backside right now. He might strain his neck if he tried to turn any further to avert his gaze from anyone else in the room.

The midwife's voice went from bossy to calming as she told the men to gently take their partner's hand. 'Your job is to support, not to fix. And not to distract, either. Ladies, we want to focus on your breathing, which will help you relax, which in turn will help tremendously with the pain.'

Nothing could help with the pain of Watson's predicament, and Mimi could tell that behind her, Alexander wouldn't be able to help stealing glances at him squirming with embarrassment.

As the midwife talked them through the various breathing techniques and encouraged the women to squeeze their partners' hands, Watson visibly winced under Geri's grip, and Mimi was jiggled by her husband's silent chuckles. She bit her own lip, trying not to join in, but they were saved by a knock at the door.

There was a brief glimpse of Mrs Law before a man in paint-splattered overalls burst in, almost pushing her aside.

'Geri darlin', I hope I didn't miss too much –. Oh, I see, I've already been kicked to the curb for someone a bit better dressed.'

Watson pushed Geri off him as politely, but as firmly as he could and leapt to his feet as if his floor cushion had caught on fire. He rushed out the door without a word.

Geri's husband made his apologies for being late and for the state of his clothing and went round the circle shaking hands.

'Please don't be sorry,' Alexander said. 'I wouldn't have missed Mr Watson standing in for you for the world.'

Laughter drove away any remaining tension in the room, and one way or another, slightly at Watson's expense, the ice had been broken.

24

___

'Come in, Louise,' Ally called, trying to keep the sigh out of her voice. Alec was sitting at a table with a second chair pulled up to it, iPad, pens, paper and sticky notes ready. Ally was joining in the emergency summit meeting from her usual post – bed. She had been dragged into another mystery: 'The Case of the Builder and the Unknown Brunette'.

Although she had counselled Alec not to mention seeing Scott the Builder with an unidentified woman, he cared too much about his sister to risk her getting involved with someone who was less invested in this relationship than she was. Louise was already planning how she'd manage her job with being in Mid-June every weekend to be with Scott. Meantime, it seemed like he might be dating other people. Or, at least one other.

Even if Alec hadn't mentioned it, the Mid-June grapevine was like a weed, and both Scott and his van were recognisable: he'd been spotted in his van with this woman, and even more oddly, not in his van, in the passenger seat of a car – the driver, inevitably, a pretty brunette.

The obvious thing to do was to ask him the question. So Ally had.

'Have you got a new job lined up for after you've finished with us? Alec mentioned that he saw you the other day with someone in the van? A woman?' she'd asked.

Scott's assistant had almost choked on his tea, then left the room, with Scott glaring at his wake.

'No, well yes, well no, just, um...showing someone around really,' he answered. Before hastily leaving too.

So much for the direct approach then and Ally had to admit that his reaction had been positively shady.

PLAN B IT WAS THEN, which was Louise tapping into an impromptu spy network, hastily set up on What's App and made up of close friends 'who could be trusted.'

'Trusted to do what?' Ally had asked.

'Tell me the truth, but not tell Scott anything about this ever. If there turns out to be some innocent explanation – which I *doubt*, by the way – I don't want him thinking I'm bonkers,' Louise had explained.

Thinking you're bonkers? Ally had thought.

Alec had been cajoled into asking his local What's App group to keep an eye out too, but Ally had demurred. She had enough going on, and had been foolish enough to think she could avoid getting pulled aboard this crazy train.

Louise entered, a clipboard under her arm, insulated coffee mug in hand. Alec had risen to pour her a coffee, and silently gestured his intent.

'It's OK, I brought my own. And I'll warn you, it's not my first,' Louise said, setting herself up at the table.

She launched straight in.

'So, let's start with looks. It's not too hopeful for me, I must say. Not only is she a brunette, with which I cannot compete, but descriptions have her somewhere between Dakota Johnson, Kate Beckinsale, and "Cheryl Cole, in a really cute messy ponytail." That final, very lasting impression, coming from my own brother. Thanks Alec, for that vote of confidence.'

'You asked for a description! I gave one!' Alec said, this not being the first time that his eye for detail had been remarked upon.

'You sure did,' Ally teased.

'My darling wife, you know you're the only ravishing brunette for me,' Alec smiled.

'Ravishing?' Louise said. 'Now our mystery woman is ravishing?'

'No, Ally is – you know what, I'll stop digging,' Alec sighed.

'Right. So, Ally, you were going to find me pictures of women that might match this description. Ones that might have an innocent explanation.'

'Yup,' Ally confirmed and reached for her phone. She had already shown Alec the pictures, gleaned from the internet and Scott's social media, and none matched the woman he saw. But to prove to Louise she had been working on this mission, she would run through them anyway.

'OK, I give you suspect number one: Moira – the lady making our curtains. She's a perfectionist and wanted paint samples from Scott, to match to fabrics.'

Ally flashed the picture of her and Alec shook his head. 'Not our woman.'

'Moira?' Louise said, confused. 'Isn't she –?' She took the phone from Ally for a closer look. 'Yes, I thought so, she's, well, old.'

'You said leave no stone unturned,' Ally said, taking back her phone.

She flicked through the gallery of suspects, reading them out, but ruling them out in the next breath: the lady who works at the timber yard – short grey hair; a woman Scott mentioned he was quoting a kitchen for – blonde; the barmaid at the Gillies – short hair, and also a lesbian.

'OK, here's one that matched the description, sort of.' She held her phone up and Alec gave a nod.

'Who is she?' Louise demanded, pen at the ready.

'A friend of his that I found on Facebook. But I also found out on Facebook that she's backpacking round Australia right now.'

'Ugh,' Louise said frustrated.

There was a knock on the door and Louise jumped up. 'Oh good, that'll be Sergeant Armstrong. I mean Tom. It's hard to stop calling him Sergeant, isn't it?'

'What?' Ally and Alec exclaimed in unison, with Ally adding an exasperated, 'Lou-ise!'

'I'll get the door,' Louise said, seemingly oblivious to the disbelief in the room, that she hadn't mentioned this invitation.

'Hi Tom, did you drive in by the back lane, like we agreed?' Louise asked, as she opened the door.

'I did,' Tom nodded. 'And parked by the old stables too, as you requested. Then your dad directed me up here. No one else saw me.'

He turned to Ally and Alec and registered their surprise at seeing him. 'Oh dear, I'm sorry Ally. Did Louise not tell you I was coming?'

'We're always happy to see you Tom,' Alec said. 'But Louise – could you please let us know if you've seen fit to ask people up to our room? Our bedroom no less!'

'I kind of forgot – I blame the coffee. Besides, this room is bigger than my whole flat in Glasgow, so it's more like a studio apartment.'

'Not the point, Louise. Not the point.' Alec said.

ONCE THE, now, party of four was re-settled in, Tom watched Louise intently, as she filled him in as solemnly as if she was giving evidence in court. Now and then the corner of his mouth would wrinkle, threatening to betray his amusement, but he was a pro and he'd quickly regain complete composure.

'What model was the other car? The time Scott was a passenger?'

'Well eagle-eyes here –' Louise bobbed her head in her brother's direction, 'only knows that it is navy or black, and a Golf or an Audi.'

Tom chuckled but took out a pad and pen and made some notes.

'So, what's the plan now?' he asked Louise.

'I was hoping you could tell me,' Louise said. 'Didn't you say Inez was Up-By in Glasgow for a couple of days with Katie?'

How else would a respected and storied ex-policeman, whose partner was away, want to spend his time, apart from helping stalk a man she'd been on a couple of dates with?

Tom got up and wandered over to the window, his back to them. Ally wondered if it was because he couldn't hide amusement any longer, but when he turned back to them, he was all business.

'Right, first thing's first. Enough with the crowdsourcing. Too much noise, and we'll be drowning in too many false leads, and accusing all sorts of all sorts. I think Ally will appreciate that too, to help prevent what's supposed to be her serene place of confinement, turning into a three-ring circus.'

'Which it feels like enough of the time as it is,' Ally said.

'OK, OK, I'm sorry, it won't happen again. So essential personnel only,' she said. 'Alec, you can stand down your What's App group. Tell them it's been a misunderstanding or something.'

'Gladly!' Alex said.

Tom returned to his chair and leaned forward, elbows on his thighs. 'I almost can't believe I'm about to say this, but the most efficient way to get to the bottom of this, is not to rely on random sightings, but to tail Scott. And since Inez is away for the next couple of days –'

Alec began at the same moment Louise clapped her hands.

'Tom, you really don't have to –'

'Oh, I knew you'd help –'

Alec shook his head at Tom, offering him a way out again.

'Och, it's fine,' Tom said with a small smile. 'I suppose as soon as I agreed to come in the back way, and park my car behind some overgrown bramble bushes, I knew I was up for a spot of subterfuge. I can make use of the fancy new camera and lens Inez bought me for birdwatching too.'

'You got lucky – not only is Inez away and I'm a bit bored without her, our old pal Constable Calum Kirkpatrick is away too. With his Spidey Senses, he would have me spotted lurking around Mid-June on reconnaissance in a heartbeat.'

'Oh yeah, Katie told me he was back down at Bletchley Park,' Ally said.

It had been the intrepid Calum who had re-discovered Mid-June's spy station after decades of its location and role in the war being guarded secret by those who worked there. Not even their descendants had an inkling of its existence. He had been recruited as the local representative to help uncover more about its history, a role that his diligence and interest made time-consuming – another contentious point with Katie.

Ally mused that she wished they would sort things out but quickly caught herself – she was already too embroiled in one romance gone awry.

By the time Tom left, a top-secret plan was in place that was far too procedural and meticulous for Louise's predicament, but they would expect no less of him.

From the desk of Iain Watson, Glenberry
Monday 4th January, 1960

A ~~letter arrived this morning whose impact I cannot begin to~~
~~Never have I opened a letter of such grave import~~
There is a letter. It is now in Mr D-L's hands, and he says he will share it with his wife. God help him. I have not wished so strongly that I could somehow spare him pain since I watched him lower his mother's coffin into the ground on that wet day in Kilmour cemetery.

25

January 1960

Mimi promised Watson that if she hadn't been pregnant, she would have worked with him to bring back the Glenberry Christmas Ball, which used to be the talk of society, and the subject of many column inches in January's *Scottish Field*. Mimi knew that it would be fun and something she'd revel in when the time came, but for now she was in nesting mode, taking more delight in the tiny hand-knitted bootees and bonnets that Geri was making for her, than in even the finest couture ballgown.

Alexander made a show of being disapproving that Christmas was now a public holiday in Scotland – incredibly, for only the second year. He went on a long rant about the Reformation and that Christmas was once seen as too Catholic a celebration for the austere Presbyterians. The Scots were banned from celebrating Christmas at all and poured their festive energy into Hogmanay instead.

'You're harbouring decrees made around the time America was discovered,' Mimi laughed. 'What about the Glenberry Christmas Ball? Sounds like your parents weren't anti-Christmas.'

'That's a class thing. If you asked Geri and Sadie if Christmas was important in their families growing up, the answer would be no. They'll all have gone off to work, just like any other day, looking forward to some time off and letting loose at Hogmanay.'

Alexander was mostly bluster though, and Christmas at Glenberry was cosy and pleasant, in a fairly splendid way of course. Mrs Law outdid herself with a magnificent candlelit supper on Christmas Eve, and seemingly out of concern that they might starve without her, packaged up leftovers. (If you could call roast pheasant, honeyed ham, and spiced pears 'leftovers'.)

The staff then left them to their own devices for two days: Mrs Law with her husband and grown-up children; Hattie with her parents and younger siblings; and Watson with friends in Glasgow.

As for Hogmanay, although Alexander threatened to take Mimi to the Gillie's Rest to show her what the fuss was all about, his head was bobbing over his dram by nine o'clock that evening.

IT WAS JUST a few days into the New Year when Alexander came to find her.

Dark days like this were easier to bear in the fresh new living room that she loved. Her new modern lamps cast a cozy light, and the electric fire was turned up high. Why on earth would one ever bother with the – well, *bother* – of lighting a coal fire nowadays, when you could have heat at the flick of a switch?

Mimi had her feet up, reading a magazine. She looked up to see him standing in the doorway, with the ashen look people only have when they have been stricken by the very worst kind of news.

Someone must have passed away.

Mimi slung her legs off the couch, sat up, and began to stand to go to him.

'No please, sit down, Mimi. I have something I have to tell you,' he said.

It must be one of her parents. Oh God.

'To show you,' he added.

To show her? It must be a telegram. She felt sick.

Alexander sat down beside her.

'I've received a letter.' He looked down at a piece of writing paper, folded closed. His hands were shaking, ever so slightly. His breathing was too, before he took a deep breath, that turned into something between a sigh and a groan on the way out.

'I think it's best if I just give you this to read.'

Mimi's hands were shaking more than his now as she took it from him.

Words jumped off the page at her as her thoughts galloped too fast for her to rein in: 'I have thought of you often... our wonderful romance... produced a son.'

Immediately, tears stung her eyes. She looked up at Alexander, who drew breath to talk. She held up a finger to stop him and began reading again properly, from the top.

12 Rose Street,

London,

S.W.16

30 December 1959

Dear Alexander,

It seems foreign to address you so formally after so
many more affectionate notes between us in days gone by.
Can you believe it has been more than eight years since we
ceased such exchanges? I have thought of you often,
wondering how you might react if I were ever to contact
you again.

Now I feel the time has come to do so, and I write with
some news you will find momentous: our time together in
London, our wonderful romance, produced a son.

My darling Charles is a healthy, handsome boy, newly
eight years old. I enclose a recent photograph of him, taken
on a visit to Hamley's to see Father Christmas. He has been
brought up with the help of my parents, but he is of an age
where he is starting to ask questions about his real father.
Therefore, I decided it was only fair to both of you that I
should write.

I have made enquiries about the journey to Scotland
and, if I have remembered the local names correctly, I
believe it is possible to travel to your estate by train. I
would be willing to do so, to allow you to meet your son
and to discuss with you the path ahead for him, and for
your place in his life.

I can be reached at the address above, and I look
forward to hearing from you soon,

Yours Sincerely,
Elsie Morris

'Oh Alexander,' was all she could muster.
He sat down beside her, and she put her head on his chest
and sobbed.

He cradled her head. 'I'm so sorry. I had no idea.'

There was only the sound of Mimi's sobs.

'I'm not sure what to say, Mimi,' he said, gently stroking her hair. 'I only knew that I had to show you it.'

Mimi lay still, listening to his heartbeat, not knowing what to say either, struggling to believe this was even happening to her.

She felt the baby kick. Oh, how excited they'd been the first time that happened. Their little secret that wasn't even a secret: stowed away in this dusty, half-forgotten place they called home, they had something that was theirs alone. A new life was growing within her and Mimi felt like the person in the world who had ever experienced that wondrous feeling.

But now she was all too painfully reminded that this was not the case: Elsie Morris had felt that wonder too.

She pulled away from Alexander, sat up straight, and wiped away her tears with the handkerchief Alexander tentatively offered.

'Tell me about her. About Elsie,' she said.

'Mimi –' Alexander began, his shoulders slumped in reluctance.

'Alexander, what did you think was going to happen here? That I wouldn't have questions?'

He nodded, conceding.

After a deep breath, he began.

Alexander and Elsie had been a thing for about six months. She was pretty and fun, and great company on a couple of jaunts to the South of France. 'We had a good time together, but I mean...not to sound cold, but –'

'Alexander, you can be honest with me. You have to be. Completely.'

He nodded and said the words he'd been struggling with: 'I wouldn't say she was particularly special to me.'

'That's OK to say. It's a relief, I'm honest. I'm not naive. I knew you'd had plenty of girlfriends. When we first met and shared our pasts, I wondered if you'd ever spent any time single.'

'That's my point – I just kicked around with her, no different to any of the other girls. Nothing serious. And I knew she felt the same. She was using me for a fun time, before she found 'the one' and settled down.'

Since he received the letter earlier that day, he'd been turning their relationship over in his mind. The timeline made sense, as far as he could remember. 'She was a nice girl, so I'd have no reason to think she was – you know – sleeping around.'

'Of course not, I'm sure she wasn't. If the age of the boy makes sense, we will not accuse her of anything, just to suit our own purpose.'

'How did it end?' she asked.

'On friendly terms. As I say, she wanted the happily-ever-after and she said I certainly wasn't it. But she said it nicely, and I knew it too. I expected I'd continue to see her out and about, you know, on the scene, but thinking about it now, I don't think I ever did. I suppose, because – well – we know why, I think.'

They talked some more about what he remembered about her: her job, circumstances, what part of London she was from. Elsie sounded perfectly likeable and normal, her relationship with Alexander no more serious than many Mimi had had.

Except that it had ended in a pregnancy. And a son.

They fell into silence again, the letter on the couch between them.

Mimi thought of Elsie finding out she was pregnant, after she'd broken ties with Alexander. Why hadn't she got back in touch with him and told him? Because she knew he wasn't her happily-ever-after? How very brave.

Mimi would be wrong to feel jealous and that Elsie had robbed her of any of her expectant joy. Elsie Morris had gone through this alone, with no one to smile at the neat rows of bootees and bonnets, in a tiny drawer, in a freshly decorated nursery, as she and Alexander had done this morning. Elsie hadn't had Alexander there, hand on her belly as the baby kicked, making jokes that it was the next Tommy Docherty or some other football player Mimi didn't know, and that he'd be sure to play for Scotland.

Had Elsie wanted the baby? Had she considered looking for someone who might, 'help her'? Mimi shuddered at the thought, given some of the horror stories she'd heard about women opting not to continue with their pregnancies.

'You have to write back to her, Alexander,' she said, breaking the silence.

Alexander put his head in his hands and cried. Mimi had only seen tears in his eyes once before, when the doctor confirmed to them that she was pregnant. Another thing Elsie had missed out on.

'Oh Mimi, I don't deserve you. I know that's what I have to do, I knew immediately, but I don't want to hurt you.'

'You haven't done anything to hurt me. This happened long before I even moved to London. You have a son. You must want to meet him, surely. I respect you for telling me, and I'll respect you even more for living up to your responsibilities.'

'Mimi, you're amazing.'

'I'm not,' Mimi disagreed quietly. 'This wasn't easy news to hear, and it will be hard to come to terms with. But for now, we both know the right thing is for you to write to Elsie Morris and arrange to meet your son.'

MIMI WAS SITTING ALONE, staring into space, which felt like all she had done for the past several days. Alexander had written to Elsie Morris the very day he received her letter. All they could do was sit and wait.

When they were with each other, there was a tension in the

air that prickled like static, waiting for a spark. Mimi refused to be that spark, but she couldn't quite get her emotions in line with the calm she had mustered in telling Alexander that she wasn't hurt.

Nothing had changed, she tried to tell herself: she was always aware that Alexander had led quite the playboy life before they met, and she also knew that he was blissfully happy in this new chapter of his life, back at Glenberry, with her. But this news had rocked her more than she cared to admit.

She felt strangled, claustrophobic in her own body. They had promised that they would not tell another soul about Elsie Morris and her son until they knew more, but she had to think of her own sanity. And feeling like this couldn't be good for the baby either.

For a change of scene she got up to stare out of the window. There was a dusting of snow on the great lawn and the clouds were low, threatening to follow up with a heavier fall any minute. She heard a crunch of footsteps on gravel, and expected to see Watson or Alexander, or both, calling a day on their estate rounds. But it was Peggy, so bundled up in her coat, scarf and hat that from above, Mimi couldn't see any of her face.

Mimi frowned, wondering if she had forgotten an arrangement they made. It was a pleasant surprise anyway, and nice to have a friend who felt she could drop in unannounced.

As she spruced herself in the mirror, her reflected eyes looked tired. She wondered if Peggy would notice. She also wondered, if pressed, if she would confide in Peggy. Peggy was a case of still waters run deep, and she knew she could trust her to listen and not judge, to counsel but not lecture.

Mrs Law delivered Peggy, still wrapped up, the chill air still clinging to her clothes.

'You're so cold!' Mimi said. 'Let's go into the living room, I have the electric fire on. Here, give me your things.'

Peggy unwrapped her scarf and took off her hat and looked steadily at Mimi, saying nothing.

Mimi's heart sank as under the hallway light, she saw Peggy's scraped, swollen and tear-stained face.

'Oh my God. Peggy. Who did this to you?'

26

In a break from the Louise show, Jill came to visit. Ally relished handing her the biscuit tin and watching its contents land, then sink in.

Jill's reaction did not disappoint. From stunned silence to a volley of questions and speculation: 'What's the value in today's money? How much?! Maybe one of Alec's sisters has them and doesn't know they're real? Maybe one of Alec's sisters has them and does know they're real...'

Ally also brought Jill up-to-date on where she was with Watson's journals, and Elsie and Charles Morris. Not much further forward, unfortunately. Watson was tight-lipped on this particular subject.

There was an abrupt entry on the 4th of January, 'There is a letter...' Then the matter was brought simply to a close when he mentioned Elsie and her son's departure on the 22nd of January. Even though he hadn't mentioned their arrival.

'Oh and something weird going on with Mimi's friend Peggy being "despatched" to Glasgow, whatever that means.'

Watson seemed constrained more by sadness and helplessness, than discretion. His entries were strained, making only brief reference to tensions in the castle and admitting that he had never looked forward more keenly to his days off.

'All I've managed to get is that Elsie Morris did visit Glenberry, arriving sometime after 17th January and leaving on the 22nd,' Ally explained. 'Whatever happened in between is anyone's guess. Watson's left us high and dry.'

'Ugh, come on, Watson,' Jill huffed.

'I know, I've told him off along the way too. He seems to clam up when he's uncomfortable. There was some kind of embarrassing incident at an NCT class – he mentioned it but then changed his mind. I think I remember Fiona Sinclair saying something about it at the Strawberry Fair, so I guess she'd be able to tell me if I really wanted to know...'

'What about her? Any thoughts on grilling her again?' Jill asked.

'I've thought about it, but those ladies had only just become friends. What are the chances Mimi would have opened up about something like this? Especially in those days. I can't risk asking her about it in case she really doesn't know anything. I'd be giving away a secret Mimi decided at the time not to share with her.'

'True, I wouldn't have thought of that. God, it's frustrating, isn't it? And now missing Cartiers too.'

Jill went back to staring at the valuation certificate.

After a moment, she gasped.

'Uh oh,' thought Ally. What far-fetched answers had she come up with now?

'Maybe they paid Elsie off with the Cartiers,' she said, wide eyed.

'What?' This was a leap, even for Jill.

'Why is that ridiculous? You already figured out a time-frame for when they vanished, and Elsie Morris's visit fits in with that. Maybe Mimi and Alexander decided to give her them as hush money, a one time pay-out to never darken their door again, letting them preserve the family line and Glenberry for their own child.'

She was right about the timeline, Ally had to admit. But she had come to know Mimi and Alexander through Watson's journals, and from reminiscing with Sandy when he brought her tea and goodies, using it as an excuse to skive for a bit. The couple were good people, with the immovable sense of duty of the Douglas-Lauders and the moral responsibility Mimi had learned from none other than Rose Delacourt.

'I just don't see them sending Elsie packing, seemingly never to be mentioned again, if they really believed Charles was Alexander's son. Pay out or not.'

'OK, well maybe they didn't believe her. Maybe she was lying – a proper grifter – and Mimi bit the bullet and got rid of her with a bribe. Quite a bribe, mind you. The jewels seemed to be a secret between just Mimi and Rose, so no one would have noticed them missing. They all just thought they were gaudy diamantés. Mimi was married, pregnant, and happy. Maybe she decided it was OK to let go of her "insurance policy" to get rid of a fraudster.'

'As you say – that's quite the payout. If she was a grifter she absolutely hit the jackpot.'

'Or maybe she just stole them,' Jill shrugged. 'Maybe we're overthinking it, and she just – stole them.'

Ally stared up at the ceiling. It was hard to keep her thoughts straight being hit by Jill's runaway train.

But Jill kept going. 'Look, you said yourself that Alexander and Mimi were too moral to have chucked them out on their ear if the wee boy, Charles, really was Alexander's son. So it only makes sense that Elsie was lying all along. I don't know exactly how, but there's no doubt in my mind that those Cartiers ended up in the grubby paws of Elsie Morris. Maybe that's why there's no trace of her anywhere on the internet.

Changing her name was a small price to pay. She never had to work another scam in her life.'

Although Jill had crossed over into painting Elsie as a gangster in a movie, Ally found herself following some of her logic. The theory wasn't completely outwith the realms of possibility. In fact, it was fairly within them.

Sandy called through the door, knocking.

Jill quickly opened the closest drawer and shoved the biscuit tin and papers inside.

He had tea and scones. There had been a lot of scones recently, to allow them to compare the merits of the various preserves gifted to them at the Strawberry Fair.

'Who and what do we have today?' Ally asked.

'We have Mrs Turnbull's strawberry jam versus Mr McCall's rhubarb and gooseberry,' Sandy replied.

He chatted with them for the rest of Jill's visit, critiquing the jams and musing about adding a second storey and a turret onto the old playhouse for the twins.

When she was alone again, Ally mindlessly picked up her phone.

There were several Instagram alerts and she was feeling a bit behind with all that, with everything else going on, so she decided to have a look and catch up.

Sandy and Susan's friends, as well as some of the wider circle of Mid-June stalwarts, knew that Ally ran the account, and she was used to getting encouraging messages from them. Of late they had turned into messages wishing her well with the pregnancy and excitement about the twins. Ally read them and replied to them all and ignored the few that were likely salespeople fishing.

In liking and replying to engagement, she was, well, happily disengaged. After a few loops of the scroll, though, she found herself pausing on a user called 'Mags123'. She frowned at the screen, vaguely recognising the name, and went back to the would-be fishing DMs she'd ignored. Sure enough, there were two questions from that user:

> Mags123: Hi there, just wondering if this
> account is run by a family member?

> Mags123: Hi there, I'm wondering if this
> account is run by a family member? It
> seems like it might be. If so, please can
> you get back to me?

Ally went back to her posts. Mags123 had been interacting with posts for a couple of weeks. Two days ago they had commented on one.

> Mags123: @Glenberry_Castle I sent you a
> DM. Can you take a look?

She went to the profile. It was private, but she enlarged the profile picture for a better look. Two smiling young men, tall, dark and handsome. One was in a graduation gown: black wool, a flash of scarlet lining. St Andrews.

It was stereotyping that an HR department would pull her up for, but these were the sons and profiling was easy: female, middle-aged, middle-class, and – judging by her sons – attractive and polished.

The messages were fairly oblique; maybe it was just a persistent salesperson.

Hell, she had nothing to lose. Where was she going?

> Glenberry_Castle: Hi there, yes, the
> account is run by a family member. Me,
> Ally Douglas-Lauder. Thanks for following
> along!

To her great surprise, the message was marked as Read almost instantaneously. Well this was intriguing. Now she may as well stick around.

She didn't have to wait long.

Mags123: Hi Ally, I love the account. I'm so interested in the history of the family and Glenberry. You depict it really well.

Glenberry_Castle: Thanks, have you visited?

Mags123: No, but I'd love to, someday soon.

Glenberry_Castle: I hope you do! At the moment, I can't offer to show you around, but the staff at our gift shop are great and they can provide you with a map and everything else you need to know.

Mags123: Thanks Ally. All the very best, Mags.

Glenberry_Castle: No problem, Ally.

Ally went back to scrolling, hoping the mindlessness of it might lull her over into a nap.

It did.

When she woke up, there were more alerts. Social media might be easy, but it was endless. There was a stream of DMs.

Mags123: Ally, you mentioned that you couldn't show me around right now. I've gathered from some of the well-wishers who frequent your account that it's because you are expecting. Congrats! I wish you all the best.

Mags123: The thing is Ally, you may be the right person to approach about this. My father has a special connection with Glenberry and I promised him I'd arrange a trip with him.

Mags 123: When I told my dad a few days ago that a gap had opened up in my schedule to come up from London next week, I said I'd see what I could find out about visiting Glenberry. To be honest Ally, it's too delicate a matter, and too close to my dad's heart, for a conversation with your gift shop staff. Sorry to burden you with this, but you might, in fact, be the best member of the family for us to meet first.

Up from London. Delicate matter. Close to her dad's heart. Jill wouldn't believe this!

Ally hadn't realised until now that she had formed a clear picture of Elsie Morris. The face she had given her shifted slightly from its 1960's look, to an up-to-date one, and a little older, to become the face of Mags123.

Because Mags123 could only be one person: the daughter of Charles Morris, and the granddaughter of Elsie Morris.

And sixty years after her grandmother did, she wanted to visit Glenberry.

~

From the desk of Iain Watson, Glenberry
Friday 8th January, 1960

Heavy snowfall this evening. Mr D-L and I began to shovel it in silence, until it was apparent we were fighting a losing battle. We shall resume when it has given us its worst.

The couple look tired and drawn as they await a return letter. If it's possible for a woman in the plump of pregnancy to look drawn.

Mrs Peggy McPherson is spending the night. I lit the fire for Mr D-L in his old bedroom.

27

Peggy met her husband Jim a couple of years after the war. He had served in the signal corps and returned to civilian life as a GPO telephone engineer, which was what brought him to the Glenberry area. He was tall, handsome and brave, but mostly woo-ed Peggy with his cheeky wit, always delivered with a wink.

He stayed in a room rented to the GPO by one Gladys Niven, a widow who scared local children with her resemblance to the Wicked Witch of the West, both in looks and demeanour. Everyone knew and feared Gladys. Even her good deeds performed in accordance with her grim piety had an air of severity: the flowers she arranged for the church mostly featured thistles, and meals of boiled cabbage taken to the sick were delivered with a moral lesson, not comfort.

Peggy had made a joke about this to Jim when she found out where he was lodging, and he had replied with the surprising take that Gladys was 'a pushover'. Sure enough, one rainy night when Peggy and Jim had not wanted their date to end, Jim, with loud ouching and quiet cursing, picked some of Gladys's favourite thistles from the roadside and wrapped them in his newspaper. Despite it being past the hours where any guests were allowed, and that female guests were forbidden altogether, Jim charmed Gladys into letting them in. It was on the proviso that they sat in the kitchen with the door to the hall open, but it was an impressive achievement, nonetheless.

When the area was all hooked up for the telephone, Jim's next jobs for the GPO were in the Highlands and Islands. Peggy's heart ached and she realised that this must be love.

On the Saturday after his first week away, as Peggy sat in her mother's house pining, there was a knock at the door and there was Jim, down on one knee, offering her a ring.

Life was fine. She missed him when he was away, but they made up for it when he returned every month, always with a thoughtful gift: knitted mittens from Skye, a tin of shortbread from Oban.

There wasn't much entertainment in the remote areas, so the men simply worked in the day, and drank at night. When he was home, there weren't many hours of the day when he didn't have a drink in his hand. His wit became harsher with a drink, cruel even. Sometimes he would cry, his demons from the war getting the better of the stoicism that had been instilled by the 'Keep Calm and Carry On' propaganda. In the morning, he'd seem to remember nothing of either his malice or maudlin.

When baby Jim came along he was smitten with him, and even joined in duties like bathing and settling him, stopping short of nappy duty of course. The baby was such a light in his life, Peggy dared to hope it may have banished out his darkness.

But gradually, the heavy drinking returned, as well as the ugly jibes, the ranting and the pathetic sobbing.

The first violence was throwing a teacup at her, when she was asking a simple question about what shirt he wanted her to pack for him. He did not apologise. It was like he had known all along this would come. And Peggy may have too.

. . .

MIMI TRIED to be as good a listener as Peggy herself: she listened and did not judge; she was sad, not scandalised.

'There's something else I have to tell you Mimi,' Peggy said.

'You know now that you can tell me anything,' Mimi replied.

'I'm pregnant.'

It had not been consensual.

'Oh Peggy,' Mimi said, closing her eyes to take this in.

'I can't have this baby. For so many reasons,' Peggy said.

'I know,' Mimi replied. 'It's OK, I know.'

PEGGY MAY HAVE ENDED up staying the night anyway, since Glenberry ended up snowed in, and that was the excuse they gave to Alexander and to Peggy's mum, who was looking after young Jim. Mimi banished Alexander to their old bedroom in the main castle, and Peggy and Mimi chatted until late.

At Mimi's persuasion, Peggy agreed to an emergency meeting of the Ladies' Group the following day.

'Will you help me explain things to them?' Peggy asked. 'I can't face telling the whole story again by myself.'

'Of course, if that's what you want. But I think this makes sense to tell them. Neither of the two of us has any idea where to begin, to get you...help. Might Geri have an idea? She's hardly ever even left her village, but somehow she makes me feel quite naive and unworldly.'

'THAT BASTARD!' Geri spat, once Mimi had finished. She got up and went to sit beside Peggy, putting her arm around her.

'Oh Peggy. My friend. You're entitled to a good cry,' she said, her voice changing with a switch to kind and soft. Peggy nodded her thanks. There were a few silent glances among the women as they all took this in. Mimi felt sorry for all of them that they'd had to hear the awful, violent story of their friend, but especially young Sadie.

Flora spoke first. 'So, you don't want to have this baby?'

'I can't. I'm heartbroken about it, but I can't,' Peggy mustered. 'But I have no idea how to...where to...you know...'

'That's OK, I understand. And you also you feel like the time has come to leave your husband?' Flora asked.

'I have to. For my son's sake, if nothing else.

'I know some of this isn't my husband's fault. He has trauma. They called it shellshock after the First War, but this time there's not even a name for it. No one's talking about it, but it's there and it's very real. And in my husband, it's getting worse. I don't recognise him anymore.

'I don't know what he is capable of –'

She left the unspoken thought of the threat to her son hanging in the air.

'Please know that you're not alone anymore, Peggy,' Flora said. We are going to figure this out. We are five intelligent, resourceful women, and we are going to work something out.'

She might as well have rolled up her sleeves and pulled out an operations map. Maybe she had been a spy in the war, not Peggy. She was gentle, but pragmatic. 'First things first. Geri, you and I are born and bred here. What do we know about any help women can get for unwanted pregnancies?'

'Around here? Only that awful place run by the nuns, where they send young lassies, then whip the babies away from them as soon as they're born. I've heard it's filthy too. As grim as a Dickens book.'

She said it her own brand of no-nonsense, not as gentle as Flora's, and Sadie flinched.

'Sorry everyone,' she added, 'it just upsets me, these poor wee lassies.

'But for the other thing – I mean, if you don't want to go ahead with the pregnancy at all – well, I've heard of a woman up in Glasgow who does that. She's in Partick.'

Partick, thought Mimi, and all of a sudden she wondered if she could possibly know the street. The image came back like a shutter click: the women in their windows on a sunny day, watching Mimi, everything about her out of place and a black eye blooming, thanks to her run-in with Derek Leslie. More than one had asked if she needed help, and then the old lady with the pram saying, 'Well, if you change your mind, we're here.'

It all made sense now.

'I may know where she lives,' Mimi said quietly. 'I didn't realise it at the time, but I might have been there.'

'What on earth took you to Partick?' Geri asked. 'You must have been quite a sight there.'

Mimi smiled. It felt like days since she had. 'Yup, I sure was.'

'This woman, how do you know about her?' Flora asked Geri.

'I'd rather not say too much, but I'll be able to get her exact address, and find out how to contact her, from a cousin of mine,' Geri said.

'Is it safe?' It was the first time Sadie had spoken.

'As safe as it can be given the laws against it,' Geri answered. 'I believe she keeps an immaculate house and is very kind. She's been known to let young women stay with her for as long as it takes for them to recover. She doesn't just run a grotty production line, like some of the stories you hear.'

Sadie nodded, and fell back to her thoughtful silence, letting the older women go back to logistics.

'How long do you think you need to pack up, Peggy? Is your husband back at work up north again for now?' Flora asked.

'Yes, he won't be back for a couple of weeks. That's not the rush. The rush is...the other thing.'

'Absolutely,' Geri said, all business. 'The sooner the better. Easier all round.'

'I'll help you pack Peggy. Do you have a suitcase? I have plenty, and trunks as well, that you can borrow,' Mimi offered.

'Trunks?' Geri laughed. 'We don't all have the array of clobber and glad rags that you do! Am I right, Peggy?'

'The loan of a suitcase would be perfect, thank you,' Peggy said.

They needed dates. And a firm plan.

'Geri, is your cousin you mentioned, on the phone?' Mimi asked. 'You could phone her now. I'm proud to say that I talked my husband and Watson into us getting an extension line into the apartment. It's in the kitchen.'

'My God, you're like yon Doris Day, with your trunks of clothes and two phones! Aye, I could give it a try.' Geri hoisted herself up and headed to the kitchen.

Meanwhile, the others backfilled the logistics.

With all the snow, trains had been reduced to one service per day, and even that was iffy. Flora wouldn't hear of that anyway, and said she'd be driving Peggy right to the door of the woman she had to see and would look after Jim while she was in there. Mimi insisted that she would go too.

Geri came back, a kind smile to Peggy not succeeding in hiding her mixed emotions. 'I got you an appointment, pet. In two days' time.'

28

How had Ally managed to become so embroiled in this drama between her sister-in-law and her builder?

She could tell by the bubbles, that Scott was already texting her again, so she waited. She longed for the days when he was just texting her about choices of doorknobs for the new kitchen.

Louise said that if Alec had any sense of family loyalty, he'd fire Scott and not pay him a penny more.

'Louise, have a heart, we need our place finished for the babies arriving. Only Scott can do that for us on time. Good news is, we're nearing completion and then you'll never have to see him again.'

That had just prompted a dramatic new round of sobs and tears.

The bubbles became text.

Scott the Builder: I'm really upset about
this Ally.

Wow, he had a cheek.

Ally: You're really upset about it?! Think of
Louise!

Scott the Builder: Please, I need to show
you some swatches from Moira anyway.
Can I come up?

Ally deliberately took her time replying. Let him stew.

Ally: OK, fine, come on up.

TOM HAD REPORTED BACK with the results of his surveillance operation the day before. Ally had been expecting the whole thing to be a misunderstanding and that there would be a perfectly innocent explanation. Unfortunately, that was not the case.

Tom entered command central, aka Ally's supposed place of respite, with a shake of his head.

'Ally, I wish it was better news,' he said, but was interrupted by Louise flying into the room via her own secret entrance.

'Jeez, I forgot that thing was there. I think I'm jumpy from sneaking around the last couple of days, you nearly gave me a heart attack,' Tom said.

'Sorry Tom, Ally usually makes me knock –' Louise began, as if that was a somewhat unreasonable request of Ally's, but with a glance at Ally's expression, added, 'For obvious reasons. Of course I should knock. And I usually text or walkie-talkie first too.'

'You have walkie-talkies?' Tom asked, intrigued.

'No, it's just what my dad calls our mobiles,' Louise

explained. 'What have you got there Tom? What did you find out?'

'I brought my laptop with the photos I took, Louise,' Tom replied. 'But I'm afraid you're not going to like them.'

Ally's heart sank, as she watched poor Louise's face cloud over with the dread of hearing the bad news that she had been hoping was all in her head.

'Let's sit,' said Tom.

He opened his laptop and got straight to it. They were now able to very clearly put a face to the no longer elusive brunette.

The first series of photos, taken in quick succession, surveillance style, was of the woman and Scott standing by a car, on the passenger side. The woman was animated and tipping her head back laughing. As Scott went to open the passenger door, she stopped him, with a hand on his wrist, and her hand remained there for the next several frames, until Scott got in the car and she shut his door for him.

Even in still photos taken through a zoom lens, you could tell the mood was flirtatious.

'Ugh.' Louise made a sad face at Ally and said quietly, 'I hoped I'd be wrong.'

'I know, me too,' Ally nodded. This caper had taken a wee sad turn.

'Where were those pictures taken, Tom?' Ally asked.

'At a house just on the way to Berry. You know the big white one on the right?' Tom replied.

Ally nodded. The house had a renovation coming up that Scott had been hoping to bid on, but that detail seemed inconsequential now, faced with these pictorial PDAs.

'Their next stop, was I believe, the house of that lady who makes the curtains. Moira, is it? It's a quaint wee cottage with roses around every door and window?'

Ally nodded.

'Scott went in, and the woman stood outside taking photos of the cottage,' Tom explained.

He clicked through the photos, confirming his story, and then Scott exited with a parcel wrapped in brown paper, tied with string. He was holding the flat parcel in both hands, palms up, like you would hold a pizza box. The woman opened the passenger door for him with a smile and stroked the parcel in his hands.

Louise harrumphed and Ally had to agree. It was hideously intimate.

The two ended the day at The Gillie's Rest, where, Tom noted, Scott's van was parked. Tom left soon after they went in.

'I had to get back and feed the neighbour's cats, or Inez would kill me. And I have to admit, sitting sentry outside a B&B felt a little sordid.'

'*Sordid* is the word alright,' Louise said with a sigh. 'What about yesterday?'

'I headed to the Gillie's early, assuming that the woman stayed the night there, and she had. Scott showed up and they had breakfast together, before they went their separate ways.' He nodded towards his screen at the photos taken through the window of the Gillie's Rest.

'At least she seems to be managing to keep her hands off him for a hot second,' Louise said.

Tom cleared his throat and kept going.

The couple emerged and this time stood by Scott's van. More touching of Scott's wrist as the woman stood close – too close – and looked up at him chatting. Then she reached up and ran her fingers through Scott's hair, laughing.

Ally wanted to believe that it looked like Scott was pulling back slightly, but didn't have time to complete the thought, because Louise shut Tom's laptop, just short of slamming it.

'Sorry Tom, I can't watch them kiss goodbye,' she said,

moving from her chair to sit beside Ally on the bed, positioning herself for a sympathetic back rub.

'They only hugged goodbye; there was no kissing.' Tom's tone conveyed that he knew this was small consolation.

'There's just one more thing,' he continued. 'Once Scott left, she went back inside the Gillie's. I thought I'd get out the car and take an amble along. I got there just in time for her coming out with an overnight-type bag. She was on the phone. To Scott.'

Louise's eyes were in danger of rolling into her head. 'Well, we've seen all the PDA's, I shudder to think of the sexting that must go on.'

'Sexting is texting Louise, she was talking on the phone,' Ally pointed out, probably not very helpfully.

'Well dirty talk, whatever. Either way eww,' Louise huffed.

'No dirty talk, thank goodness,' Tom said and took out his notebook. 'I wrote it down when I got back in the car.

'OK, I quote: "Scott, you know I loved you the minute I clapped eyes on you. And now that I've seen Mid-June, everything is even more perfect. I know it's a lot and it's happened so fast but please –"

'Scott must have interjected here, then she said, "OK, I'll let you go. I've told you how I feel. It's over to you now. Bye."

'She said bye a few times. The way people do.'

'I'm surprised they didn't go for the old, "you hang up, no you hang up…",' Louise said in a silly sarcastic voice.

'You didn't ask at the Gillie's about her, did you?' Ally asked.

'No, I wasn't sure how much we actually wanted to know about her, now that, well, we know.'

'Oh we know! We know alright!' Louise said. 'And it seems we'll get to know plenty about her when she moves to Mid-June. Since she's fallen in love with it, as well as Scott.'

Louise's tone had changed. Worryingly.

'Thank you for everything Tom, I really do appreciate it, but

I need to be alone right now,' she said grimly, then left by the door she'd come in.

'I feel so bad for the wee soul,' Tom said, 'but man, that secret entranceway must be driving you mad! You must be desperate to get back into your own place.'

ALLY HAD some idea from Louise of how her confrontation with Scott had gone, and now it seemed she was about to hear his side of things. She looked at her phone.

> Scott the Builder: I'll be there in ten.
> Thanks Ally.

Her phone was low on charge, so with great effort she hoisted herself over to the charger. She couldn't wait to be back in their own apartment for small joys like sockets galore, and chargers within reach of the bed: then she'd feel like a princess in a castle.

∾

I have seldom looked forward more to my days off and a jaunt to Glasgow.

I have seen very little of Mrs D-L this past week. It pains me to think of her sequestered in the new quarters we designed to give her light, only for such a dark cloud to hang over her now.

As for my time with Mr D-L: it has been sadly, but inevitably stinted, such as we have never known, even with his years of absence. That pains me even more.

I am taking the train up to Glasgow this evening instead of tomorrow, because another large snowfall is forecast overnight. At the moment it seems arduous, but I hope I will be the better for it in the end.

29

All their worst fears had been realised.

They were packed and ready to leave first thing, but the weather forecast had been correct. They awoke to the great lawn a blanket of white and the pine tree branches bowed with the weight of the heavy dump of snow that had happened overnight. If it had been any other day, Mimi's heart would have been gladdened at a taste of the crisp, cold and glistening winter mornings of New York. Instead, it was Jim who rejoiced: 'We can't go to Glasgow to stay with your friend now Mummy – it's too snowy! Can I go out to play? Please?'

Peggy had insisted that Alexander be granted the courtesy of sleeping in his own bed, in his own home, instead of banished to the wilds of the castle proper, as he had been a few nights prior. She and Jim had been perfectly comfortable in the nursery. She had also given Mimi permission to fill Alexander in on the headlines, if not the gory details, of her situation.

As Jim ate his porridge, eyeing the clean white wonderland that awaited his footsteps, the three adults pondered. They could wait until another day, but they didn't know how long it would take for all the roads to be cleared. And as for the train, their little part of the world was so sparsely populated, that with the recent rise of the motor car, rumours were swirling of the train line being retired altogether, so it certainly wasn't a top priority for clearing in a snowstorm. They focused on infrastructure logistics to avoid mentioning the appointment that Peggy had to keep or rearrange.

Alexander had already talked Mimi into packing an overnight bag. This journey and its purpose were long and stressful enough, and there were so few hours of daylight at this time of year. He managed, in the face of this unstoppable force of womanhood, to persuade Mimi that they should stay at the Central Hotel overnight. He'd called the manager already and told him to keep two rooms.

The telephone rang. It startled them all as it was such a rare occurrence. Alexander had forgotten it was even there.

'Flora? Hi, yes good morning to you too.' Mimi was surprised by Flora's chipper tone. Perhaps she hadn't looked outside yet.

'I know you'll be thinking the worst, but I just wanted to call and let you know that we are going ahead as planned. Well, we might be a tiny bit later, ten minutes or so, but we'll be there!'

'We?' Mimi asked.

'You'll see. Tell Jim he's in for an adventure. Be ready in half an hour.'

Alexander and Peggy looked at Mimi expectantly.

'Commander Flora Sinclair has issued her orders, and we shall mobilise as planned, despite the snow,' she said. 'We've to be ready in half an hour.'

'Boo,' Jim said. 'Do we have to go? I want to play in the snow.'

'According to the radio, there's snow where you're going too,' Alexander said. 'And do you know how many hills there are in Glasgow? Seven! It's built on seven hills like Rome was! Let's get you dressed and I'll take you to Mrs Law's kitchen and see if she has an old tea tray that you can take with you to use as a sledge.'

He took Jim's hand and Mimi's heart swelled.

She hoped they'd have a boy.

Or a girl. Alexander would be such a sweetie with a girl.

She had just been counting her blessings all around over the last few days, with the less fortunate circumstances of the pregnancies of poor Elsie Morris, and now Peggy.

Just as she couldn't be more in love with him, he stuck his head back into the kitchen and said, 'Central Hotel! You're staying there. Please don't fight me on this, Mimi. I'm not happy that you're travelling at all today, never mind both ways.'

He'd left to go back to helping Jim by the time she said, 'Roger that.'

'OK, well let's get our bags then. I'm going to bring a couple of blankets, and maybe even a pillow too, so that Jim can get cosy and have a wee sleep in the back seat. Unless Flora's new plan involves a helicopter, it's going to be a long ride. I'm glad we'd decided to start out so early, so that you can still make your...appointment.'

The Ladies' Group had closed ranks around Peggy and made no bones about the fact that she had to do some things that were brave – and dangerous. But they still hadn't figured out a way of being forthright in their language. They couldn't find the words to use. The correct terms were so harsh. Not to mention, could have them arrested. A couple of Mimi's wealthy friends in London had 'had things seen to' and were frank about it, but even they only used euphemisms, for fear of getting their esteemed Harley Street doctors into trouble.

Jim came back from Mrs Law's kitchen with a waxed paper package of warm biscuits, and two flasks: one of tea, one of coffee. Mimi was thankful that Mrs Law had not so much at raised an eyebrow at their impromptu houseguests. Nor at her trip to Glasgow, in the middle of winter, by car. A car driven by a woman no less.

They gathered in the hall. Alexander stepped outside in his wellies, eyeing the gate for Flora's arrival, while the ladies and Jim stood inside. For once, the gargantuan front door being open did not mean that a draft whipped through the hall. Outside was still and muffled by the snow, and although the sun had barely risen, it was going to be a sunny clear day after a week of gloom. They struggled to keep Jim from dashing out. The snow was a cruel temptation for a small boy, but they didn't want his boots to get cold and wet ahead of their journey, so Alexander scooped him up and told him to listen.

Instead of a car engine, they heard a distant scraping sound. It got louder, as whatever it was approached. From her sheltered position in the hall, Mimi watched Alexander grin and Jim's eyes open wide with wonder. He gasped, and his mouth fell open. Curious, Mimi and Peggy stepped onto the outer threshold and craned their heads around the entranceway.

There were two cars, not one. The first, tall, boxy and loud, was just visible behind the wall of snow it was pushing, which creaked under its own increasing weight.

Flora's husband, Fergus, stopped the car just in front of Alexander and Jim, Jim's mouth still gaping. 'Good morning sirs,' he said and shook Alexander's hand. 'And You must be Jim? Do you like my car, Jim?'

Jim nodded, while Alexander said, 'What on earth have you come up with here? A snow plough? It's genius. And I like the car too. Land Rover Series Two – I've been thinking it's time for me to invest in one.'

'Love the Land Rover. Highly recommend it. And the boys on the farm and I made the plough out of an old trough. It's been a Godsend for clearing our own roads and paths, and frankly, for some of the roads in from The Glass Pass, so my supplies don't get held up.'

'Have you asked the council for money for your troubles?' Alexander asked.

Fergus just snorted. 'Chance would be a fine thing. But talking of The Glass Pass, I'll tell you our plan for this morning: the girls will follow along behind me, until we get over The Glass Pass, then I expect the main road up from there will have been cleared.'

As the men talked roads, cars and homemade ploughs, Flora's more familiar car pulled up behind the Land Rover.

'Look at the couple of numpties I found ankle deep in snow, making their way here.'

'I – I mean, we – couldn't let Peggy leave without saying goodbye,' Geri said getting out of the passenger seat, with Sadie following from the back seat. Geri's face was softer than usual, no cheeky glint in her eye, just glassy-eyed reassurance. She went straight to Peggy on the step and gave her a long hug. Then she held both her hands in hers, as they said quiet farewells out of earshot.

Sadie interrupted them with her contribution for the journey of some homemade shortbread, and a flask of hot Ribena. Then she held out a gift simply wrapped, but with a sprig of dried lavender entwined in the knot in the string. 'There are two lavender bags inside too – I've heard the scent is calming. And an embroidered handkerchief. I'm not as handy as Geri, but I'm learning.'

More hugs, and stifled tears and sobs, ensued.

Geri tried to compose herself and put a hand-knitted hat on Jim's head, with a smile that he saw, but still tears in her eyes that she made sure he didn't. She had talked her sons into 'donating' a few toys to a wee boy who needed them more than they did. Jim scratched the itchy wool hat right off his head and used it to store his three new toy cars in instead.

The men scraped Alexander's own car free of snow so that he could take Geri and Sadie home. 'I'll join in the cavalcade behind you,' Alexander said. 'Let's get these ladies, and young Jim, packed up and on their way. I'm relieved to have convinced our wives to stay at the Central Hotel tonight.'

'Me too,' Fergus replied. 'Thanks for organising.'

'Listen, if I had my way, I'd have been a lot more involved in this whole thing. But I've been put firmly in my place that it's women's business.'

'Me too,' Fergus said again.

Flora gave Fergus a warm hug goodbye.

Alexander looked at Mimi tentatively, but she didn't hesitate. She stepped into his arms and squeezed tight. She felt his chest give with relief.

It was enough.

It had been quite the week.

30

S cott looked weary, his good looks marred by heavy under-
eyes. No bags, shadows or wrinkles just a heaviness.

Ally found herself feeling sorry for him and thought again
what a nice guy she'd believed him to be, until this whole
'pickle' he'd got himself into. She wished, yet again, that it
would turn out to be just that: an innocent pickle. It was hard to
see how that could be though: Tom's evidence was fairly
damning.

'Ally –' It was the only word he managed before he looked
to the ceiling and blew out a long, defeated breath. He went
from looking at the ceiling to hanging his head, looking at his
shoes. After one more sigh he tried again.

'Ally, look, I really like Louise.'

Hmm. Funny way of showing it, Ally thought, but said
nothing.

'I mean, really like Louise.'

Ally waited. She was happy to let him do all the talking.

'I know how this must look.'

*So do I. Like you led Louise on when you already had some other
chick in Glasgow.*

But she kept her silence – it was working. Besides, he'd had the hairdryer treatment from Louise earlier.

'I'm not seeing anyone else, I promise.'

Contrary to all evidence.

'I tried to tell Louise, but she stormed off.'

Because all he'd offered was: 'There's an innocent explanation that I can't tell you right now.'

'Honestly, Ally, there's an innocent explanation, but I can't tell Louise right now.'

And there it was.

'I wish I could, but I promise, I'm not dating anyone else. I was really excited to be dating Louise. She's so...hot...'

Hot? He was trying to get around her sister-in-law by being reductive?

'That's terrible, sorry, I'm panicking. I just mean, it took me so long to believe she was flirting with me because Louise is the talk of the town – the gorgeous, single, youngest sister at the castle.'

Well, that was certainly true.

'Our first date though, was so...so...sweet. There's so much more to her than just the cute girl who grew up in a castle. We took this selfie...'

Scott patted his pocket for his phone.

'Shit. I've left my phone in the van. I have to go and get it, I'm expecting a call. Sorry.'

And with that he was gone. As soon as he shut his door, there was the familiar random scratching, purporting to be a secret knock, at the other one.

'Louise?' Ally asked.

'Of course,' Louise said, coming in. 'Who else would it be?

'Scott just this minute left. Did you hear him?'

'He was here? No, I told you I don't listen at the door! I texted you if I could pop in but – oh your phone's over there charging. So Scott's just left?'

'Yes! He was here to talk about you.'

'Really? What did he say?'

Ally tried to remember the ramblings that had played out merely two minutes ago. 'He said the same as he said to you: it's not how it looks.'

'Sure Scott, sure. That's all he's got?'

'That's what I thought,' Ally agreed.

'Anything else?' Louise asked.

'He said you're hot, but that there's more to you than just the girl in the castle. He was starting to talk about your first date,' Ally listed.

'Aww. He did? He was?'

Louise softened for a second, but just a second. She regrouped and regained her indignation fast.

'He's probably only here to give you the same shit that he told me. Or was going to tell me before I stormed out.'

She pondered.

'Maybe we could let him tell you the full story, whatever it is. I'll listen through the door. I can hear him out, without him having the satisfaction of knowing I'm hearing him out.'

Bizarrely, Ally understood Louise's logic.

There was a knock at the door. Scott was back.

'OK, only this once, I'll be listening from behind my door, OK?' Louise whispered as she left.

Ally nodded quickly, with no time to consider if she had a choice. 'Come in.'

'Sorry about that. It's terrible timing, but I'm waiting on a call,' Scott said.

'That's OK, but you might struggle in here, reception is terrible. The Wi-Fi you've been using at the apartment doesn't stretch to here,' Ally said flatly. Then, 'Scott, what's going on? Louise is upset, you're upset, but you seem to be saying there's no need for any of that.'

'There really isn't Ally, I just can't tell Louise exactly why right now. Soon, hopefully, but not right now.'

'Who's the handsy brunette Scott?'

'What?' Scott frowned.

'Well, I know Louise told you. We saw pictures. That woman and you were all over each other.'

'We were not. Vi...she's – ugh. OK, the woman you "caught" me with, she's a bit OTT. What it is...there's a project that we're working on.'

'Whoa, hold on, I asked you outright if there was a project or a new client and you said no. Now when you've been caught and it suits you, you're saying there is.' Ally shifted as the babies kicked, sensing her getting worked up.

Scott rubbed the back of his head, sighing, and walked to the window. He must have hit the magic spot for the room's sporadic phone reception, because his phone buzzed and pinged.

Ally heard him give a 'grr'. She'd give him that. He was genuinely exasperated.

'Sorry Ally, again, the timing of all this is shit, but I've got to look at these,' he said.

'It's OK. Look if you go out into the hall there, and stand by that window, you'll get better coverage.'

Scott left, making enough of a bang with the door that Louise knew it was safe to spring through hers.

She whispered fast.

'Did you catch that? He nearly said her name! Starts with "Vi". Victoria? Vivienne?'

'I didn't catch that,' Ally whispered back.

'I know, because you interrupted him! Just as he was about to talk about some project.'

'Because we're calling BS on a "project". I'm one of his "projects" and you don't see me holding his hand and ruffling his hair.'

Ally hated the sound of whispering, she found it unsettling and apparently the babies did too, because she could barely follow this frantic exchange over the babies' thumpings.

'We have to be quick, Ally. What's your strategy here?'

'My strategy? I'm supposed to be on bedrest, and I've found myself in a play! Or an episode of Frasier!'

'Frasier? You need to get out more, less daytime Channel Four for you.'

Scott knocked.

Louise jumped up and pantomime tip-toed to her door.

Scott was flustered when he returned.

'Look, Ally. This isn't exactly how I imagined this playing out – declaring my love for Louise to her sister-in-law first. I'm not good at this stuff at the best of times. I think Louise is great. Amazing. I've never met anyone like her. We had such a good time together hunting for that old fireplace. And the way she talks about her job and those wee kids she teaches – she's so passionate.

'Ugh Ally, I don't really want to monologue to you, but I just want you – want her – to know that I want to look after her. To cherish her. I just need a chance to show her.'

His phone rang. An ugly ringtone interrupting a beautiful speech that was in danger of winning Ally over. She wondered if it had worked on Louise.

He left.

Louise entered. Looking like a human heart-eyes emoji.

Safe to say, it had worked on Louise.

'Ally. This is torture. That phone needs to stop ringing for a hot second so that we can get the whole story, it can all be a misunderstanding, and I can fall into his loving arms forever.'

Louise needed this wrapped up with a bow and Ally had to get off this love rollercoaster.

'Louise, when he comes back, don't leave. I'll tell Scott to give me his phone, or turn it off, and we'll get this sorted once and for all. Then you two can either call it a day or head off into the sunset together. Or just down the secret passageway to your room. And leave me alone to sleep.'

A knock at the door.

'Right, ready? You're staying put,' Ally said. 'Come in, Scott.'

'Actually, pet, it's me.'

Inez poked her head around the door with an apologetic smile.

'Well, actually – it's us.'

Filing in behind her was a sheepish-looking Tom, then Katie, who gave a small, awkward wave.

And finally, none other than the pretty brunette, queen of the PDAs – 'Vi.'

31

The journey was not easy but making it through the Glass Pass was an adventure with Fergus ploughing them their own path through a winter wonderland. On the other side of the pass, Jim fell asleep and the women fell into silence for the most part. They'd said all there was to be said.

Following Fergus's written instructions, they found their way to the edge of Partick. Its thoroughfares had been cleared of snow, but the local streets had not. They would have to park on one of the main roads, and walk in to the address Geri had given them.

Sure enough, it was on the very street Mimi had walked up that bright summer's day. Standing at the bottom, looking up the incline of the street, it was just as busy with children playing as it had been in the heat of that day, except their games and clothes were very different. The children were dressed mostly in grey but with colourful woollen hats: on a rainy day it would have been drab, but today, in the brief window before the sun fell behind the tenements, it was a scene from a Lowry painting.

Looking at the street numbers, the flat they were looking

would be on their left. 'Number 15, one floor up, in a green wally close,' Geri had told them. They made their way up gingerly, gravely aware that two of the three pregnant women were being extremely cautious.

They stopped at the close entrance.

'Do you want us to come up with you?' Flora asked Peggy.

'No, I'll be fine. I think the plan of you looking after Jim out here is fine. It's not too cold, is it?'

'Not at all. Jim maybe we'll go back to the car and get your tin tray and ask these kids if you can share these snow ramps they've made?' Mimi said to Jim.

Then she turned to Peggy. 'You're doing the right thing, for you and your son. Everything is going to be OK. I know it.'

The three women exchanged brief but firm hugs, before Peggy walked into the dark close.

Mimi tried not to look at her watch, to avoid confirming that time was passing excruciatingly slowly. She had no idea how long 'these things' took, so keeping track of how long it had been, was pointless.

She tried to absorb herself in the children playing. The snowmen were mostly being built by girls and threatened with destruction by boys. A small row of snow bricks and an upturned tin used to make them was evidence of an abandoned attempt at an igloo. Building igloos had been Mimi's favourite part of a winter storm, but it did require New York-sized dumps, not just the few inches Glasgow had today.

Just like in her hometown, the domed metal lids of garbage cans made perfect shields for the many older boys involved in the running battle of a snowball fight. The smaller boys were mostly busy either sliding down the hill on trays, or building ramps, for an extra thrilling finale.

'Why are they mostly in their school uniforms?' she asked

Flora, for something to talk about. 'Do you think they cancelled school at the last minute?'

'They're in their school uniforms, but those are the warmest clothes they have. These kids won't have many others. School uniforms and maybe one other set. When you're at church you can spot the Glenberry families who're a little more comfortable, because their kids aren't in school uniforms. They have a little more money for a Sunday best outfit.'

'I'd noticed, but I'd never thought it through properly,' Mimi said. 'I think things were tougher here – after the War I mean. We never had rationing in The States. I felt quite naive when I was first told about it.'

'It was worse in the cities. Down in Glenberry a lot of bartering and swapping went on. Having a farm, we were more fortunate than most, so I can't say we suffered much during rationing. But you're right that up here it was pretty stringent.'

There weren't many mothers outside on the street. The older kids kept an eye out for the younger ones, but every now and then a child would call 'Maw' up into the red sandstone canyon and remarkably their mother would appear at their window, with a 'Whit is it now?'

The women would acknowledge Mimi and Flora with an almost imperceptible nod and a small smile. Mimi had no doubt that this time they knew why these strangers were here – standing on the street watching children play, while their friend was at Number 15, one floor up, in a green wally close. She hoped that their heavy wool coats disguised their bumps, or they might look like some kind of grim queue, waiting their turn. Maybe the women on this street had seen such a queue before though.

Jim sat on his tray at the top of one of the longest slides, waiting for an older boy to give him a shove. 'Is this one of the seven hills Mr Douglas-Lauder told me about? That Glasgow's built on?' he asked Mimi, breathless from all the fun.

The boy answered instead. 'You think this is a hill? You should come and try the street up there – it's *really* steep!'

A woman trying to clear snow from her front step with just a broom, shouted, 'Oy! What have I told you? You're not to take any of the wee ones down Gardner Street. If you want to break your own neck that's one thing, but I won't have anyone else's mammy crying to me about their wean getting hurt because of you.'

The boy shrugged and aimed Jim at a snow ramp that made Mimi nervous enough, never mind whatever Gardner Street held.

On the banks of snow against the fences, there were stripes of yellow. Mimi nodded towards them and said, 'I guess they're not allowed to go trailing snow in and out of their mum's houses.'

'Och, you know boys – I'll bet none of them actually needed to go to the toilet. That's just part of the fun.'

Yuck. Maybe Mimi wanted a girl after all.

All of sudden a girl, around ten years old, was dragging a slightly younger boy towards them, who was bleeding profusely from his nose.

'Lean forward,' she told him. 'Mum'll kill you if you get that on your new school coat. 'Maw!' she called up. 'Can you chuck down a rag or some lavvy paper? He's got a nosebleed again.'

The trail of stark crimson on white was jarring. Mimi's breath caught audibly and wobbled on the way out. Flora touched her arm and both women fell into silence.

The thing was, they actually had no idea what the process was. The 'process'. Such a sterile way to tiptoe around whatever it was Peggy was being subjected to. There were rumours and whispered suggestions: knitting needles; bleach; gin; rubber tubes; warm water. Even the words didn't bear thinking about, never mind conjuring the part they played.

Mind you, even childbirth itself seemed to be cloaked in

secrecy. It was part of what the NCT was trying to change. Geri had told them a story about a woman she'd been in the labour ward with, who thought the baby was going to come out through her belly button. The nurse had told her, 'Hen, it's coming oot the same way it went in.'

But Geri wasn't convinced that the woman was even sure how the baby *had* got in.

A woman came to the door of number 15, the green wally close. Her face was grave.

Mimi felt her legs go weak.

'Are you Peggy's friends?'

'We are,' Flora replied. 'How is she?'

'She's fine,' was the reply. 'But I think it's best she stays with me for a couple of days. I like to look after the women who come to me, not send them on their way and risk – well, risk infection or something. It's better for us all if I look after her here.'

'What about her son?' Flora asked.

'Of course he'll stay with me too. My daughter will be back from her job up the road soon, and she will help me look after him. She's young, bonnie, and very good with children. He'll love her. All the kids do.

'Peggy said you have her suitcases in the car. Can I send a couple of these wee tearaways down to get them? To save you two ladies, in your condition.'

A couple of young boys were duly given instructions and despatched. Mimi tried not to hug Jim too tightly, too urgently. 'You're such a good boy, Jim. You're going to stay here for a couple of nights and then you'll go to stay with your mum's other friend. Your Gran will be up soon too; we'll make sure she gets on the train OK.' He was rosy-cheeked and smiling from playing in the snow and didn't seem at all nervous about going with this woman. Mimi was thankful for that at least.

'Peggy isn't expecting that small green bag there.' Mimi

gestured towards a case one of the boys was holding. 'Can you be careful with it please and tell her it's just a few things I thought would be useful?'

'We will,' the woman said. 'Right Jim, do you like Bovril? I think that's what you need after all that sledging. Let's go up and see if your mum would like one too.'

MIMI AND FLORA received a VIP welcome at the Central Hotel and agreed to freshen up in their rooms before a bite to eat in the bar. Personally showing Mimi to her room, the manager told her all about the plans for a major overhaul of the hotel. 'Every room will be ensuite – people have less taste for shared bathroom nowadays. There will also be a telephone in every room and proper central heating throughout.'

'Well, I wish you luck. I just undertook a significant re-do of part of Glenberry, and it's no mean feat. I might take a walk around and take in the old place as it is now, so I'll be able to appreciate the changes when you make them.'

'Please feel free. Make yourself at home Mrs Douglas-Lauder.'

Mimi wandered the residents' hallways aimlessly, then on the ground floor inspected the echoey ballroom and the private dining room, which had the stuffy air of a private gentleman's club. There were a few doors marked Staff Only, and she was about to turn back, but noticed a stairway, going down.

There was a basement?

As she got closer, she heard the sound of muffled merriment.

A speakeasy? How fun!

The air thickened with smoke as she descended, and the laughter became more distinct. A comedy show. As she got nearer, she could hear it was quite a blue comedy show. Nearer still, and she caught the rhythm of the words she hadn't heard since London: Polari.

So this wasn't the sort of speakeasy where she'd be welcome.

All the same, she couldn't resist a peek.

She paused at the doorway and listened. She was close enough now to make out individual voices, and as one particular joke's crescendo ebbed, she heard a familiar, quieter chuckle linger on. She leaned forward and looked in.

At one of the cocktail tables, his face lit by the spill of the spotlight, sat Watson.

Mimi smiled.

Then left.

'A ROOM each was far too generous of Alexander. I'd have happily bunked in with you,' Flora said. 'And talking of kind gestures, what was in the little package you left for Peggy? It was very thoughtful of you. I was so focused on logistics, I didn't think of a gift like the rest of you did.'

'Just a few things I thought she might find useful, and a small toy for Jim,' Mimi replied.

'Mrs Douglas-Lauder!' came a cheerful greeting from behind the bar. 'What will you be having for that growing bump, then? A Guinness? Guinness is good for you, after all. And the baby – it's the iron, they say.'

Used to having champagne here, Mimi had a brainwave.

'How about a Black Velvet? Have you tried one Flora?'

'I've never heard of one,' Flora replied.

'It shouldn't work, but somehow it does. Guinness and champagne, both of which are definitely good for these little ones.'

She patted her belly and nodded at Flora's.

'You don't look convinced, but you'll like it, I promise. It was invented so people could mourn Prince Albert, even while drinking champagne. The Victorians took their grief very seriously, didn't they? It felt like every corner I turned in London, there was some memorial to him or a tradition that was established by Victoria to remember him.'

The stress of the day made Mimi talkative, even before the bubbles took effect. Over prawn cocktail then grilled haddock, she and Flora chatted easily, mostly telling stories from their pasts. Mimi had been sad to lose a friend today, but in the glow of champagne cocktails and shared confidences, she felt she was gaining another one.

'Good for you, for tying down the Laird that they all said *couldn't* be tied down,' Flora laughed. 'I think if he and Fergus shared a dram or two, they'd have a few more dalliances and exes to talk about than us.'

Mimi's eyes filled with tears.

'Oh no, what have I said?' Flora reached out and put her hand on Mimi's

'Oh Flora, can I confide in you? I have a feeling I going to need a friend. We are to have a visitor to Glenberry. Two visitors in fact.'

~

From the desk of Iain Watson, Glenberry

Sunday 17th January, 1960

I have returned to Glenberry this afternoon to find out that Mrs D-L and Mrs Flora Sinclair despatched Peggy and Jim McPherson to Glasgow. I am not to mention this to anyone, as Mrs McPherson's husband must not find out her whereabouts.

Mrs Law either knows, or suspects, more then she is letting on. It's not like her to hold back, so it must be bad, as she was quite subdued.

But then, she has now been brought up-to-date on the matter of the letter from Ms Elsie Morris: she had to be, as the woman and her son are to visit Glenberry.

Heaven help us all.

Postscript: It emerged in my rundown with Mrs Law that Mrs D-L stayed at the Central Hotel on Friday night. I was rather unsettled, given I was nearby that night, but I saw and chatted to Mrs D-L over dinner service and she neither said anything, nor showed a glimmer of awareness, so I am confident that I am in the clear.

Postscript: The comedy show was the tonic I needed, but unfortunately no miracle cure. Things weigh heavy at Glenberry.

32

Right behind Inez's party of four was Jack the Jack Russell, who ran to Louise's side and emitted a continuous growl, lower than Ally had ever heard from him. And it was directed at 'Vi'.

'I can explain,' Tom began.

'No, I can explain,' Katie interrupted.

'No, please, let me,' said 'Vi'.

Inez held up a hand, awaiting silence. 'I think I'll manage this. You three eejits can speak when you're spoken to, only. And we should tell the story fast before Jack has a go at your ankles, Viv.'

Viv. The brunette causing all the trouble was called Viv.

By the twinkle in Inez's eye, Ally could tell she was about to thoroughly enjoy telling the story, and just like that, the knot in Ally's shoulders loosened. Whatever this was, Inez had it.

The whole thing had started the day when Ally had first been put on bed rest and Katie had come by with Inez and Tom to cheer her up, but had got waylaid with a tour of the apartment instead.

Katie nodded at this point.

'I never even saw you, Ally. Alec and I both got caught up in all the amazing things you were doing. You have such a good eye, and I can get really into that stuff. Then when I met Scott... well...'

'Well what?' Louise asked brusquely.

'Well, he's straight out of central casting, isn't he?'

Louise couldn't deny that. It was exactly what she'd said to Ally.

Katie thought of Viv, her colleague who was looking for the right candidates – location and leading man – for a home makeover show. Katie thought that both Mid-June and Scott might fit the bill, and when she told Viv, Viv did too.

'I had to use all my wiles to get Scott to even come up to Glasgow to talk to us about it', Viv said. 'This was out of the blue for him obviously – he was a bit like a rabbit in the headlights.'

Viv confessed that she'd persuaded him by saying this was a long-shot: nothing concrete, just possibilities. A concept. A 'stretch target' of hers that she just wanted to be seen to be proactive about.

But her boss loved Scott and she was despatched to Mid-June to a) look around for potential episode fodder, and b) win Scott over.

Viv was interrupted by none other than Scott himself. He took in the ensemble, and they could all see that rabbit-in-the-headlights look for themselves.

'Scott, Viv's just explaining to us what's been going on. Why didn't you just tell us about the TV thing?'

'I didn't ever think it would come to anything. Viv told me – Louise, this is Viv by the way –'

'We've been introduced,' Louise said flatly.

Scott repeated what Viv had admitted, that her idea was such a long-shot it was practically just a caper for him: a paid trip to Glasgow and a nice meal out with some people from the

BBC. He hadn't told a soul, mortified that people would think he rate himself so highly that he could be on TV.

But then Viv appeared in Mid-June and it seemed like the ball had started rolling before he'd even said yes. Before he'd even had a chance to properly think it through.

'All of a sudden, Viv had been driving round scouting out locations. And of course, my guys managed to figure out what was going on –' He looked at Viv conveying to the room that his team might have had help 'figuring it out'.

'Anyway, you can imagine, I'm sure, the slagging I've been getting. They printed off an application for Love Island for me.'

The group hid their amusement in a variety of ways.

Scott realised it would be a different kind of mortification if things ended up falling through and he didn't get the gig after all. The gig he wasn't even sure he wanted. So he had even more reason to keep it a secret.

'Small chance of that with you around though Tom, or should I say, Inspector Clouseau.'

'Eh yeah about that Scott –'

'You done me bad, man.'

'I done you bad, I'm sorry.'

'Don't get me started,' Inez said.

Inez, Katie and Viv had arrived at Inez's house to find Tom deeply engrossed in photos on his laptop. His surveillance photos. He looked up to say hello, expecting only Inez and Katie and looked like he'd seen a ghost.

'I slammed my laptop shut, I got such a fright. And I'm sure you can imagine how that looked,' he said.

The group once again found their own ways of trying to hide their amusement.

'Louise?' Scott asked.

Louise's posture had taken longer to soften than Ally's and she wasn't quite there yet. Neither was Jack.

'But all the touching?' she asked. 'The familiarity?'

Viv put up her hand.

'All on me. Sales – what can I say?'

'I can confirm,' said Katie.

'Maybe we could talk alone Louise?'

The group made various concurring sounds that it would be a good idea.

'OK Jack, stand down Wee Man,' Louise said. She scooped him up and rather than answer Scott, said, 'Now Scott's going to come with us for chat, be nice to him – for now.'

She started walking towards the door to the passageway to her room. Scott was confused and even more so when she opened it and appeared to gesture him into a wardrobe.

'Go,' Ally said.

As he reached the door, Viv, apparently unable to stop herself, despite everything, said, 'Wait Scott –'

Ally swore she heard Jack *and* Louise growl.

'What happened on the phone? Did they give you firm terms? Did you agree to the contract?' Viv asked.

'They gave me terms, yes. I told them I'd have to talk it over with my girlfriend.'

Louise caught her breath.

'And – curtain,' Ally thought.

33

The weight of anticipation of Elsie and her son's visit was heavy between Mimi and Alexander, too daunting to tackle aloud. Instead, Alexander asked how things had gone with their trip to Glasgow. Mimi wasn't ashamed to share everything with him. She was beginning to wonder who was being served by the conspiracy of silence that surrounded any part of femininity that wasn't outwardly pure and decorous. It certainly wasn't women. Womanhood was challenging, turbulent, messy, and literally bloody. The Bible may have sidestepped this with Immaculate Conception and declaring menstruating 'unclean' for seven days, but this was 1960: wasn't it time we were more honest about things?

The problem was that there were parallels with Elsie, which hung plainly in the air. Mimi couldn't help wondering if Elsie had considered having her pregnancy 'taken care of'. If she had found her own 'number 15, with a wally close', but changed her mind once she saw whatever the conditions or instruments looked like. In her expectant state, and with Peggy's dilemma and brave decision so fresh, she couldn't help turning her imagined tribulations of Elsie over in her mind.

Elsie was arriving in a couple of days and apart from Mimi saying now and then, 'You're going to meet your son,' with an attempt at an encouraging smile, neither of them addressed the elephant in the room. What was that US military phrase? 'How do you eat an elephant? One bite at a time.'

Elsie and Charles' visit was so momentous that it was impenetrable. So instead they focussed on just getting the practical things ready for guests. Less, eating an elephant one bite at a time, more, putting one foot in front of the other.

Alexander broke the news to Mrs Law, who quickly had an arsenal of lambastings at the ready by the time Mimi next saw her.

'If this, "Miss Morris",' she said, saying the name through gritted teeth, 'was open to having relations before wedlock with *your* husband, who's to say how many others there were? Once you've crossed the Rubicon after all...'

She let the implication hang in the air.

'Times have changed,' Mimi said. 'Sex before marriage does not make someone immoral. They may just have slightly different morals than you. And besides that, he wasn't my husband then.'

Mrs Law gave a humph. 'We have no way of knowing if Mr Douglas-Lauder really is –' she began.

'Mrs Law, I think I know what you are about to suggest, and as I told Alexander, I refuse to cast aspersions on this lady, just because her revelation doesn't suit us. Alexander has been perfectly honest with me that they did kick about together, in the timeframe that would have produced an eight-year-old.'

'"Kick about together". Is that what we're calling it now?' Mrs Law grumbled.

'Well, it's how I sometimes talk about my ex-beaus.' Mimi smiled, aware she was teasing Mrs Law now, mortifying her on purpose. But there was an underlying point, this could easily could have been her.

'It's very admirable that you are giving this woman the benefit of the doubt, but I'll have my eye on her that's for sure, until we find out exactly what she wants here.' Mrs Law rubbed her cloth over her workbench furiously, trying to scrub Elsie Morris away.

Maybe the joke would be on Mimi, and Elsie Watson would sail in, claiming her son's spot as the Laird-in-waiting, vying to rekindle Alexander's affection, to oust Mimi and become Lady of the Manor herself.

Elsie had told Alexander he wasn't 'the one' but who knows what could change once she saw him again? Or once she saw Glenberry for the first time? Mimi knew nothing about their particular circumstances, but she knew London. They had the Clean Air Act now, after the deadly Great Smog, but there was a reason it was still called The Big Smoke. What mom wouldn't prefer the clear, pure air of Glenberry, where the only threat to visibility was when a westerly wind swept in an atmospheric sea haar.

Anyway. Such musings would get her nowhere.

'*Any-way,*' she said emphatically, drawing to a close the topic, both aloud and in her own mind. 'Hattie has prepared our old bedroom for them, hasn't she? I'll go up and make sure everything is ship-shape.'

Mimi had her doubts about their guests being in the main part of the castle alone, as she thought it might be scary for the young boy, but the new apartment was out of the question. Their old bedroom made sense since it was the most recently lived in and aired. There was a basket of soaps and lotions for Elsie, and one of small toys and candies for Charles.

She had done all the practical preparing she could, if none of the emotional, so she straightened up the bed one last time and looked around, remembering her first day here. That heart-sinking dismay seemed so foreign to her now that she was so content in her new life and burgeoning family.

She found herself crossing her fingers as she left the room.

ALEXANDER HAD Watson fetch Elsie and Charles from the train station, so that he and Mimi could greet them into the castle together, as a united front. Standing at the entrance, there wasn't much of a warning from the hum of the engine from behind the gates, before the crunch of the gravel beneath its tyres, as it entered them.

Mimi nudged Alexander as the car drew to a halt. 'Go and open her door,' she whispered.

'Oh, of course,' he muttered.

Mimi would look back and realise that Elsie's grand entrance at Glenberry made perfect sense, in that it wasn't grand at all. Far from the femme fatale bouncing out of the car, with sweeping hugs and air kisses, that Mrs Law was no doubt picturing, Elsie was demure.

Alexander was frozen with nerves, not knowing how to greet her, but Elsie removed a glove and held out a handshake.

'It's nice to see you again, Alexander. Thank you for having us.' She was struggling to look him in the eye, so her introduction of Charles was actually somewhat of a relief in watching the awkward exchange.

'This is Charles. Charles, this is Mr Douglas-Lauder,' she said, putting her hand lightly on the boy's head.

This time Alexander offered his hand first. 'It's lovely to meet you, Charles.'

The boy returned the handshake, then looked at his shoes.

There was a lull. Then Elsie said, 'I've explained to Charles why we're here.'

'Oh right. Good-oh. Thank you,' Alexander replied.

Alexander introduced Mimi. She had never seen him so nervous.

Inside, Mrs Law had laid out a spread of a light supper.

Enquiries were made as to the ease and comfort of Elsie's and Charles' train journey, and reciprocally as to Mimi's health and the baby's due date. Charles looked around in wonder, but back to his shoes whenever he felt the conversation was in any way including him.

Mimi felt sorry for the boy, who seemed naturally shy anyway, and now plonked into this overwhelming place and situation. Although Elsie said she had explained things to him, how much could an eight-year-old really understand? Mind you, what did Mimi know about eight-year-olds?

Alexander caught him looking at a model of a Tall Ship and took him over for a closer look. Mimi and Elsie sat in silence, pretending that looking at the man talk to the boy about the ship counted as interaction.

Seeing them stand beside each other, Mimi thought there was a resemblance in stature.

'Charles is nice and tall,' she commented, getting up to offer Elsie some shortbread. She had no idea if he looked tall for his age or not but knew that it was polite to err on that side.

Elsie accepted, replying, 'He's not actually. I suppose because he's quite thin like Alexander, you would think that. He's actually on the small side compared to other eight-year-olds. It would be nice if he eventually reaches his father's height, but I'm afraid my own dear dad is only five-feet-four, so I suppose it could go either way.'

'And his dark hair must be from your family,' Mimi commented. 'Your hair is so beautifully glossy.'

'Thank you, that's kind of you. Yes, both my parents are very dark. My mother's maiden name is Rossi – Italian. But you'd never know by the sound of her. She's as East End as they come.'

It was the most talkative Elsie had been. It was funny she mentioned accents, because Mimi was consciously trying to re-develop her ear for the London accent: its proud brashness, born from bricks, buildings and pavements, whereas Mimi had got used to soft Scottish lilt, born of rolling countryside and rustling pines.

The evening was every bit as awkward as one would expect, and it was a relief when Elsie asked Charles, not so subtly, if he was feeling tired.

34

———

As it happened, Ally hadn't had a moment to respond to Mags, née Morris. But she'd had no intention to reply quickly anyway, and every intention of making her sweat. She'd also hoped that sleeping on the veiled, yet all too clear, revelations from Elsie Morris's granddaughter, might help. *Chance of either would be a fine thing*, she thought several times throughout the night. Sleep was hard enough right now, without this new twist in the tale weighing on her too.

There was no doubt in her mind that Mags was Elsie Morris's granddaughter. And maybe thanks to Jill, maybe because she had added two and two together to get five, there was also no doubt in her mind that Elsie Morris had been, at best, a chancer, at worst, a scam artist.

What wasn't clear was why would Mags want to return to the scene of the crime.

Ignorance perhaps? Somehow they didn't know that Elsie had fleeced Mimi of her beloved inheritance. Her own insurance policy.

Or greed? Had three generations – four, let's not forget her clever little St Andrews grad – somehow burned through their ill-begotten gains and come looking for a top-up?

This latest affront from the past curdled up her fury that Derek Leslie, Mimi's assaulter, had got away with *his* crime for a second time. She was in no mood to let something similar happen again. Charles and Mags Morris better look out.

She had looked out the photo of the boy with the sledge – Charles Morris – and now studied it again. Looking at the boy's stature, she convinced herself he looked like Mags's sons.

Then she had an idea.

It would have to be a carousel, a collection of photos. She hastily put together a collection of similar photos from the stack, all with kids in, all in black and white. She came up with a fairly perfunctory caption and posted.

Rather than sit and stare at her phone, she, slowly and cautiously, went about freshening up for the day. Clean pyjamas – the luxury! Who did she think she was?

Back in bed, she took a deep breath and picked her phone.

> Mags123: Oh my goodness, Ally. My dad
> just called me because your latest post
> has a picture of him it. He's the boy with
> the sledge. He was quite emotional.

Sure Mags, it was a coincidence. But I got you. I know who you are.

> Glenberry_Castle: Oh wow! When was it
> taken? There's nothing on the back of it.
> Mags123: Winter 1960.

Yup, I know.

> Glenberry_Castle: How does he know?
> Does he remember it?

> Mags123: He does. The reason he
> remembers is partly why we got in touch
> in the first place.

Here we go.

> Glenberry_Castle: It was?
>
> Mags123: Yes. He remembers it very well.
> Because it was taken on his last day at
> Glenberry. In fact, his last in Mid-June, as
> it's called now.

And there it was.

Ally couldn't play this game of cat and mouse any longer. Time to nip the latest iteration of this generational scam, firmly in the bud.

Her hands trembled as she replied.

> Glenberry_Castle: I'll be frank, Mags. I
> was pretty sure that was your father in
> the picture. I know more than you think. I
> know your father is Charles Morris and
> your grandmother was Elsie Morris. I'm
> appalled that you expected me to
> welcome you to Glenberry after what
> she did.

She'd run out of steam, not words, so she pressed send.

She needed to take a beat. Her heart was racing and the babies were a-flutter. If she was allowed to, she would be pacing, but instead she reorganised her pillows, trying to get comfortable and somehow calm her breathing.

When she picked up her phone, she wasn't surprised to see a reply. But she was dumbfounded by what it said.

Mags123: Ally, I'm sorry but there has been some confusion. I have never heard of Elsie and Charles Morris. I apologise that I have caused you stress. I feel terrible. I'll tell Dad that this is not a good time and let's forget about it for now. He only has good intentions. I don't know who Charles and Elsie Morris are, but my dad's name is Jim McPherson, and my grandmother was Peggy Allan, at one time, Peggy McPherson.

Mags123: She was a good friend of Mimi Douglas-Lauder and someday we'd love to tell you what a very good friend Mimi was in return.

35

Mimi couldn't stand it anymore. She felt like she could burst, which was an unsettling feeling for someone who was pregnant. The two days Elsie and Charles had been at Glenberry felt like an eternity.

The first morning had been spent tramping around the grounds, all five of them: Mimi, Alexander, Watson, Elsie and Charles. As best they could anyway, because the snow had melted to slippery slush and the damp air seeped through their clothes into their bones. They dipped into the warmth of the kitchen for a mid-morning cup of tea, to Mrs Law's chagrin. She was incapable of throwing a civil glance in Elsie's direction.

At lunch, Elsie wondered if Alexander would like to show Charles around the castle on his own. 'To show him where you used to play, when *you* were a boy growing up here.' The emphasis was clear.

Alexander glanced at Mimi, who quickly smiled and said, 'That's a great idea, I could use a lie down anyway. Are you happy left to your own devices, Elsie?'

'Well, I'd love to see the renovations you said you've done in your new apartments, but if you're too tired...'

That was a little bold. 'Umm, sure. Why don't we all meet up there for afternoon tea? Alexander can bring you both along, once he's shown Charles all the good hiding places in the turrets and up in the old tower. You're lucky Charles, I don't think I've seen them all!'

But Elsie didn't wait for Alexander, and let herself into the apartment. At the most inconvenient time as it happened. Mimi hadn't quite reorganised everything after her trip up to Glasgow and so, unable to nap when she lay down, she decided instead to put away the last bits and bobs from her overnight bag and a few things that had ended up lying around in her rush to leave. She was startled by Elsie standing in the doorway, right as she was securing the front panel of her hidden cubby back into place. In her condition, she couldn't bounce up and ignore the fact she had been on her hands and knees, so she took her handkerchief from her pocket and gave it a little polish and said, 'Thank goodness, it rubbed away. I thought for a moment that the beloved oak panelling had been damaged by the installation of my new fireplace. Watson would have my guts for garters or banished to the old tower.'

She got to her feet. 'Well, here you are then, first stop on the tour of the new digs I twisted Alexander's arm over.'

Again, it was hard to read Elsie, as she showed her around. Mimi was feeling guilty, yet defensive, about *everything*, but Elsie was impassive, beyond complimenting Mimi on her good taste. It was only in the new nursery, with its cream and lemon gingham wallpaper and matching bedding, that Mimi thought she might have caught a fleeting glimpse of something – envy, resentment, regret?

'Hullo?' Alexander called from the small hallway that led into the new apartment.

The women met them there. 'Come in, come in. Mrs Law is bringing tea to the living room for us. Let's go and sit down.' Mimi said.

Charles squeezed in tight beside his mother on a settee. She stroked his hair and bent her face down to his to ask gently, 'How did you like exploring the castle, darling? Was it exciting? Can you imagine spending summers here?'

Alexander and Mimi darted a glance at each other. This was the first hint of any intention Elsie might have. Summers at the castle.

OK, Mimi thought. *Could be worse.*

'It was fun,' he said, so quietly he could barely be heard.

Alexander cleared his throat. 'So, Elsie, when you say summer's at …', but he was interrupted by Mrs Law bustling in with the tea tray, ascertaining immediately where Elsie was sitting, so she could studiously and obviously avoid looking in her direction.

Unexpectedly, she then said, 'Mrs Douglas-Lauder, may I have a word with you in the kitchen please. It's on a household matter.'

This would be a first, Mrs Law deigning to consult Mimi on a 'household matter'.

Once in the kitchen, Mrs Law made a point of making sure the door was closed firmly behind them and that she had her back to the door, so that if there was any danger her hushed tones would travel, it would be into the room, not out.

'I have to tell you something that Hattie overheard today, when your husband was showing that young boy around your home.'

'You have an interesting way of putting that Mrs Law, and I hope you've not had Hattie following them around, but go on.' Mimi smiled patiently.

'The Laird was trying to make conversation with the boy – he's awfully shy, is he not? Too shy, I think.'

'He's only eight, Mrs Law. Any young boy would be feeling intimated in this position he's in. What were you about to tell me? Alexander will kill me if he's left on his own in there too long. It's all so awkward as it is.'

'Well, that's just it – it's about his age. The Laird was talking to him about the loch and asked if he could swim, and the boy said, he learned to swim last summer...'

A long pause to make clear the punchline was coming.

'Then he said to your husband proudly, *"when I was only six".*'

Mrs Law pursed her lips, letting the words sink in.

'I'm not really following,' Mimi said.

'Well, if the boy is eight now, he'd have been seven last summer, not six.'

'Surely that's an easy mistake to make?

'Not when you're eight. Or rather *seven*! Every month counts at that age. I'm not happy about any of this.'

'Well, you've made that really clear Mrs Law, and continue to do so. I'll bring it up with Alexander tonight.'

AFTER ANOTHER EXCRUCIATING evening meal for the motley crew of four, Mimi and Alexander were back in their apartment, Mimi seeing to her nighttime beauty routine.

'How was your time with Charles?' she asked.

'Hard to say. He's very quiet, isn't he? Are all eight-year-olds like that?' he said.

'Your guess is as good as mine. Neither of us has anything to go on I suppose, not having been around children very much,' Mimi said.

Alexander sighed. 'I can't say there's any pull there. Is that bad? I mean any pull to bond with him. Any paternal instinct, so to speak. I've been scared to mention it to you. I don't want you to think badly of me, or that I won't feel it when our wee one comes along.'

'I think that'll be different. This poor little kid Charles has been – what's the word? It's so unkind to say, but, foisted upon you. Out of the blue. I don't think you can be expected to have feelings for him right away,' Mimi said.

'I suppose I just hoped I'd see something of myself in him, or my family. Some glimmer of recognition that would spark a bond, or something. I don't know.'

'Mrs Law brought something up this afternoon,' Mimi began tentatively.

'Oh yes, I've been meaning to ask you what that was all about. I was enjoying your moral support after my "alone time" with the boy, and then she spirited you away to the kitchen for a secret confab. That was all I needed right then.'

'Do you recall talking to him about swimming?'

'Yes, it was one of the times he was somewhat animated. He was proud that he had learned to swim last summer.'

'Anything else?'

'Eh, no. Think that was it. Should there be?'

'Did he mention what age he was last summer?'

'I can't recall, but he'd be seven, wouldn't he? If he's eight now?'

Mimi sighed. 'Well, Mrs Law said that Hattie said – God, I can't believe I'm beginning a story that way – that Charles said he was six last summer, which would make him only seven now.'

She waited for Alexander to do the procreative maths.

'You don't think...'

'No, actually, as you know, I don't think – I've said all along we can't invent a nefarious persona for Elsie to suit our purpose. *But* we do have to have to get to the bottom of what she actually wants with us. And when I say "we" I mean, you and Watson, and when I say, "with us", I mean with you. I think after breakfast tomorrow, you and Watson should sit down with Elsie and ask her exactly why she's here.'

. . .

SAID summit had taken place and for some unfathomable reason Alexander still seemed to have no answers.

Which was why she was where she was now. In Flora's car, on her way to an emergency meeting of the Ladies Group at Flora's house.

'Thanks for coming to pick me up,' Mimi said. 'I couldn't be in the car with Alexander, even for the short ride to yours. I need a break from that pressure cooker, but I'm not feeling like giving him one.'

'Oh of course, it's no problem at all. I picked up Sadie and Geri first and dropped them at the house. I filled them in on everything, as we agreed on the telephone,' Flora said.

'How did they react?' Mimi asked.

'Exactly as you'd expect. Imagine Sadie's jaw dropping and eyes opening wide, in innocent horror, and Geri folding her arms over her bosom and shaking her head in indignance, muttering away about Elsie. You get the picture.' Flora smiled.

Mimi smiled too. 'Sounds like Mrs Law has Geri on her side then. Mrs Law told me something about young Charles yesterday. I'll tell you when we get to yours and we're all together.'

'YOU KNOW for a lassie who's lived on two continents and who's never been dependent on a man, you can be very trusting sometimes, bordering on naive,' Geri said, exasperated.

'It could have happened to anyone, I'm not going to judge –' Mimi began.

'So you keep saying, and I'm not judging this woman for getting pregnant either, or for having sex with your husband. Sorry Sadie.' Geri had got used to peppering her conversations with apologies to Sadie for various reasons. 'But I *am* judging her for coming up here and pretending this child is his, if it's not. What if she just looked through her address book and just came up with the richest old flame and decided to try her luck?

Do you want to be lumbered with her and this wean for the rest of your life, if it's actually nothing to do with Alexander? And even if it is his, you need to get her to show her hand and speak up about what it is she's after. Sounds to me that she'll just be hanging around like a bad smell otherwise.

'You've got to put a stop to this Mimi. No offence, but Alexander and yer man Watson are sounding a bit haunless over the whole thing. Give me a shot at her – I've always said I should have been in the interrogation unit during the war.'

'Well, you're right about my husband and Watson,' Mimi agreed.

'So, seriously, can we meet her?' Geri asked.

'What good do you think that would do?' Mimi asked.

It was Flora who answered. 'Women's intuition. Times four. Geri's right, so far it sounds like Mrs Law and Hattie have been a lot more use than the men in your house, so let's see what more of us can find out.'

'Exactly. Over the years, I've learned to never underestimate what a group of women can achieve together,' Geri said.

'OK, what do you suggest?' Mimi asked.

'Let us come over to yours tomorrow morning and just include her in our get together.'

Mimi's mind was swimming. She had been so determined to be very modern about this, and fair to Elsie, and this felt like a hijack.

Or a witch-hunt.

A witch-hunt, of an unmarried mother, at the castle. So much for modern.

36

I t was far from ideal, but Alec and Sandy had done a great
job of creating a living room within her bedroom, where
they could all meet with Jim and Mags. It was quite presentable
and not at all like a church hall meeting, as Ally had worried. A
small settee and two pairs of armchairs had been comman-
deered from various rooms in the castle to accommodate the
six of them: Jim and Mags, Sandy and Susan, Ally and Alec.

Ally had suggested inviting Flora, but Mags had said just
the family was probably more appropriate for now. (Jill had
suggested inviting Jill, but Ally had assured her she'd fill her in
on everything as soon as she could.)

Ally had had a few conversations by phone with Mags. The
first had been mostly her profuse apologies for jumping to
conclusions and her awful false accusations. Then in the next
couple of calls to figure out logistics, Mags said over and over
how excited her dad was to be visiting Glenberry and meeting
Mimi's family. Ally assured her Sandy was looking forward to it
just as much, intrigued about this apparently very strong bond
in his mother's life that he knew nothing about.

Ally had gone back through Watson's journals for mentions

of Peggy. There was her involvement in the Strawberry Fair incident, mention of their burgeoning friendship and then an abrupt stop when Mimi and Flora 'despatched' Peggy and Jim to Glasgow.

Obviously Ally couldn't join the greeting party outside, and she was a little fluttery as she waited.

Then she heard tyres on the gravel and car doors. The greetings that followed were muffled, but distinctly warm and jovial. When the party filed in a couple of minutes later, Sandy and Jim brought up the rear, already chatting up a storm.

Things were going to be fine.

Jim shook hands with Ally, Mags gave her a hug, and they all found their spots.

Jim waited until everyone had settled, then cleared his throat. 'I had a little opening speech in mind, but I'm afraid that Sandy already heard it on our way up the stairs. Sorry, I couldn't help myself.' Jim chuckled and rubbed his hands together.

'I suppose I just wanted to begin by letting you all know how highly my mother, Peggy, spoke of Mimi throughout her life. Always with deep admiration and affection. It was as if Mimi was somewhere between a movie star, a sage, and a saint.

'Although their friendship in Mid-June was brief, its legacy lasted *more* than a lifetime. Which I'll get to later. Meantime, I know that this has come a bit out of the blue for all of you. There's so much to say. I thought, with your permission, I'd start at the beginning?'

'Jim, feel free to take the floor, we are all ears,' Sandy assured him. 'I'm dying to hear about this friend of my mother's. All we have so far is the picture of both of our mothers at the Strawberry Fair, and the one of you holding a sledge with my parents in the snow. We are all historians in one way or another, so we would actually love you to start at the beginning.

And take as long as you want – we want to hear the whole story.'

'Be careful what you wish for,' Mags said, smiling, as she pulled some things out of a bag. 'He brought notes. And props.'

She handed Jim an Amazon cardboard box, which he put beside his chair, a bright yellow card folder, which he placed on his lap, and his notes, which he held on to.

'Believe me, I'm doing you a favour – at my age it's hard not to ramble. And I enjoyed taking the time to jot things down, remembering my mother and all she achieved.'

'Good for you, Jim,' Susan said. 'I'm sure she'd be honoured, as we are, that you came to visit and tell her story. As Sandy said, we're all ears.'

Peggy Allan, Jim began, was born Margaret Victoria Thomson in the village of Berry in 1922. Her father died when she was very young, and her mother, a tiny but formidable woman, brought her up as a single mum. She was only ever known as Peggy – Jim was a young man before he found out that Peggy was a diminutive of Margaret.

Peggy's account of her early life sounded like a picture book: days that were slow but had purpose, neighbours who kept an eye on one another, children safe to roam freely. Jim wasn't sure if his memories of Mid-June were his own, or inherited from repetition.

He frowned. 'For example. I think I remember being at the Strawberry Fair, but it was such a fixture in my mum's memories that maybe mine were second-hand.'

At the mention of the Strawberry Fair, Ally's chest tightened. She too knew how strongly you could feel something second-hand.

Jim reminded them that when Peggy was growing up, the First World War was referred to as the Great War, because people thought it couldn't happen again. But it did, when Peggy was seventeen. She went straight to work for the Auxiliary

Territorial Service. There were no photographs of her in uniform, or none that survived anyway. So when Jim tried to imagine her in those years, he borrowed the image of the young Queen when she served, composed and purposeful, with the same striking blue eyes as Peggy.

Peggy married Jim McPherson, a telephone engineer who was in Mid-June to install the new system. Once the work was finished in Mid-June, he worked all over the country and came home only on weekends.

When Jim Sr was home, Jim Jr was often sent to stay with his grandmother.

'I believe he suffered from PTSD from fighting in the war – not that it was called that then. He took it out on my mother. But I think it got worse and worse. Well, I know it did. So bad that she made the very brave decision to leave.

'Now, the memories of us departing Mid-June for good...' Jim paused thoughtfully, and nodded. 'I'm confident those memories are my own. They are so clear, and they've stayed with me all these years. But, fortunately, not for the reasons you might expect. They were happy memories. I got to stay in a castle, there was snow and sledging, a warm kitchen with a kind cook, and all sorts of delicious food. The day we left, I got gifts, and there was a shiny new Land Rover with a homemade snow plough, which carved our very own path through a winter wonderland.

'Then we got to Glasgow. Partick. Just one street up from where I ended up growing up. There was more snow and more sledging and I made friends that I had for life, that very day.'

Jim stopped and took a deliberate breath.

'But we were there, not just because my poor mother was escaping her abusive husband, but because there was someone on that street who performed abortions.'

There was a small 'oh no' from Susan, and Sandy shifted uncomfortably in his seat.

Jim allowed them a moment, almost apologetic that he'd had to break that news to them so many decades later, before he went on.

The ladies of Mimi's NCT group had sprung to Peggy's aid. They had stepped in when she had nowhere else to turn. Her safety had been secured not by luck, but by planning, discretion, and courage. There was a friend who knew who to call to find as safe an option as possible, another who insisted on driving them from Glenberry to Glasgow, despite the dangerous road conditions, and of course Mimi.

In their brief friendship, Mimi and Peggy became close quickly, both in need of a friend for their own reasons. Mimi took Peggy in when she showed up battered, bruised, and pregnant. She made sure Jim had nothing but fun in his stay at the castle, never letting on for a second that there was anything to worry about. She gave Peggy a suitcase to pack her things and another full of gifts: some of her own work clothes for when Peggy found employment, a set of clothes for Jim, pyjamas for both, plenty of toiletries, and a small amount of cash.

As he was telling this part of the story, Jim picked up the Amazon box and put it on top of the yellow folder on his lap. He looked at it, choosing his words.

'But there was one surprise in there that, well, was just – extraordinary.'

He looked down at the box and paused.

'It's hard to know quite how to break this to you. You see, Mimi had told Peggy about a woman she knew. Part of New York society. A suffragist in fact…'

Ally stopped listening. She couldn't focus. Her brain was going at a rate of knots.

She knew it already: Jim had the Cartiers.

Mimi had given them to Peggy, and they were right there in that unassuming brown box.

If she could calm her mind a little, it would all make sense.

Of course Mimi gave the Cartiers to Peggy, a woman in distress like lots of the women Red Rose helped in her lifetime.

Jim was handing the box to Sandy.

Sandy and Susan were looking at each other, baffled.

Sandy pulled out a small, flat, crimson leather box, and Susan gasped, her husband still none the wiser.

Giving the process the reverence it deserved, Sandy placed the red box carefully on his lap, handing the Amazon one to Ally.

Which was empty, devoid of a second crimson box.

Jim had only brought one of the Cartiers.

37

Mimi broached the subject at dinner.

'I have this swell group of expectant moms that I've got to know, coming over for tea and coffee tomorrow morning. I hope you'll join us.'

She could feel Alexander's surprised look, that she hadn't mentioned it to him first. She also knew he would have no complaints. Firstly, because he would know better, secondly because she'd bet that he would be glad of some breathing space for the first time in a few days.

'One of them is bringing her son for Charles to play with. He's around his age,' she added.

'One of Geri's children?' Alexander asked. 'Good luck Charles!'

'Hush your mouth! Geri's kids are adorable, they're just a little *energetic*, shall we say. You haven't met her eldest, Robert, who is surprisingly mild-mannered. It must come with the responsibility of being the oldest of three, soon to be four.'

Robert was coming strictly to occupy Charles, so that Elsie was free to engage with the others, and not for any of the subterfuge reasons Geri had suggested. She had wanted to prime Robert with questions to catch Charles out about his age.

'We are not bringing in a child on a spying mission, and we are not subjecting a child to being the object of one,' Mimi had said unequivocally.

'Spoilsport,' Geri had huffed. 'You'd have been a useless spy.'

THE THREE WOMEN, plus Robert, arrived en masse. Mimi hastily introduced them and added, 'Robert, is eight, just like you,' knowing there was a high chance it would cause Geri to try to catch Mrs Law's eye.

With it being a slightly bigger group, they used the reception room in the main castle, rather than the apartment. Watson was attentive until they were settled, with tea, treats and toys.

Elsie enquired as to how far along the women were in their pregnancies and what number child it was for them.

'And Charles is your only...I mean, your first...I mean, your only child?' It was so unlike Sadie to speak up first, and she blushed bright red that she'd made such a mess of it.

'He's my only child yes. We live with my parents. They love him to bits. And he adores them,' Elsie replied.

There was a short silence.

'That's nice,' Flora ventured. 'My parents are nearby, and the children love when they visit.'

The boys were warming up in their play, circling their toy cars closer, gradually progressing from parallel- to co-play.

Flora soldiered on, trying to get the conversation flowing. 'Gosh, Mimi organised a childbirth practice class here just before Christmas, in this very room.'

'Och, what a laugh that was,' Geri joined in. 'Watson had to stand in for ma man at first. He was like a deer in the headlights!'

Sadie gave a quiet giggle behind her hand.

Geri continued explaining things to Elsie. 'Our American friend here has been trying to help us see the merits of a new modern world, where we women are more open with each other about things. No more secrets about childbirth. I think wee Sadie has her doubts though, don't you Sadie?'

'No, I'm glad actually, that Mimi got us all together. I've learned much more from you and that midwife who was here that evening, than from my mum or Bobby's mum – or even my GP. You should see Bobby's face when I tell him some of your stories about having your babies. And what happens afterwards. I didn't know much, but he really knew nothing.'

Mimi was touched. 'Oh Sadie, you've made my day saying that. I'm so glad I sent out those cards to you all and that we have our Ladies Group. Soon-to-be, Mothers and Babies Group. And imagine if we had never heard the story of Geri's last baby being born in the ambulance?'

She laughed. 'Geri, you have to tell Elsie the story. Or just re-tell it anyway to give us a laugh again.'

Geri didn't need much encouragement and regaled them with tale. Her children had been born at home, but with the last one, she thought a break at the cottage hospital sounded quite nice, not to mention sparing her children the sights and sounds of childbirth. But as she went into labour, there was a power cut. She had children crying by candlelight, saying, 'Mummy, you scare us when you make that noise like a pig,' and her panicking husband bringing her sopping wet towels, because he thought he'd seen it in a film. The ambulance took an age, then it was another age to load Geri into it, over dangerously slippery floors in the dark. All that, only for the baby to be born as soon as they closed the ambulance doors.

Mimi watched Elsie laugh along with Flora and Sadie and

realised she hadn't seen her laugh before. She wondered if she had even seen her properly smile, apart from the smile you give when you shake someone's hand or say good morning at breakfast.

Then Elsie said, 'Well, I didn't have a power cut, but –'

She paused at a knock at the door – Watson. He had a box of toy soldiers and tanks for the boys, who were now hidden away together in a far corner of the room. Watson gestured his intention and joined the boys, quietly explaining the toys to them.

Elsie continued. 'I went into labour with Charles right when we were in the worst of it with the Great Smog. The midwives had to walk from their convent to our home, which was only about half a mile, but they couldn't see two feet in front of themselves. So my father organised the neighbours to line the streets, flashing their electric torches to light the midwives' way.'

'That's quite wonderful,' Flora said. 'A bit of the old Dunkirk spirit.'

'Well, it didn't make for a particularly private birth, because all the neighbours then gathered in the street waiting for news! But you should have heard the cheer that went up when my dad went out to tell them Charles had been born. It was as if he'd announced another Royal baby at the Palace gates.'

Elsie was relaxed. Her face looked so different – softer, prettier, with her guard down. Mimi felt bad for her again. Coming here had been such a difficult thing to do that it had even shown on her face.

Their chat continued, and after a while, the next time Watson returned it was to retrieve the empty trays.

'Mrs Douglas-Lauder, may I have a quick word with you please?' He said it casually, but with a bob of his head indicating he meant in private.

'Of course. Excuse me ladies.' Mimi gathered a few

remaining items to help Watson and followed him to the kitchen.

Mrs Law's arms were folded and her face set. She nodded her head towards Watson, urging him to speak up.

He obeyed her silent order. 'When I was in the room a little earlier, I overheard Miss Morris talking about the night that her son was born.'

'Yes?' Mimi said curiously.

'She mentioned that it was during The Great Smog.'

Mimi nodded.

'When I came down to the kitchen, I asked Mrs Law if she could remember what year the Great Smog occurred.'

'And?'

'I could not,' Mrs Law said.

Mimi was slightly exasperated and completely baffled.

'But, Mr Watson thinks it was in December 1952!' Mrs Law couldn't wait to get the words out. 'Meaning – that wee boy isn't small for his age at all. He's only seven, just as I told you.' She was equal measures triumphant and aggrieved.

Mimi's her heart leapt, though she would be ashamed to admit it to anyone.

'Is my husband home?'

'He has taken the opportunity to go to The Gillie's Rest for a pub lunch,' Watson replied.

'Ok...But, Watson, you only *think* that The Great Smog was 1952?' Mimi asked.

'Yes, I'm afraid I can't be sure. Obviously it was big news all over the country, but I'm struggling to pin it down exactly. It may well have been 1951, making the young boy eight years old, as Miss Morris claims. But I just have a feeling that's a bit too long ago.'

'A feeling?' Mimi said. It wasn't much to go on.

'Well, my context is a trip to London, which I took in 1953, and the smog seemed so fresh in local's memories. I'm sorry, I wish I had more to go on. I probably wouldn't even have registered at all if it we hadn't already had our doubts about the boy's age.'

'Well how can we find out for sure? It was before I moved to London, so I have no clue,' Mimi asked. 'Oh! Surely we can consult the set of encyclopaedias in the library,' she realised. Why hadn't they already thought of that?

'We already thought of that,' Mrs Law said flatly. 'They only go up to 1940.'

It seemed this had been a topic of conversation and consternation.

'That's slightly misleading,' Watson said, sounding a little on the back foot. 'The set was bought in 1940, by Mr Douglas-Lauder Senior. He saw it as an act of patriotism that the household should have a proper repository of knowledge, particularly in regard to our history and geography. I know it's of scant use to point it now, when we're seeking to verify something whether something happened in 1951 or 1952, but at the time it was an investment meant to last a lifetime.'

'And someone didn't see fit to keep the investment up to date, and didn't purchase the annual supplements,' Mrs Law interrupted, tightening the grip on her folded arms, as Watson shuffled his feet uncomfortably.

'Well, there's nothing we can do about that right now,' Mimi said. 'Any other suggestions?'

'Would any of your Ladies Group be able to help, do you think?' Watson asked.

Mimi thought.

'Well, we can rule out Sadie, she'd be too young to be paying attention to the newspapers seven or eight years ago. Maybe Geri? No, let's start with Flora. Farmer's pay attention to the weather and seasons, don't they? Oh, I don't know, but we could ask.'

She looked at Watson and Mrs Law who just looked back at her expectantly.

Right. It was up to her to come up with a ruse to get Flora out of the room too.

FLORA LOOKED AT MIMI QUIZZICALLY. 'Mrs Law wants to ask me something about her stew for tonight's evening meal?'

'I know, go figure. Wonders will never cease,' Mimi replied.

'Well, I'm not sure what nuggets of culinary wisdom I'll be able to contribute, if any, but OK. So, I should just head down to the kitchen?'

'Yes, she's there. It's a real head-scratcher apparently.'

Geri knew something was afoot and frowned at Mimi, also quizzing her.

Mimi gave a small 'not now' shake of her head, and asked, 'What have I missed up here anyway?'

As she tried to rejoin the conversation, she caught herself bobbing her knee anxiously, and worse, Sadie and Geri's eyes being drawn to it, so she stood and went to Charles and Robert and asked them about their games instead. She almost suggested taking them on a wander through the castle so she could locate Flora and find out what was taking them so long, but thought better of it. What was taking them so long though?

After an interminable amount of time, it was Watson who appeared.

'Mrs Douglas-Lauder, you are required in the kitchen.'

38

'I can't believe it,' Susan said. 'We were just talking about the jewellery in Mimi's wedding picture the other day, weren't we, Ally? I just always assumed they were diamanté.'

The brooch was exquisite; breathtaking, the most beautiful piece of jewellery Ally had ever seen. She was trying hard to join in the moment of awe, but why was no one else wondering where the matching bracelet was?

'And this is where Mimi's and Peggy's – and I suppose Rose Delacourt's – legacy comes in,' Jim said.

As Jim saw it, they landed exactly where they were supposed to be. They got a room and kitchen one street down, with a painted close, not a wally one – the flats got more basic as you went down the hill.

Jim described a happy life of community, with mothers supporting each other in the complicated dance of raising children and making ends meet. Peggy became close to the woman who had 'helped her out' and became part of the quiet network of women who did just that: helped each other out, friends or strangers, in uncountable ways.

'There was a pawnbroker –' Jim began to explain.

Sandy interrupted. 'You're not going to tell me your mother pawned a Cartier – in Partick?'

'Well, I think being in Partick probably helped, actually. Pawnshops were just a necessary part of life – of surviving. The items pawned were usually things like winter coats, or perhaps wedding rings, so my mother took the brooch along in a worn velvet pouch and left the Cartier case at home. The pawnbroker assumed, as you all did, that it was costume jewellery.'

He explained that pawning the jewellery helped Peggy get her footing until she got a job, but by that time, she was already helping other women in need. Women like herself who had very little, but not lucky in having a friend like Mimi.

Jim said his mother also realised that the safest place for the brooch was actually in the pawnbroker's safe, so she left it there. If someone needed financial help from their informal support services, she'd go and ask for a loan against it, even though it lived there permanently.

When the pawnbroker learned what the loans were for, he refused to charge interest, and if he'd had a windfall, he would refuse repayment at all, moved by the stories Peggy told him.

Jim went to Glasgow University, just along the road, where he met Mags' mother, Donna. Peggy and Donna got on like a house on fire.

Donna's own mother had been very much involved in second-wave feminism, in the 1960s. Peggy hadn't ever thought too closely about it, but she came to realise that she and all her friends were very much the epitome of feminism in action. But Donna convinced her to do even more.

One day Jim came home from a football match to find them at the kitchen table, up to their elbows in paint, making banners from old sheets. They'd decided that they were heading to Cathedral Street, to protest outside the Sheriff Court. A woman, a battered wife as they were called in the seventies, was up for stabbing her husband. The poor woman had suffered at his hands for years and had somehow managed to muster the strength to protect herself with a knife, purely in self-defence.

'My mum and Donna made it onto the telly!' Jim said. 'It was the headline news on Reporting Scotland every night of the trial. I brought some newspaper cuttings to show you.'

As he looked them out, Mags followed up. 'My mum and Gran said that, depressing at it was that they had to be there, there was an amazing solidarity outside the court. It didn't fade through the whole case. Unfortunately, though, it might actually have worked against the woman, because the judge said he refused to be intimidated by "a hysterical mob of female agitators".

'The woman was sentenced to two years in prison, with her children passed back into the care of her violent husband.'

Jim picked up the story again with a silver lining in their time at the gates with their fellow 'agitators'.

A delegation of women from Edinburgh made the journey every day. They were part of a collective that had set up two or three shelters around Edinburgh, that took in victims of domestic abuse, or 'battered wives'. It was the very initial stages of Women's Aid Scotland.

Peggy realised that she and her friends and neighbours had been providing this service, informal and unlabelled, for years. She struck up a relationship with the Edinburgh crowd and ended up going to visit their shelters to get an understanding of how they were run and an idea of how to institute their own operations.

The long and the short of it was that Peggy became one of the key founders of the organisation that became Women's Aid.

Jim's folder contained newspaper clippings from over the years of Peggy in her new element as Women's Aid grew in size and stature, and he passed them around.

Ally looked at a page that was more modern-looking than

the others, all of its pictures in colour. There was a picture of an older but still very recognisable Peggy, at a microphone on a podium, with the headline: STALWART OF WOMAN'S AID SCOTLAND CALLS FOR REPEAL OF MARITAL RAPE IMMUNITY LAW.

Ally looked at the date of the paper. *1990? Surely not.*

Mags caught her expression and said, 'It's unthinkable, isn't it? It wasn't until the next year that rape within marriage became a crime.'

Mags pointed out a man in the corner of the picture. 'On a happier note, that's her husband. She was remarried by then. He was a lawyer. They met when he was doing some pro bono work for Women's Aid. He was a lovely man.'

There was a lull in the storytelling while Jim proudly showed off his mother's accolades, before he said, 'I was keen for you all to know what my mother achieved, after some brave women from Mid-June helped her escape an abusive relationship. And that pretty brooch was along for much of the ride, helping out whenever it was called upon.'

Jim smiled as he told them that the pawnbroker became the first recipient of the 'Woman's Aid Recognition Award', which was displayed proudly in his shop, even though it was just a simple certificate signed by Peggy. When the stakes got higher, and financing was needed for Interval Houses and such, Peggy's husband arranged more legitimate means of using Mimi's gift as collateral.

They never had a certificate of provenance – housing it back in its red box worked well enough for their purposes. When it was retired from duties and back in Peggy's care, her husband joked he was relieved not to have an up-to-date valuation because he wouldn't be able to afford the insurance.

As they laughed at that and had a quick speculation about its value, Ally cleared her throat. She had to come clean.

'We have a certificate of provenance,' she said. 'Scott found it when we ripped out that old electric fireplace.'

'You do? Is that why you were asking me about the brooch?' Susan asked.

Susan seemed to have forgotten that Ally had been asking about both pieces of jewellery. She, like everyone else, was so focused on the dazzling piece now sitting on a coffee table in the middle of the ensemble.

Ally couldn't show them the certificate and reveal they had discovered only half Mimi's bequest. Not right now. She didn't want to burst the happy bubble.

'Yes, I have it and was trying to find out more before I told you all about it. Hope you'll forgive me – it was just some amateur sleuthing to stave off the boredom. With this pregnancy brain fog I can't remember right now where it is, but I Googled the up-to-date value, and I do remember that. It's kind of hard to forget.'

That much was true.

They all looked at her expectantly.

'Somewhere between three and four hundred thousand pounds.'

She thought Sandy and Jim might fall off their chairs.

39

Mrs Law and Flora were sitting at the kitchen table, and Mimi sensed the answer to her question. There was a lightness in Mrs Law's face, relief in her posture.

'It was 1952,' Flora said. 'The Great Smog was December 1952. Fergus checked the farm records and it was there: my father had made a note about the effects on farmers Down South. So Charles is seven, not eight. He can't be Alexander's son.'

Mimi sank down into one of the chairs too. Watson stood awkwardly. All four were silent.

Mimi looked at Mrs Law, half expecting an 'I told you so' lecture, but Mrs Law nodded, gave Mimi a small smile, then burst into tears.

'Oh Mrs Law,' Mimi said and reached for her hand.

'I'm just so happy for the Laird,' she said, trying to quell the tears with a corner of her apron. 'And for you. And for your baby. You're just starting out and this was just too much to bear.'

'What do I do now?' Mimi asked.

'I thought I'd be wanting to storm up there right now, give

her the evidence that she's lied to us, and throw her out into the cold. But...what makes someone go to these lengths?'

'I know,' Mimi said. 'We can only assume it's been done out of desperation. Where is Charles's real father?

'Well, I know this much, I'm not going to go up there now and expose her in front of everyone. We gain nothing by humiliating her. Flora, can you take Geri and Sadie home please? Feel free to fill them in once you've left. I don't think you'll have a choice – Geri is champing at the bit.'

VERY UNHELPFULLY, Alexander seemed to have got caught up at lunch at the Gillie's Rest. Mimi drummed her fingers on the teak arm of her sofa. She knew who she wished she could talk to. But even if she was still around to telephone, her old friend Rose Delacourt would have been out demonstrating against nuclear testing or something, saving the world as always.

'What would you do, Rose?' Mimi thought.

She thought of the numerous stories about Rose helping prostitutes and unmarried mothers. Of the young girl she took in after she had knowingly had an affair with her married employer, only to be abandoned by him and disowned by her parents when she fell pregnant.

Rose would not hurry to judge Elsie. She would be less focussed on the lie, more concerned about the desperation that led to it.

MIMI INSTRUCTED Watson to have Charles entertained in Mrs Law's kitchen, so that Elsie could come to the apartment alone. Mimi took an armchair, Elsie the couch.

'The only way to do this is to get straight to the point,' Mimi said. 'You said that Charles was born during the Great Smog. We checked the date: the Great Smog happened in 1952.'

Elsie wasn't shocked to be caught.

'Yes,' she said.

There was no defiance in her voice. Just tired acceptance.

'That means,' Mimi continued, 'that Charles cannot be Alexander's son.'

Elsie's mouth tightened, but she did not look away.

'No,' she said. 'He isn't.'

'Why –' Mimi began, but Elsie interrupted sharply.

'You called me brave,' she said. 'Do you remember?'

Mimi nodded.

'You thought I'd chosen this life. Chosen to soldier on bravely with a pregnancy, and raising a son, even though I had no husband. Quite the trooper in your mind.'

She gave a short, humourless laugh.

'I wasn't brave. I thought he would marry me – Charles's real father. We made plans, we set a date at the registry office. Then the week before, a friend delivered a note from him. He wasn't ready to settle down. He was moving to Canada. He'd already set sail by the time I got the note.

'I'm not worldly and modern. I'm abandoned and ashamed.'

'Ashamed? Elsie, you certainly shouldn't be ashamed. The coward who left you is the only one who should be ashamed.'

'It's hard not to be embarrassed at being tossed aside.' Her voice was flat. She said it like it was just a matter of fact, as if she was talking about someone else.

'Can I ask, why Alexander? What made you think of him?'

'Because although we weren't together long, and it was just a fling, I could tell he had a good heart. That if he thought he had a son, he'd want to do the right thing by us. By Charles I mean. You have to understand that this was all for Charles. To secure his future. And maybe even to have a father figure in his life – I did mean that part. It wasn't all about financial security.

'I didn't know about you. That Alexander had got married.

And then, when I arrived you were pregnant too. But by then I was too far along this path I'd decided to take.'

Elsie's hands were clenched in her lap now, knuckles pale.

'Every time I thought about stopping,' she said, 'about telling the truth, it felt like pulling the ground away from under him. From Charles. I told myself I was already too deep, that it would be crueller to undo it than to see it through.'

Mimi sat back in the chair.

'I'll go,' she said. 'I'll go in the morning. Or now if you want. I could stay at the inn you mentioned.'

'No,' she said. 'Stay until tomorrow. My husband knows none of this yet. I think it should be you to tell him. I think you owe him – and me for that matter – that.'

Elsie nodded.

Right on cue, they heard the door open and Alexander's buoyant voice.

'Mimi?' he called from the hallway as he shed his winter layers. 'You'll never guess who I ran into at the Gillie's Rest.'

He appeared in the doorway, cheeks flushed, eyes bright, clearly having enjoyed some good ale and good company, not to mention a break away from the tensions in the castle.

Then he took in the room, and slowed.

'What do we have here?' he asked, realising the scene was not of a cosy social call.

'You'd better sit down, Alexander. Elsie has something of a confession to make I'm afraid.'

~

From the desk of Iain Watson, Glenberry
Saturday 23rd January, 1960

Elsie Morris and her son, seven years old, born during the Great Smog, departed today.

40

November 2019

Alexander Iain Douglas-Lauder and Isla Amelia Douglas-Lauder were eight weeks old, and Ally's days had taken on a new, relentless rhythm. Feeding, changing, settling, then starting again. Nights blurred into mornings, mornings into afternoons. Somewhere in the midst of it all Glenberry had pulled off a successful music festival and Ally and Alec had moved back into the renovated apartment.

Louise was back at the castle for a long weekend and had taken the twins out on a walk around the grounds while Ally sorted through some remaining things in their old room. Most of it was going back into the library. It would be there when she needed it, as opposed to taking up space amongst the baby clutter.

As she re-placed a pile of Watson's journals into the despatch boxes, she was relieved to realise that Elsie Morris hadn't been top of her thoughts in weeks. She remained convinced that Mimi's Cartier bracelet had left Glenberry with Elsie, but more than that, she had come to terms with it.

Whether Elsie had stolen the bracelet, been given it, or been paid off with it, from what she'd learned about Mimi and Red Rose, she knew they would have viewed its new ownership as independence for someone who needed it.

It was a different matter when her thoughts strayed to Charles. That was still unsettling. But maybe it was destined to be another of Mimi's secrets that Ally inherited and held close.

Just one more time...

She'd take one more look for what she already knew wasn't there, before she stacked the boxes back on their shelves, to be left alone again for who knows how long.

She re-read Watson's brief entries around the issue of Elsie Morris from 'There is a letter...' to '...departed today' and the frustratingly few facts in between. Just his own tortured help-lessness.

'Elsie Morris and her son, seven years old, born during the Great Smog, departed today.'

When was the Great Smog? She reached for her phone to scratch the mild curiosity itch. December 1952. Yup, that made Charles seven at Christmas 1959, when Elsie wrote to Alexander.

Wait, what? She looked from the journal to her phone.

They backed each other up.

But...

Ally hurried back to the apartment.

Tucked inside a book at the bottom of her bedside table, was Elsie's letter itself. Even though she could probably still recite the letter, she had to double-check. And there, plain to see in black and white, even if the ink was fading and the paper thinning, was Elsie's claim that Charles was eight.

She had lied about his age to place the pregnancy during her relationship with Alexander.

Watson had left her clues after all. He'd almost spelled it out.

When they moved back in, Alec had organised a surprise for Ally: an oversized framed print of the photo of Mimi, Alexander and Baby Sandy at the Central Hotel. Ally had been thrilled and it was pride of place in their foyer.

She went for closer look. Behind the couple and their baby, the three stars of *Singin' in the Rain* shone out from the poster in their yellow raincoats, apparently mid-song. Beneath them read: MGM'S TECHNICOLOR TREASURE in red.

But beneath that, Ally was right in thinking there was more detail in this particular version on the poster.

Banner-style, on the diagonal, obscuring the stars' names, read:

WORLD PREMIERE – RADIO CITY MUSIC HALL, NEW YORK, NEW YORK

And on the second line, the date:

MARCH 27, 1952

Wow. There it was.

The premiere that Mimi and Alec attended, but famously *didn't* meet, was nine months before Charles Morris was born. Not only were Alexander and Elsie no longer an item, but he was also off on his extended jolly in New York and the Hamptons.

There was no secret illegitimate heir of Glenberry.

In the same way she'd silently apologised to Watson on her return from her aborted confrontation with Derek Leslie, did so again for not deciphering his abrupt entry earlier. But she also thanked him, for the peace she had now she finally got it.

She should call Jill and tell her.

As she reached for her phone it buzzed in her pocket. Louise, with two crying babies in the background.

'Oh good you're there. It's all kicking off here Ally. Help!'

· · ·

THERE WAS a party for Scott at The Gillie's Rest. A screening party. He wasn't best pleased about it, but his pals and the guys that worked for him couldn't resist going over-the-top: to congratulate him, but keep him in his place at the same time. His new show, *Scott's Home Fix*, wasn't airing until the new year, but BBC Scotland's early evening magazine show was running a segment previewing it.

Susan had offered to stay home with the twins, telling Ally and Alec to go and enjoy the fun. Jim McPherson was back at Glenberry for a couple of days. He and Sandy were becoming good friends. Ally drove, and they picked up Flora on the way.

Flora, of course, had been overwhelmed to meet Jim, and he had been delighted to share his mother's impressive stories all over again.

They joined Inez, Tom and Katie at a table. Calum had just got back from his duties in London and would be along later. Louise was already at the bar with the rabble of Scott's friends, who were mercilessly winding him up.

'Jim, tell these guys the theory you have about your mum,' Sandy said. 'You'll like this one, Tom.'

Jim didn't need asked twice and leaned in.

'My mother, Peggy Allan, formerly Peggy McPherson, and Peggy Thomson before that, amongst her many, many achievements in her life, served in the Auxiliary Territorial Service during the war. Like the Queen. And also like the Queen, she learned mechanics and how to drive.

'She never gave much away about her exact duties; in fact she could be downright elusive. Now, I used to think she kept her stories shrouded in mystery so that my young boy's brain would invent its own heroic war tales, but there may be more to it than that...'

He paused and smiled, a twinkle in his eye.

'Go on then, you have us all in the palm of your hand,' Sandy said.

'Well, you're all locals, so you're probably aware of the same rumour as me. The one that Churchill and Eisenhower held a secret strategy meeting just a little south of here to finalise the D-Day landings.'

Tom nodded and said, 'Yes, at Knockinaam Lodge, so the rumour goes. It's a hotel now, but I believe it was a private residence at the time.'

'That's right,' Jim said. 'And as a copper, what do you make of that theory?'

'Personally, I can't see any reason to discredit it. The location makes perfect sense to me. It's remote and secluded, but still accessible.'

'Exactly what I said!' Sandy said enthusiastically. 'And you what's always struck me Tom? It's a bit of a coincidence that Eisenhower was given an apartment inside Culzean Castle, just up the coast from here. I'm convinced that's related to the Knockinaam thing.'

'Interesting,' Tom said, nodding.

Jim picked up his story. 'Among the mysterious half-tales she would tell, there was one about her meeting Winston Churchill. But she'd tease me, saying she couldn't possibly tell me why, and joke that it was because she'd had to sign the Official Secrets Act. When I learned about the Knockinaam Lodge thing, I thought well, maybe –'

He paused for effect, letting his audience catch up with his thinking, but Sandy jumped in: 'Peggy must have been Winston Churchill's driver!' He said it as a definitive conclusion, as if the flimsy preceding evidence supported it.

'Well that would be quite a claim to fame, yes,' Tom said, adding, '– if that was the case.' The evidence was a little *too* flimsy for him.

'Why have I never heard that story about Knockinaam Lodge?' Inez wondered.

'Because,' Tom answered, 'as we, of all people, know very

well, the people of Mid-June who lived through the War were made of special stuff. They knew how to keep a secret.'

'Ah yes!' Jim said eagerly. 'You two were in that group that had to take shelter at the old World War II spy station a couple of years back, weren't you? I read all about it at the time. That whole secret war, the one fought on the home front, is fascinating, isn't it? Brigades of civilians carrying out covert missions right under everyone's noses. And the tech at stations like that one – it was so simple, but so sophisticated at the same time.'

He went on. 'I'd love to go up there for a look around – to picture them picking up enemy radio signals to send down to Bletchley to be deciphered.'

'Well, you'll meet Calum later – he's your man to organise a tour with,' Tom said.

There was a ting, ting, ting of a fork on a beer glass, and the room, loud with pre-match bravado, settled into a half-listening hush. Scott's mate grinned, clearly enjoying himself.

'Right. Most of us know that Scott headed up to Glenberry Castle a few months ago for some honest graft – dust, sweat, and a pregnant boss that could make grown men weep.'

He winked across at Ally, who raised her glass in reply.

'What he didn't plan on was coming back down with two things: one, a beautiful girlfriend –' he raised his glass towards Louise, 'and two, the news that his face is apparently deemed suitable for national television.'

A ripple of laughter followed.

'So tonight, as we watch our Scott pretend he's not terrified while explaining lintels to the nation, just remember – this is the same man who once spent a full afternoon arguing with a wheelbarrow. We're very proud, slightly confused, and fully prepared to deny knowing him if this all goes horribly wrong. Cheers, Scott.'

It was a short, rowdy watch, with jeers and words of 'advice' shouted at the screen.

A few minutes later, the TV was switched off, the jukebox on, and regular Gillie's activities resumed, and Calum arrived. He kissed Katie on the cheek, was introduced to Jim, and waved hello to the others.

'Sorry I'm later than I thought,' he said, sliding into the bench beside Katie. 'It got so close to the beginning of Scott's segment, I thought I might as well wait and watch it with my mum.'

'That's OK,' Katie replied. 'You know I don't get jealous of your mum. Those people that you spend all your time with at Bletchley Park, however, they're a different story.'

'Ah yes,' Jim said. 'I've been told you're someone I'll enjoy talking to, Calum.'

He wasted no time in grilling Calum, who filled him in on his liaison role between Mid-June and Bletchley.

'Gosh, what an interesting job to have. I'm a little envious,' Jim said.

'What mission have they sent you back with this time?' Alec asked.

'Well, the archivists have come across some documents that reveal the names of the people who worked up the hill at our Y-station. The next step is to try to track them, or their families, down,' Calum explained.

'So they did send you back with a list of names?' Alec asked.

'They did. I was looking at it on the journey. The requirements for the job were really stringent. The women – it was mostly women – had to pass all these tests. They had to be pretty clever to be asked into the program, never mind the onus of keeping what you were doing completely and absolutely secret. They were essentially the cream of the crop, but they never received any personal recognition, because they had signed the Official Secrets Act.

'Anyway, because of all that, they had to cast a wide net, so most of the girls came down from Glasgow. I only have a few local names.'

'Oh yeah? Are you allowed to tell us?' Jim asked.

'Of course, that's exactly what I'm supposed to do – get the names out there in case anyone remembers them. There were two women who stood out. They have an amazing list of accolades between them.'

'So our wee Y-station up there really made a difference?' Inez asked.

'For sure,' Calum nodded. 'These two women were the two on duty when a wolf pack of U-boats tried to force a passage through the North Channel into the Firth of Clyde, heading for Clydebank. Had the U-boats made it, it would have been catastrophic. But thanks to these women, they were intercepted, and no-one was any the wiser about the near miss.'

'That's incredible. Can you remember their names?' Jim asked.

'Yup. Geraldine Robertson and Margaret Thomson. But they were known as Geri and Peggy.'

Jim's hand struck the table loudly as he fell back in his chair, eyes fixed on Calum in shock. Sandy put his hand on Jim's shoulder. There were various splutters of disbelief and stunned laughs around the table.

Calum looked on, bemused, with no idea as to why the names had landed so momentously.

It was Tom who clued him in. 'Well Jim, it seems like your mum, Peggy, didn't have the time to drive Churchill to Knockinaam. She was too busy saving the world. Literally.'

Sandy started to get up. Flora was in tears. His eyes were sparkly too.

He knelt by her chair and hugged her.

Calum wasn't the only one bemused this time.

Ally realised neither of them would be able to get the words out. 'The thing is,' she smiled, 'Geri was also a friend of Mimi's. She was one of the playgroup.'

'Oh my goodness,' Inez said. 'I'm in danger of tearing up myself. I've got goosebumps. What a remarkable group of women you were, Flora.'

She handed Flora a napkin as a makeshift tissue and as she dabbed her eyes, she started to giggle.

The giggle spread around the table, no one sure why.

'I just wish you all could have met them,' Flora said. 'And you'd know why I find it so astonishing. Peggy maybe, but Geri? A spy? Well, I never...'

'You'll need to tell me all about her,' Jim said. 'I can't wait to get to know my mum's fellow spy. Ladies and gents: I think a toast is in order. To Geri and Peggy?'

'To Geri and Peggy,' they cheers-ed.

❧

From the desk of Iain Watson, Glenberry
Wednesday 13th July, 1960

It is time once again for the Strawberry Fair.

On its eve, I find myself... at ease. The past year has had its moments, to say the least, but now Glenberry is thriving in a way I could scarcely have dreamed of. There is a particular happiness in seeing the D-Ls so besotted with Baby Sandy, as we all are, and so... settled.

In fact, it is hard for me to put into words the joy and contentment I feel.

Tomorrow is a hard day's work for all, but I have every confidence it's going to be one of my favourites yet.

41

———

11th July, 1960

Dearest Mimi,

Just a short note, I know you'll understand why it's hard for me to be in touch more.

A baby boy! I'm sure you're madly in love with him and I hope you are both in good health. Do give my love to the rest of the girls too.

We are doing well here. One day I hope I can fill you in on everything, but your gift to me has already helped in ways you couldn't imagine, and would make you, and your friend Rose, very proud.

I couldn't resist writing to wish you luck in your second Strawberry Fair. According to legend the sun will shine that day, as it always does, though not as brightly as you, my fabulous friend,

Much love,
MT

Mimi was thinking of Peggy's letter as she got ready for the Strawberry Fair. She had selected her outfit in advance this year: a pale blue silk dress, belted loosely at the waist, chosen to match Baby Sandy's clothes and pram.

She was intrigued by Peggy's mention of her 'gift', and more so by the reference to her old friend Red Rose. She smiled at her reflection. She had suspected from the start that there was more to Peggy than met the eye.

Mimi could only hope that Rose's bracelet, wherever it was now, had been used for good too. She hadn't been surprised when Elsie left and the bracelet was gone. In the hope of a better life for her son, Elsie had leapt into the complete unknown, trying to claim that Alexander was his father, with no idea what the consequences might be for either of them. Compared to that, taking a glittering object she had once caught a glimpse of in the apartment felt almost incidental.

Mimi almost wished Elsie had taken the letter from Red Rose as well, if only so she might have understood the true value of the bracelet, and the intention behind it. The thought of a shady second-hand jewellery dealer being the real end recipient of Rose's goodwill made Mimi feel sick.

Alexander appeared, holding Sandy.

'You look stunning, darling. Are you ready to wow them all over again?' he said.

'You're kidding, aren't you? Look at that perfect handsome baby you're holding – I won't get a look-in.'

Mimi and Watson had organised sherbet lollipops for the children again, and she had asked Mrs Law's counsel on other gifts.

'Perhaps wee mindings for the older ladies who gave me the rolling pin last year?'

Mrs Law waved the idea away at once.

'Give them their moment,' she said. 'They'll have been knitting up a storm for wee baby Sandy. It's been months in the planning, I'll warrant. If you make sure to head for their group first with the baby, that'll be quite enough.'

She paused, then added, with gentle authority, 'Accept their gifts, admire the workmanship and you'll make their day for the second year running.'

As Mimi stood in the same spot, about to embark on her second Strawberry Fair, she almost wished she could feel again the remarkable, overwhelming emotion of her first. But then she looked at her husband, his hands resting on the handle of the pram, offering her an arm, and knew being part of this piece of history would always feel special.

The rhododendrons, once again in full, unapologetic bloom meant they couldn't see the driveway from their position on the gravel in front of the castle. The blurred sound of laughter, engines, and voices in good spirits, swelled beyond the gates, and Mimi felt the flutter of anticipation.

Sandy slept on, oblivious to ceremony, his small chest rising and falling beneath a crocheted blanket Mrs Law had declared suitable for the summer air. Mimi glanced down at him, then towards the driveway, and already felt like she was stepping into a memory.

'Ready?' Alexander asked.

She smiled.

'I think so.'

As they passed through the gates, the noise gathered and sharpened, just as it had the year before. The sight beyond them was unchanged: the same steady stream of people moving towards the castle with baskets and buckets, children darting ahead, tractors idling at the roadside. It was just as exciting, but Mimi felt entirely at home.

Mimi and Alexander didn't make it far into the oncoming parade. The first wave of people swarmed them for a look into

the pram, and with overlapping congratulations, compliments
and enquiries as to Mimi's and Sandy's health.

'Would you look at that,' a woman said. 'Just as handsome
as his dad.'

'Aye, a bonnie wee thing,' her husband said. 'Well done to you,
Missus. And Mr Douglas-Lauder as well.' He pressed a cigar into
Alexander's hand. 'A small token, for doing the hardest bit.' He
earned himself an elbow in the ribs from his wife for his cheek.

They'd manage a few steps, before another pause, Mimi
fielding unfamiliar, and yet very familiar, questions. How many
weeks is he now? Is he sleeping through yet? Are you getting
any sleep?

Advice was offered freely and with confidence, much of it
contradictory, all of it kindly meant.

Lots of – in fact, most of – the adults subtly tucked something into the side of Sandy's pram, but in the busyness, Mimi
didn't have even a second to look under the blanket or ask
Alexander what was going on.

Then one woman held up a silver thimble. 'For luck and
hard work,' she said, as she placed it in the pram.

Mimi couldn't resist a look. She pulled back the blanket,
and the pram was scattered with silver coins, mostly sixpences
and shillings, with a few half-crowns.

'Another Scottish tradition I forgot to tell you about,'
Alexander smiled. 'Silver. For luck.'

Finally, the same group of older men who had brought up
the rear last year, filed towards them.

'You've no made it as far up the drive this year,' one
commented. 'Everyone was stopping for a look in the pram, I
suppose.' He proceeded to do the same. 'You'll blink and he'll
be off up those woods with the rest of them.'

Mimi laughed, though the idea made her throat tighten
unexpectedly.

The men walked through the gates, but Mimi held Alexander's elbow back, needing just a moment with him before he headed out on berry-picking duties.

'Still extraordinary?' he asked.

Mimi nodded, smiling.

'Yes,' she said. 'Just a little differently. Maybe even better.'

WHEN ALEXANDER LEFT her just inside the gates, she followed Mrs Law's instruction and made a beeline for her rolling pin friends.

Sure enough, it was hard to pick a hand first, there were so many held out to her, all holding small, wrapped parcels.

'Would you like a seat, hen?' one of them asked.

'I'd love that, thank you. Can I park the pram beside you? I think he's stirring a wee bit. Can you give it a wee shoogle maybe?'

'Och, you're like Grace Kelly, but with a Scottish accent,' the woman replied.

'Maybe not the accent, but I've been picking up a few words I suppose,' Mimi laughed. 'Shoogle's a good one. I like clipe too. Mrs Law is always asking me not to clipe on her to Mr Watson. But don't clipe on me for telling you that!'

Mimi opened the gifts one by one, admiring colours chosen, the intricacy of the pattern, the evenness of the stitches – she'd never have the patience, she said. And to top off the women's glee, Baby Sandy started to fuss enough that he was lifted out of the pram and passed around.

Geri appeared.

'Are you auld girls hogging this wean – our new Laird-in-waiting? I could give you one of mine if you want.'

Mimi hoped that Geri knew the women, calling them old girls, but you couldn't always be sure with her.

'Mimi, we're all plonked down over there when you're down with your rounds,' she said.

Mimi looked in the direction that Geri was pointing, and Flora and Sadie waved brightly at her from a set-up of chairs, picnic blankets and prams.

Mimi's waved back, beaming.

'Ah, look at that,' said the woman bouncing Sandy on her lap. 'I'm glad you've made some friends at Glenberry. Even if one of them is our Geri here.'

'I have,' Mimi said. 'I have.'

PART III

~

From the desk of Iain Watson, Glenberry
Friday 4th April, 1969

By coincidence, not design, my last entry at Glenberry is ten years to the day after Mrs D-L first arrived at the house. I took a perusal back through my entries, and my goodness, I was guilty of mistaking suspicious vigilance for care!

As we know now, Mrs D-L's instincts have been, from the outset, directed toward the welfare of the house rather than her own advantage. And as I know now, stewardship is not preserved by guarding the gates alone, but by recognising when it's right to open them.

Personally, I never could have dreamed of gaining such a close ally, with such tact that she asked no questions that did not need answering.

And here we are today, shortly to take the train together, her depositing me at Brighton as though I were a twelve-year-old boy bound for his first term at boarding school. It is a kindness I will not pretend to resist.

I may only be there for the summer theatre season: it will be interesting to see if the changes in the law in England have made things any easier for us, and we shall take it from there. Mr D-L already has dates in the calendar for me to come back and assist with estate goings-on, and Mrs D-L is threatening to refurbish and redecorate one of the cottages for me, to tempt me back as often as possible.

I have no doubt I will feel the draw, no matter what.

In the meantime, Glenberry, my demanding but patient old friend, I leave you in loving hands.

42

____

April 1969

Mimi and Alexander were both dreading their goodbyes. Mimi, so much so, that she had come up with the ploy of accompanying Watson on the train to Brighton, even though she knew she was just delaying the pain.

Alexander was quiet after their final meeting in the library.

'How did it go?' Mimi asked. 'What did you say? What did Watson say? I just can't imagine after all these years...'

'All I can think of now are all the things I didn't say, and there are too many of them. Perhaps I'll write him a letter.'

'I think he'd like that.'

THE MORNING OF THE JOURNEY, the household moved around with exaggerated normality, fooling no one. Mimi drove Sandy to school as normal and came back to find Mrs Law sobbing in Watson's awkward arms. She could barely look, so instead she watched Alexander pack her overnight bag and Watson's two modest cases into the car. Two cases. That was all. Having spent almost all of his adult life living at Glenberry, he'd accumulated very few possessions.

THEY SETTLED into their comfortable first-class seats and surmised what the offerings from the tea trolley might be, fairly sure they'd be breaking into the lunches that Mrs Law had packed for them instead.

The train carried them south through a Scotland that was now very dear to Mimi. The landscape was familiar, but still able to take her breath away.

She watched Watson in the window's reflection and wondered how he was feeling. She hoped the nervous thrill of his new life outweighed any melancholy about leaving his beloved Glenberry behind.

'Do you have any idea how nervous I was arriving at Glenberry?' Mimi asked.

Watson seemed surprised at the question, out of the blue.

'I've been reminiscing a lot,' she said by way of explanation.

'I remember you seeming quite poised,' he said.

'Even when I was a bubbling mess on my first night, over the wedding present?' she asked.

'Well, there was that.' He smiled.

'You were so wary of me,' she teased.

'With good cause. You were American after all,' he teased back.

'We've had some good times, Watson,' she said.

He didn't answer, just smiled and nodded.

'Remember the NCT class? Where you had to stand in for Geri's husband?' Mimi asked.

'I do, but I'd rather not,' he said briskly.

'Oh, would you rather I remind you of the other compromised situation I got you into?'

'Which one would that be? There have been so many,' he said.

'The Christmas Ball? The game of Twister my cousin brought from the US?'

Watson groaned. 'That would have been entirely avoidable had I not been led to believe it was an innocent children's game. It most certainly was not, especially under your cousin's direction. I became far more well-acquainted with Lady Fairbairn than I care to remember.'

Mimi laughed. 'Not to mention her brother, who always managed to engineer being tangled up with you. I think he liked you. Shame you were already taken.'

Watson gave an embarrassed roll of his eyes, and they fell silent for a moment.

'How is he?' Mimi asked softly, almost a whisper.

'Very well, I think. He's excited to show me around and introduce me to everyone he's met already. His repertory rehearsals started last week.'

'Great. That all sounds great,' Mimi said quietly again. It wasn't something they talked about freely. It was just the way it was. Maybe in Brighton he would gradually be able to loosen some of his restraint. At least the law had changed in England, so there should be less looking over his shoulder. Though old habits die hard.

Watson broke their reveries. 'When did you –' He changed his mind and started again. 'I was wondering what made you finally ask?'

Mimi was glad he didn't ask his first question: when did she know. She had suspected very early on, and then got confirmation the night she saw him at the basement bar under the Central Hotel. But it would be unkind to tell him that, to make him question who else had seen through his careful facade throughout the years.

She answered, 'You mentioned his name just that wee bit too often. It wasn't that I was sleuthing, more that I picked up on it because it was sweet. I remember doing much the same with Alexander, dropping his name in contexts where he was scarcely relevant.'

'Not that you were as blatant as I was of course,' she added.

BRIGHTON GREETED them with all its salty seaside grandeur. Mimi had never been before and she laughed to herself that Watson was swapping stern, mossy old Glenberry for the fantastical gleaming domes of the Royal Pavilion, grand hotels and elegant terraces.

The newly rented apartment was small, but bright and homely already: books stacked wherever they would fit, theatre programmes pinned to the wall, a script open on the table, dense with notes. So relaxed and informal, not words one usually associated with Watson.

Mimi eyed the geometric wallpaper. 'Look how modern this is,' she said. 'How about this for the Grand Hall? I could be doing all sorts of updates without your beady eye on me.'

Watson gave her a mock-stern look.

'I'm just kidding, I'd never dare. But I can't wait to get my hands on that wee cottage that's going to be home for you – both of you I hope – when you come back to Glenberry.'

They were to meet Watson's partner in the pub next door to the theatre when he had finished rehearsals.

Mimi was nervous. She didn't want to let Watson down.

But his partner greeted her with such openness that she felt welcome, and better than that, immediately at ease and content for Watson.

The evening blurred into laughter and wine and the pleasure of seeing Watson be someone she hadn't seen before, and yet entirely himself. He was Iain. Known and proudly introduced by his Christian name, not his surname.

He was the apple of someone's eye. Cherished.

'I don't know how we're going to live without you, you know,' Mimi said to him as they watched the merry antics of the theatre folks. 'But I've met someone who simply can't.'

'Oh, you'll all manage just fine,' he said.

'I will. But, oh boy, I'm going to miss you. Every day.'

'I know. I will too. Every day.'

'Will you call?'

'Certainly.'

'I bet you don't. I bet you're too busy with this lot. With your exciting new life.'

He smiled. 'I'll call.'

'And I'll see you again soon at the Strawberry Fair, of course. Will you bring him?' Mimi looked towards his partner, who was trying to start up a chorus of Do-Re-Mi.

'I haven't decided...'

'Isn't he intrigued about Glenberry?'

'Very.'

'Then please bring him. For me? For Sandy?'

'Oh, that's a low blow, using your child to get to me,' he said.

She laughed. 'Can we call it a date then, Iain?'

'It's a date,' Iain said.

The End

APPENDIX A

Glossary of Scottish words

- auld: old
- boilings: traditional hard boiled sweets
- burn: a stream
- clipe: tell on, or tattle
- close: the entry to a tenement house and the common stairs
- dunt: a thump
- eejit: an idiot
- flit: to move house
- haar: a cold sea fog
- haunless: (handless) awkward, clumsy, incompetent
- joiner: a skilled carpenter who makes and fits wooden items
- lavvy: a lavatory
- Mid-June: fictional area of Scotland named in the 1990s, after a Billy Connolly joke
- nae wunner: no wonder
- oose: dust or fluff around the house
- sledge: a sled
- shoogle: to shake or wobble
- to skive: to dodge or shirk work
- steamie: the communal laundry building
- Up-By: term used when travelling north
- wally: porcelain, china, glazed earthenware or tiling
- wee minding: a small gift
- well-kent: well-known
- yous: you (plural)

APPENDIX B

A Brief Timeline of Social Change

Scottish dates of interest

1958 Christmas Day becomes a public holiday in Scotland (abolished since 1640)

1974 Boxing Day (December 26) becomes a public holiday in Scotland

Women's suffrage and rights, UK

1918 Women over 30 gain the vote (with property qualifications)

1928 Women gain the vote on the same terms as men (over 21)

1958 Women permitted to sit in the House of Lords

1961 Contraceptive pill available on the NHS for married women only

1967 Abortion legalised in Great Britain under the Abortion Act

1975 Sex Discrimination Act outlaws discrimination, including in banking and credit

1991 The legal exemption for rape within marriage is abolished in the UK

2019 Coercive control and psychological domestic abuse criminalised in Scotland

Women in the workplace

1944–46 Marriage bar lifted in teaching and the Civil Service, though informal restrictions persist.

1950s–70s Maternity bars widely enforced; many women required to leave work when pregnant or after childbirth.

1975 Employment Protection Act introduces limited maternity leave and job protection.

1975 Sex Discrimination Act outlaws discrimination in the workplace

2016–17 UK debate over workplace dress codes after a woman was sent home for refusing to wear high heels; petition and parliamentary scrutiny highlight ongoing gender equality issues.

Women's Aid Scotland

1973 First local Women's Aid groups established in Scotland
1976 Scottish Women's Aid founded as a national coordinating body

Gay rights, UK

1967 (England & Wales) Male homosexuality partially decriminalised; age of consent set at 21
1980 (Scotland) Male homosexuality decriminalised; age of consent set at 21
1994 Age of consent lowered to 18
2000 Age of consent equalised at 16
2014 Same-sex marriage legal in Scotland

Women's suffrage and rights, US

1848 Seneca Falls Convention, launching the organised US women's rights movement
1920 Women gain the vote nationwide
1963 Equal Pay Act passed
1964 Civil Rights Act (Title VII) bans sex discrimination in employment
1965 Legalised contraception for married couples
1973 Roe v. Wade legalises abortion nationwide
1974 Equal Credit Opportunity Act allows women to open bank accounts and obtain credit without a male co-signer
1978 Pregnancy Discrimination Act makes discrimination on the basis of pregnancy illegal
1993 Marital rape criminalised in all 50 states (date varies by state; this marks completion)
2022 US Supreme Court overturns Roe v. Wade, ending federal constitutional protection for abortion rights.

ALSO BY LEE CAREY

The Glass Pass

ACKNOWLEDGMENTS

The Glenberry Wives only came to life because of the the support and enthusiasm I received from friends, family, and readers of *The Glass Pass*. You made the whole giddy experience of publishing my first novel a joy. Every time you sent a text, took the time to write a review, or invited me to your book group, you truly made a dream come true. Thank you from the bottom of my heart.

Buoyed by the success of being a bestseller in my own social circle, I somehow found myself appearing as a panellist at the Rye Watershed Literary Festival. Many thanks to the organisers and fellow participants for their warm welcome. Chris Shoemaker at the Rye Free Reading Room was moderator extraordinaire on a very Gilmore Girls autumn evening. Insightful and enthusiastic, he has promised to take on a permanent role when my tours take me all over the world.

From a technical point of view, thank you to Barbara Saxon for her invaluable insights into the police service – of which I had none. A huge thanks to my brilliant beta readers, Elaine Lynch, Anna Sandford and Graeme Sandford, for their time, honesty and encouragement.

And finally, to Graeme, Gregor, Anna, Kirsty, and my extended family — you are just the best. I'm so lucky to have you all. Making you proud is everything.

COMING SOON

Life by Chance

In a slightly magical place called Moniack Mhor, I began a slightly magical novel, Life by Chance. If you loved *The Very Long, Very Strange Life of Isaac Dahl*, by Bart Yates, *Theo of Golden*, by Allen Levi, and if you watch *It's a Wonderful Life* every Christmas, look out for Life by Chance.

ABOUT THE AUTHOR

Lee hails from Glasgow and now splits her time between there and New York. The *Glenberry Wives* is her second novel, following *The Glass Pass*. She is delighted to be publishing this novel in the same summer that Scotland wins the World Cup.

Lee is an optimist.